# HE'S SO SICK

KNOT PUCKING MINE OMEGAVERSE

SINCLAIR KELLY

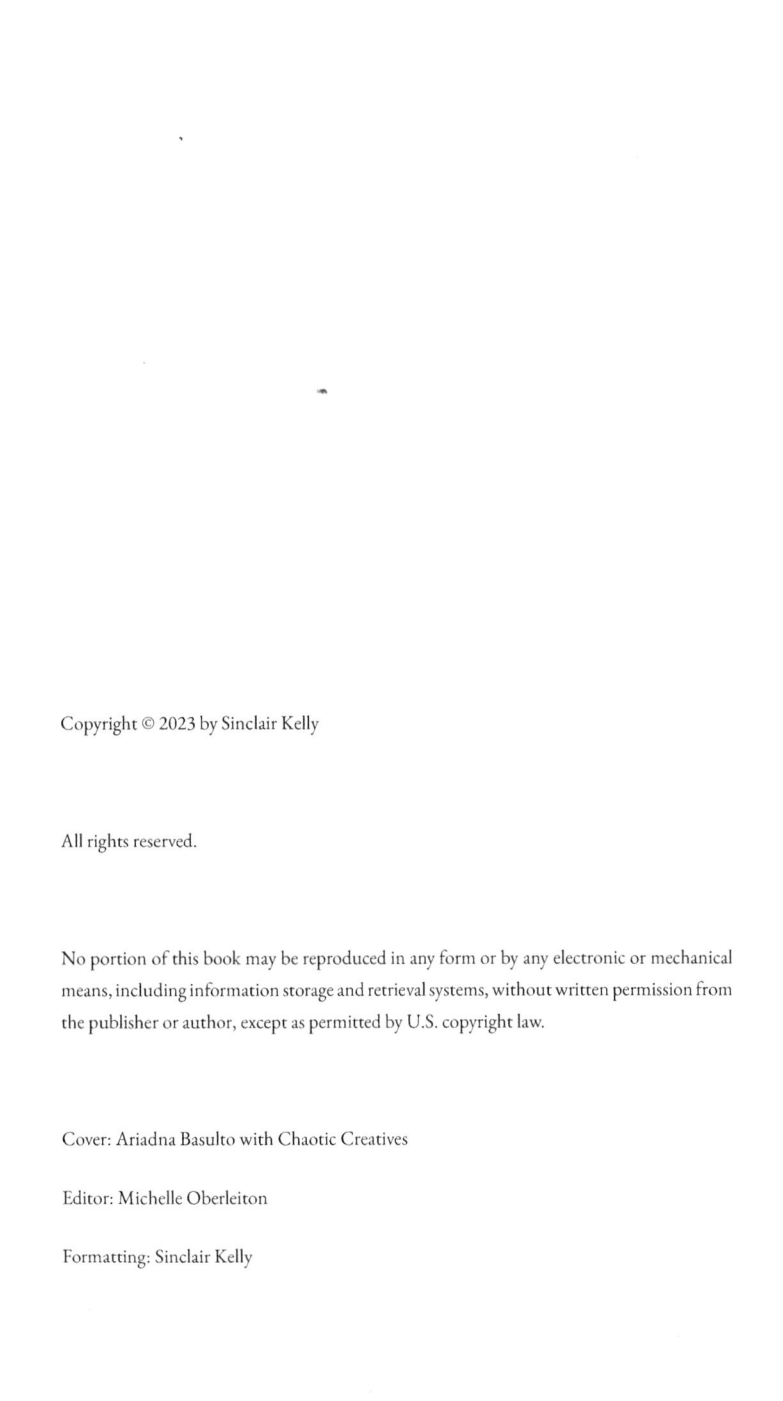

Copyright © 2023 by Sinclair Kelly

All rights reserved.

No portion of this book may be reproduced in any form or by any electronic or mechanical means, including information storage and retrieval systems, without written permission from the publisher or author, except as permitted by U.S. copyright law.

Cover: Ariadna Basulto with Chaotic Creatives

Editor: Michelle Oberleiton

Formatting: Sinclair Kelly

## DEDICATION

This book is dedicated to
all my hockey girls
who love a fictional man
that's good with his stick.

# Contents

| | |
|---|---:|
| Player Roster | VII |
| 1. Nash | 1 |
| 2. West | 8 |
| 3. Porter | 17 |
| 4. West | 25 |
| 5. West | 36 |
| 6. Huxley | 44 |
| 7. Nash | 50 |
| 8. Porter | 56 |
| 9. West | 66 |
| 10. Huxley | 77 |
| 11. Porter | 83 |
| 12. West | 94 |
| 13. West | 102 |
| 14. Nash | 109 |
| 15. Huxley | 117 |
| 16. West | 124 |
| 17. West | 133 |

| | | |
|---|---|---|
| 18. | West | 142 |
| 19. | Porter | 148 |
| 20. | Ziggy | 155 |
| 21. | West | 166 |
| 22. | West | 175 |
| 23. | Nash | 183 |
| 24. | West | 190 |
| 25. | Nash | 199 |
| 26. | Huxley | 207 |
| 27. | West | 215 |
| 28. | Ziggy | 226 |
| 29. | West | 234 |
| 30. | Huxley | 243 |
| 31. | Porter | 255 |
| 32. | West | 265 |
| 33. | West | 272 |
| 34. | West | 280 |
| 35. | West | 290 |
| 36. | Ziggy | 296 |
| Epilogue - Nash | | 301 |
| About the Author | | 306 |

# WESTERN CONFERENCE ROSTER

## PHOENIX HEAT

Barrett Matthews | #19 | Center
Porter Hanson | #9 | Right Wing
Flint Campbell | #5 | Left Wing
Nixon Brooks | #24 | Right Defenseman
Rafferty Sorensen | #74 | Left Defenseman
Huxley McCarren | #33 | Goalie

## CHICAGO STORM

Nash Daniels | #55 | Center

# 1

## NASH DANIELS

West Carter is a little fucking brat.

"What do you mean you granted her time on the rink? What the fuck could she possibly be doing out there?"

My anger flares, and my gut flips. After the call I just had, I need to get my ass out on the ice and work off this stress, or I'm going to be a hot fucking mess for practice later. But I can't. Because of *her*.

"I didn't ask fucking questions, Daniels. Her dad and I go way back, and I've known her since she was a baby. When she showed up at my door a little over a year ago, asking for a favor, what the hell was I supposed to say?"

"You tell her to fuck off, Coach. The ice is for players, *not* pampered princesses."

His eyes narrow dangerously. "Look, I agreed she could use the ice on any of our practice days as long as she was off in time for it to be cleared before we started. She even offered to pay the zamboni drivers for the extra resurfacing work, but they agreed to do it for free any time she was here."

I blink. "What the actual hell?"

I've heard the stories. She's hockey's sweetheart, her daddy's pride and joy. The media adores her, but she's just another privileged heiress with nothing better to do than waste other people's time. Those men work hard for little pay. Why the hell should they agree to work for her for free when she's got money coming out of her ass?

"She's got ties throughout the league, Daniels, and has the respect of many important people. You'd do best to remember that."

I roll my eyes. "What you really mean is that daddy's little girl uses her money and connections to get her way."

"It's not like that. She's a good kid."

"She sure as hell doesn't look like a kid to me. Maybe she'd let me share her ice time if I—"

"Listen to me. Leave her the hell alone. That's an order."

"But, Coach—"

"You heard me. You can take an extra fifteen before the rest of the guys get out on the ice. Now get the hell out of here before I decide to make the team do extra warm-ups and blame it all on your inability to listen to instructions."

I open my mouth, then shut it. It's no use. Once Coach has made up his mind, there's no changing it. Stalking out of his office, I barely manage to stop myself from punching the wall in frustration. Panic is knocking at my door, and I freeze in the locker room and run both hands down my face.

*It's fine. Everything is fine.* Only, it's not.

The worry in my gut shifts to fury. This is *my* arena. *My* rink. Who the fuck does she think she is? Coach said to leave her alone, but he didn't say I couldn't watch, right? I deserve to know why I can't skate on my team's own damn ice. With my mind made up, I grab my bag and head for the tunnel that will lead me to the rink, cursing entitled chicks that think they can do whatever the hell they want.

Rationally, I realize my anger has very little to do with her and everything to do with my personal hell, but no one's ever said I was rational. No, they call me a shit ton of other names that aren't nearly as polite.

I didn't earn the nickname Nash "The Beast" Daniels because I was friendly, that's for damn sure.

I don't play hockey to make friends. I play to make money. To *win*. Let the fans think whatever the hell they want. I don't care.

As I approach the wide opening that leads out onto the rink, I hear the distinct sound of steel blades racing across the ice. My heartbeat quickens, and the natural high I've only ever achieved with a stick in my hand lights a fire in my blood. Leaning against the opening, I cross my arms over my chest, and watch a figure fly across the rink with a stick in her hand. She's in full gear, from a helmet down to the pads, with an old Phoenix Heat jersey on.

Surprise rushes through me. I had assumed she'd be skating in circles, or maybe practicing fancy moves learned during expensive private ice skating lessons. I had no idea she actually knew how to play the game. That's something the press never mentions. My eyes narrow on her expert stick-handling, the way she effectively moves the puck across the ice like she's done this a million times before.

As she slides to a stop, her arms pull back and whip forward, executing a perfect slap shot into the net. She doesn't cheer or bounce around like a cheerleader with too much caffeine. She straightens, her shoulders heaving up and down, probably from the exertion of traveling at speeds usually only us professionals are known for.

I can't see her face from where I'm standing, but I don't need to. I've seen enough newspaper and magazine articles about West Carter, daughter of the owner of the Phoenix Heat hockey team and billionaire heiress. She's got big blue eyes and lips that any man alive would love wrapped around their dick. Not to mention a body with curves that would bring most men to their knees. She's gorgeous. There's no denying that. But I don't play with pampered rich girls like her. They just scream trouble. Add in the fact that she's an Omega, and that's a double hell no. Omegas come with needs and commitments, not to mention *packs*—all of which I don't have any inclination of dealing with. I'm best suited for a life of solitude.

She skates forward, grabs the puck, and makes her way right over to where I'm still propped up against the boards. She doesn't seem to notice me, at least not until I open my mouth.

"Nice shot, princess."

To her credit, she doesn't startle. The only sign she was caught off guard is the slight pause of her feet on the ice. She skids to a stop, spraying ice into the air before stepping onto the solid ground just outside of the rink.

"Nash Daniels. I don't believe we've met." Her voice is smooth, cultured, and only slightly out of breath.

I'm about ready to lay into her for stealing away my ice time when her delicate hand reaches up and lifts the helmet off her head. Her long pink hair comes flying out as she shakes it off her face, and I'm hit with her scent—sugar plums and cinnamon—and I suddenly forget every word that has ever existed.

She's holding her helmet and an old beat-up stick in one hand, while the other extends to me, hesitating slightly when her nostrils flare. She recovers quickly, patiently waiting for me to reciprocate, but I ignore it. I have to. My Alpha instincts are going fucking nuts, and I have no idea what will happen if I touch her, which has never happened in my life. I have control. *Always.* When I finally break through the mind fog her scent has created, I swallow hard and ignore the heat rushing through me.

"You're on my ice."

Her brows lift, and a smirk appears on her flushed face. The pink of her cheeks elicits thoughts I have no business thinking, imagining certain other parts of her in that same pretty shade.

"I didn't realize you own this arena."

"I don't, but the team does."

Her scent sharpens, the cinnamon getting stronger as her eyes sparkle under the bright lights above.

"Actually, this arena is owned by the city of Chicago, with operations run in conjunction with the Chicago Storm hockey team."

My jaw clenches so tightly I'm worried I might crack a tooth.

"And I was given permission from Coach Tomlinson, a personal friend of my father, to use the rink as needed. Maybe you should take your disapproval up with him."

She starts to walk past me, and for a few seconds, I let her go. In thick hockey pants and a jersey with shoulder pads that make her look as broad as a man, she shouldn't be sexy, but something about her presence has my dick standing up and taking notice. I don't want to be attracted to the stunning Omega, but I am, which sparks my inner fury anew.

Catching up to her in two large steps, my hand shoots out without my permission, latching onto her arm. She immediately freezes, her steely gaze whipping toward me over her shoulder. She takes one look at my hand then lifts her eyes to mine. They're so damn blue I swear I could drown in them.

"Is there a problem, Daniels?"

Her use of my last name grates on my nerves, but I'm still working through the mess of emotions she's stirred within me.

"What the hell were you doing out there?" I don't know why it matters, but it's the only coherent thought I have that doesn't involve her naked.

"Oh. Practicing my triple lutz, obviously," she deadpans.

I'm stepping closer without conscious effort, and her body turns toward mine as I crowd her space. Her scent is stronger here. More alluring. The slight hint of her sweat adds to the appeal rather than detracting from it. Even with her skates on, I'm still half a foot taller than her, and I find myself liking that she's so much smaller than me. Something inside is practically salivating at the chance to get up close and personal with the pretty Omega whose eyes are alight with fury.

"I have better uses for that smartass mouth of yours."

I don't fucking know why I say it. The words just come out, and now I can't stop imagining her on her knees, pretty lips spread open, waiting for my dick.

*Fucking hell. I'm in trouble.*

Her tongue comes out, licking that plump bottom lip just before she drags it between her teeth and closes the distance between us.

"You have that much confidence in your *stick game*, Daniels?"

Said stick throbs with the need to show her just how confident we are.

"Bright eyes, I'm damn good on *and* off the ice. Just say the word, and I'll prove it to you."

Her lips pout dramatically, and her sigh shoots straight to my dick.

"Unfortunately, *sunshine*, I'll have to pass. Hockey players are on my Do Not Fuck list." She brings her hand up and, no fucking lie, boops me on the nose. "Even ones who claim they're good with their *stick*."

She turns and makes her way down the tunnel, not even stopping to take her skates off. All I can do is stand there, my balls aching and my dick sore from being squeezed into my jock strap. They're not exactly made for an erection.

The entire time I watch her disappear, my instincts are screaming at me to bring her back, that she's ours. Not that they know what the fuck they're talking about. They just want to get laid. Maybe I'll find a willing Beta and take care of that after the game tomorrow. When I think back to the last time I had sex, I realize my dry spell is significantly longer than I expected.

Dragging my eyes away from the tunnel, I glance back at the empty rink. There's still time for me to throw on my gear and get some ice time in before practice, but I find that the restlessness has settled. My eyes narrow, and I risk another glance toward the darkness where the feisty Omega slipped away. I don't want to analyze this sense of calm and anticipation too closely, telling myself it was simply the distraction of her that took my mind off the shit storm my life has become.

I don't need her. I don't need anyone. I should remember that and get back to what matters. The game. The fans. The trophy that damn near has my name on it. Focus. Play hard. *Win*. That's all I've got time for, even if my brain—and more importantly, my dick—think otherwise.

# 2

## WEST CARTER

*I wonder if his dick is as pretty as he is. It's a shame, really. What a waste of a perfectly good knot.*

Lights flash across the black leather interior as the car barrels down the Arizona freeway, drawing me out of my daydreams of the hockey bad boy I can't have. The sports world is much too small, and I have strict rules. I don't do drama, drugs, or hockey players. I learned long ago, it's best not to shit where you eat. Not to mention most of these guys are practically family.

*Ewww.*

Of course, with tonight's charity ball looming on the horizon, maybe I should've made a one-time-only exception. Nash could've provided an epic distraction. My stomach has been in knots for days. Even a couple hours on the ice back in Chicago wasn't enough to pull me out of it this time. Obviously, there's no guarantee good dick would've helped...but it definitely couldn't have *hurt*. At least not in a bad way.

But I digress.

Tonight's event is incredibly important—don't get me wrong—and the entire reason I flew back to Arizona in the first place. I could just do without the annual reminder of everything I've lost.

Today is the twentieth anniversary of my mother's death, and it's hitting a little harder than usual. Maybe it's because I'm getting older. Maybe it's because I've accomplished so much already, and I wish she were here to see it. Or maybe it's simply because I miss my mom. Whatever it is, it never gets easier.

My phone chimes. Glancing at the screen, I see a text from Elle.

**Best Bae: Fuck him.**

**Me: Right? Who fucking propositions someone they just met?**

**Best Bae: Girl, that's not what I meant. Fuck. Him. Like...*literally*. He gets his knot off, and you get an orgasm from an Alpha who probably screws like an animal, if his nickname is any indication. Sounds like a win-win to me.**

I reread her words, positive I've read them wrong. It's so unlike Elle to give me the green light to ignore my self-imposed restrictions. Normally, she's the one who reminds me of the multitude of reasons I steer clear of hockey players. I'd be aghast if I hadn't been thinking the same thing mere seconds ago.

**Me: Who are you? Have you been body snatched? Prove you're the Elle I know and love by repeating my lifelong mantra.**

She sends an eye roll emoji, and I grin.

**Best Bae: Trust me. No one wants inside this mind or body. They'd flee in terror.**

**Me: Mantra. Now. Or I'm calling Cadence and she'll find you and perform an exorcism.**

**Best Bae: Exorcisms only work for demonic possessions, not aliens. Get your sci-fi tropes right, Carter.**

**Me: Elliott Mitchell!**

**Best Bae: Ugh. Fine. No dicks with sticks. Happy?**

**Me: Exactly. No. Dicks. With. Sticks. Even if they are pretty as hell and built like a god.**

**Best Bae: I weep in solidarity with your vagina.**

I snort, slipping my phone into my wristlet as the car pulls up to the curb, and straighten my black evening gown. The deep V exposes more of my cleavage than I anticipated, but I feel sexy, which fits into my plan perfectly. I'll have the press eating out of the palm of my hand, proving I'm no longer the little girl they want to portray me as.

Adjusting the bunched fabric on my left shoulder that's more for appearance than function, I make sure it looks purposefully messy. My pink hair is artfully pinned up, and my itchy black lace gloves hit mid-bicep. The tall black heels Cadence insisted I bring are already making my feet ache, and I haven't taken more than a few steps to the car. Despite what the media thinks, I'm much more at home with a pair of skates on my feet and a stick in my hand. The heiress they think they know is nothing more than a tomboy forced to play the role they've assigned to me.

At the age of three, I became the poor little girl who lost her mother. The media latched on to the story of the wealthy Alpha widower who was forced to raise his young daughter on his own after surviving the loss himself. They've followed me my entire life, even through the awkward teen years. When my designation came in, rumors swirled about which pack would scoop up the rich Omega whose story had kept the hockey world enthralled for so long, but none did. The few that were brave enough to approach me were overwhelmed by the intense public scrutiny and quickly bowed out. There were a couple other money hungry packs who didn't so much as make it past a first date. So here I am, still single without any prospects on the horizon. My daddy assured me that one day I'd find men who were worthy. I'm not so sure.

Guilt swamps me when I realize it's been months since I've seen him and even longer than that since I've been to a game. The Phoenix Heat are what saved us, what kept us from falling apart when our world crumbled. We bonded over our love of the sport, and it helped us focus on something other than our grief. That's probably why he strongly encouraged me to be his date at tonight's annual Carter Charity Ball along with agreeing to stay for a week and attend this Wednesday's game. Maybe he was worried I'd try to dip out. Not that I would. My father and I are close, and he deserves more of my time than I've offered lately.

The car slowly comes to a halt, and I take a deep breath and exhale, putting on my game face. When the door opens, the valet's hand reaches in to help me exit as gracefully as one possibly can in a ballgown. The moment my toe hits the red carpet, camera lights are flashing, the press calling out my name.

"West, we hear you're in talks with your father to step into the family business. Is that true?"

"Ms. Carter! Who was the young man you were photographed with at the café a few weeks ago? Is he with a potential pack?"

"West, over here!"

My smile is wide, and I wave but don't engage. They're vultures, waiting to devour an easy target, and I'm anything but easy.

Making my way toward the entrance, my strides are steady and confident. Anyone looking sees the twenty-three-year-old woman who simultaneously earned a Bachelor's in Communications & Journalism, along with her MBA. What they can't possibly comprehend is that part of me still feels like the little girl who misses her mama, playing dress-up in a room full of sophisticated adults. The only difference is that I'm taller, and I've got boobs and an ass.

Walking through the door, ushers guide me to the main ballroom where the sounds of low laughter and conversation filter through open double doors. Through the sea of people in the candlelit room, it's easy to spot my dad. Standing tall and commanding, he's right in the center of it all, people naturally gravitating toward him as he boisterously talks about hockey and the team.

Pushing my shoulders back, I walk forward, feeling dozens of eyes following me. The calm expression on my face is as fake as most of the attending players' teeth. What? At least eighty-five percent of hockey players lose one or more teeth throughout their careers. The sport single-handedly keeps dentists in business.

Kidding. Kind of.

I catch Dad's eye, his smile growing wide. My lips quirk up with genuine affection when he excuses himself from his conversation with the mayor.

"Darling! I'm so glad you made it," he says, stepping forward and wrapping his strong arms around me in a hug. He smells like sandalwood and cloves, and I'm suddenly so homesick I can't stand it.

*God, I've missed him. As much as I love Chicago, I love him just a little bit more.*

"Hi, Daddy."

Pulling back, his hands go to my shoulders as he takes in my dress. "When did you grow up?"

"Oh, I don't know. Maybe around the time you forced one of your players to buy my first bra? Or maybe it was when you sent the athletic trainer down to the convenience store to buy me pads and explain how periods work?"

He chuckles, then drops a kiss on my forehead. "I've missed you, biscuit."

"That old nickname, Dad? Really?"

"What? You'll always be my little *biscuit*. Unless you've suddenly sold your collection of pucks?"

His brows are raised excessively high, and I chuckle. "You know I didn't."

He grins, tugging on my hand. "Come on. I want to introduce you to some important people."

"Lead the way, Mr. Carter."

I'm dragged along from one important person to the next. Congressmen. Movie stars. Musicians. Everyone in attendance is generously opening their wallets, making hefty donations that will support a great cause. I should be grateful, and deep down I am, but on the gigantic screen at the head of the room—the one I'm vehemently trying to ignore—is a perpetually running slide show containing pictures of my mother throughout her short life. Each time I see the little girl with blonde pigtails in the arms of the woman she misses more than any other, my heart twinges.

My father founded this charity after my mother unexpectedly died from a disease no one could name back then, so it's close to both of our hearts. The money he raises each year funds research and spreads awareness of the rare Omega-only illness.

"You holding up okay?" Dad whispers in my ear between greetings.

"I'm fine."

One brow raises the way it always did when I was a kid and he caught me in a lie.

I shrug. "You know how hard these things are for me, but don't worry. I'm handling it."

"I know you will. Just wish you had someone to shoulder some of the burden for you."

I roll my eyes. "Not this tired conversation again."

"What? Maybe I want to see my daughter settle down. Want to plan for my GILF years."

My nose scrunches up. "Please tell me that doesn't mean what I think it does."

He playfully wags his eyebrows. "Has a nice ring to it, I think. Grandpa I'd like to f—"

"Ewww. Gross. Don't ever say that again." I step back, shaking off the bad juju. "Someone needs to limit your access to social media. Now, I need to find a drink if this is the sort of craziness I'm going to have to put up with all night."

His laugh rings out just as I hear a loud voice call out above the crowd.

"Sugar plum!"

I turn, a massive grin on my face when my eyes snag on Barrett Matthews, center for the Phoenix Heat and my self-appointed protector and unofficially adopted big brother.

"Loser!" I shout, ignoring the crowd who turns to watch us.

Those who've been around for a while grin, whereas others look shocked by our antics.

Barrett's hand dramatically goes to his heart. "You wound me."

I walk over, and in seconds I'm wrapped up in his arms as he spins me around. The ache in my heart subsides the slightest bit with him here. He smells like the desert after the rain, and I feel myself relaxing in his hold. He's the oldest and longest-standing player on the Phoenix Heat, so we go way back.

"Where've you been?" he murmurs, stepping back to assess me much like my dad did.

At thirty-eight, he's tall—close to six and a half feet—with brown hair and kind amber eyes. The guy always has a smile on his face, and his easy going personality has made him a staple of the Heat organization. That's why my dad has kept him around. That, and he's one of the best centers in the league.

"I know. I should've dropped in more, but school kept me busy."

"Those heathens in Chicago at least letting you get some ice time in?"

I nod. "Coach Tomlinson is a good guy."

"But beware. Some of his players aren't. You're too sweet and innocent for the likes of them."

I almost choke on my own spit. "This where you give me the birds and bees talk, B? I hate to break it to you, but I had sex a long—"

He fake gags. "No. I don't want to think of you and sex in the same context ever again."

Laughing, I say, "I did meet Nash Daniels yesterday, actually, and—"

"Steer clear of that one, West. He's the worst of them. I'm not kidding. Total fucking asshat."

"Pretty sure he's not a fan of me either. He got pissed that I was on *his ice*. Then he propositioned me."

His scowl intimidates grown men, but all I do is chuckle. "He so much as breathes in your direction, you let me know. Got it?"

"Don't worry. I shot him down. He won't be an issue."

He doesn't look convinced, but he lets it go, tugging me into his side and walking us over to a group of players congregated near the bar.

"Someone get me a Kool-Aid for sugar plum here."

I elbow him hard in the ribs, and his loud *oomph* is more than a little bit satisfying.

"Actually, I'd be eternally grateful to anyone who gets me a dirty martini."

"I got you, biscuit," Brooks—another of my faux older brothers—calls out, and I sigh.

Barrett chuckles. "What do you expect? I'm still trying to figure out what happened to the little girl who wore a sugar plum fairy recital costume while demanding I watch her pirouette."

"Spoiler: she traded it in for a ballgown and boobs."

"I can see that. So can all these other jackasses." He scans the group of players, some of which are new to me, who keep sneaking glances my way. "Time to have the hands-off talk."

"Let me know when you do that, and I'll be there for added intimidation factor," Brooks adds, handing me my drink.

The man is built like a brick wall, tall and solid.

"Seriously, guys. Growing up with all of you, I'm more than capable of taking care of myself."

"We know, sugar plum. You just shouldn't have to."

And this is why I put up with their bullshit. Because I know they truly care. Loveable jackasses, all of them.

Leaning up, I kiss Barrett on the cheek. "Thank you. I probably haven't told you that enough, but I should have."

"What the hell am I? Chopped liver?" Brooks asks.

Stepping up, I peck his cheek loudly. "Thank you, Brooks, for being the second-best cock-block I know."

His loud guffaws draw even more eyes our way.

Barrett throws his arm over my shoulder and pulls me into his side. "Welcome home, sugar plum," he whispers in my ear. "We've missed you."

# 3

## PORTER HANSON

I can't take my eyes off of her.

My body has gone still while I stare at the woman practically launching herself into Matthews' arms. Their smiles are wide as he whirls her in a circle, and when he sets her down, her laugh makes something inside me flare with longing.

*Fuck, she's stunning.*

I mean, I knew she was beautiful, but getting an up-close-and-personal glimpse of her has me adjusting my dick in my pants.

"Bro, I don't know what the hell is up with you today, but knock it the fuck off."

I tear my gaze away from my co-captain and the owner's daughter, turning to my best friend. Huxley's long, dark hair is pulled back into a knot on his head, his beard neatly trimmed. The tux he was forced to wear to tonight's event is stretched taut over his large body, and he keeps fucking with his tie. He can't stand shit like this but fully supports the amazing man who is part of the reason we eagerly signed with the Heat last season.

Maxim Carter is a legend, having played in the league before he was married and coached in it before his wife's passing. He took the reins of the Phoenix Heat and has made the franchise what it is today—a championship-worthy team that draws some of the best players in the league. Everyone wants to play for Phoenix and work under the icon Carter has become. He understands the sport, understands the players, and is an all-around genuine dude.

Then there's his daughter. Gorgeous. Smart. A media darling. Some of the older guys talk about her like proud brothers all the time, but since Huxley and I joined the team, she's been away at school in Chicago. Tonight, we'll finally get to meet the woman they gush about.

Hux shoves my shoulder. "Okay. What the fuck is up, man? You're starting to worry me."

I shake my head to fight off the brain fog that's been plaguing me all day. "Sorry, bro. I'm just feeling...*off.*"

"Off is an understatement. You were shit out on the ice the last couple of days, and now you keep lapsing into these trances or some shit. Do you need to see the team doc? Get a check-up?"

Hux is naturally sort of a mother hen, but his increasing concern has my alarm bells ringing because he's not wrong. Off is an understatement. Looking out across the room full of people that are so outside of my sphere it's not funny, my eyes narrow. What the hell is going on with me? I'm having trouble focusing. My gut feels like someone is squeezing it in their fist. Lights are too bright. My sense of smell is going crazy. Hell, even Hux's spicy black tea scent is stronger and more pungent, which is doing weird things to my head. Even worse, it's doing weird things to my dick, but I ignore *that* because…awkward.

We've been friends since we were kids. Our parents always assumed we'd form a pack one day, especially after Huxley's Alpha designation came in. I come from a long line of Betas, and without the Alpha aggression or Omega's heat, us Betas aren't hit with a huge shock like the others. We sort of slowly slide into our roles more naturally.

We never felt any pressure to formalize anything. We've also been too busy just living our lives, going to college, and then making our leap to professional hockey. Luckily, we've managed to be picked up as a pair by the teams we've played for over the years. The fans love our chemistry and camaraderie on the ice, and I'm not sure either of us would know how to play the game solo or be able to handle living apart.

"Porter," Huxley whispers, "you're freaking me out."

His amber eyes are studying mine, concern evident in his tone.

"I'm okay. Promise. I think I might have a head cold that's making me a little loopy."

He takes a deep breath, and I see his nostrils flare. "Are you sure that's it?"

I shrug, glancing back over at the group of players a little further down the bar area. Matthews' normally easy going expression is replaced by narrowed eyes when his meet mine.

*Shit. My discreet looks must not have been so discreet after all.*

Still, I can't help but watch with rapt attention when West Carter leans up on her tiptoes to kiss his, then Brooks', cheeks. My gut clenches harder with something that feels a whole helluva lot like jealousy.

"I'll be fine. Let's go introduce ourselves to the boss's daughter."

I toss back the little bit of whiskey left in the glass that had gone forgotten in my hand.

Huxley follows my line of sight and looks back at me nervously. "You think that's a good idea right now? You said it yourself. Something's off with you, man."

"C'mon, don't be a fucking worrywart. It'll be fine."

I head for Matthews and West, Huxley grumbling behind me.

"What's up, fuckers?" Matthews calls out.

West's gaze shifts until I'm staring into the biggest blue eyes I've ever seen. For a second, I'm rendered speechless.

"I don't believe we've met," Huxley interjects into the awkward silence, saving my dumb ass, and holds out his hand. "I'm Huxley McCarren. Goalie for the Heat."

Those bright blues focus on my best friend, a slow smile turning up the corner of her plump pink lips as her gloved hand meets his.

"West Carter. It's a pleasure to finally meet you."

Huxley makes a barely audible noise beside me, and I glance over. Their eyes are locked, and his Adam's apple bobs harshly while his nostrils flare. A flush is working its way up his throat. Since he did me a solid a moment ago, I'll jump in to give him a second to compose himself because she's definitely packing some massive Omega energy. Even I'm having a hard time putting words together.

"Porter Hanson. Right wing," I manage to murmur, holding my hand out.

Hers slowly slides out of Huxley's, then she faces me, eyes too wide and cheeks pink.

She clears her throat, placing her delicate hand in mine. "I-I've heard so much about you both. Daddy says you're already proving to be amazing assets to the team, and he's excited to see how you and McCarren mix things up as the playoffs approach."

Her scent hits my nose, a mouthwatering cinnamon tinged with something sweet that I can't name, and I struggle to think past the need that suddenly spirals through me.

"These two are good ones, sugar plum, but, as is my duty, I have to give you guys the speech," Barrett says seriously as Nixon Brooks—the right defensemen for the Heat—steps up beside him, crossing his arms over his broad chest.

West rolls her eyes, the grin returning to her face despite the slowly mounting tension surrounding us. "Oh hell. Here we go."

Barrett leans forward, jabbing his finger in our direction. "Eyes, hands, mouths, and most importantly…dicks. If you value yours, then you'll keep them *off* West. Am I clear?"

"Oh my god," West groans, shoving Matthews, who doesn't so much as move an inch. "It's no wonder I had to move to Chicago to get laid with the likes of you two hanging around."

Huxley's sudden growl is soft, nearly drowned out by the music and other conversation, but I hear it rumble beside me. Outside of a hockey game, I'm not sure I've ever heard that particular sound from him.

"You're still a virgin," Brooks mutters. "I refuse to believe anything else."

"Dude." Rafferty Sorensen, our left defensemen, walks up and slaps his packmate on the shoulder. "She hasn't been a virgin since—"

Brooks' big meaty fist covers Sorensen's mouth. "We don't speak of that. Ever."

Sorensen's eyes sparkle with mirth as Flint Campbell—left wing and another of Brooks' packmates—walks up, eyeing us all speculatively.

"Hey, West." He attempts to ruffle her hair, but she swats him away, so he turns to us with a grin. "Let me guess. You're getting the 'Hands Off West' talk from Matthews?"

Huxley nods, his jaw muscles clenching. He's desperately trying to keep his eyes on our teammate and not the gorgeous woman in front of us who has apparently snagged us both, hook, line, and sinker with barely any effort at all.

"You know what? Y'all can eat a dick since *I* obviously can't with the lot of you around." She takes a hefty swallow of her drink and turns, heading toward her father. Glancing back over her shoulder, she winks. "It was great meeting you, boys. I'm sure I'll see you around."

Her ass sways nicely in her black gown, and I hear Matthews growl.

"Hanson, I wasn't kidding. She's off limits."

*Fuck. Caught. Again.*

"What? I didn't do anything."

"You've been eyeing her since we walked over here. She has her own set of rules that typically keep you fuckers away, but you new guys always see that as a challenge and try shit anyways. I'm just here to tell you, that shit ain't happening on my watch."

"Look, I hear you, okay?"

"For your sake, I hope you do." With one last glare, he changes the subject. "Besides, what the hell was that on the ice today? Seems like you have bigger things to worry about than unobtainable pussy."

"He's just not feeling well. He'll get his shit together and be back to kicking ass in no time," Huxley interjects, finding his voice now that the stunning Omega is gone.

It's just like him to stick up for me. I swear he's been doing that his whole damn life. Out of the two of us, I tend to be the serious one, while Hux is the kind, caring one. Why it gives me a warm feeling in my chest this time, I have no fucking clue, but I have more important things to worry about. With our game this weekend, everyone is on edge. West was right. Playoffs are rapidly approaching, and we're in a prime spot to potentially take home the Cup. Now is not the time to fuck shit up.

My gut flips again when a sudden rush of heat swirls through my veins. I can feel sweat begin to form on my forehead and fight the urge to tug at my tie.

*Fuck. Do I have a fever?*

"Look, I'll get my shit together. The team can count on me." I glance at Huxley. "I've gotta take a piss. I'll be right back."

He nods, worried eyes following me as I walk away from the group and make my way toward the hall at the back of the room. I need five minutes away from everyone, a little time to get my mind straight and maybe splash some water on my face to cool myself down. That sensation that's been slowly creeping up on me now feels like it's barreling toward me at full speed, and I'm helpless to avoid the collision that's bound to happen.

Making it through the crowd and into the men's room, I take a deep breath and exhale. The air is blessedly scent-free, and the fog descending on my mind clears a little.

*Cool water. That's all I need. I'll get myself back under control, and I'll be fine.*

But as my shaky hands cup the flowing water and lift it to my face, I feel my erection pressing against the zipper of my pants. That shit isn't normal. I've been hard for a chick before, but this is something else entirely. I think of scorpions. Algebra. My grandma's old dried out meatloaf. Nothing works. If anything, I'm *harder* now. That's just seriously fucked up.

I hear a whine echo through the bathroom, and my eyes widen when I realize the sound came from *my* throat.

*What. The. Actual. Fuck?*
*Betas don't whine. Omegas do.*
*Wait. No. No fucking way.*
*I'm twenty-eight years old.*
*I'm a Beta.*
*I can't be...*
*There's no way...*
*I'm not...*
*Except I fucking think I might be.*
*Holy shit!*

# 4

## WEST CARTER

I'm beyond ready for the night to be over so I can head home and sleep the rest of this god awful day away. Walking out of the bathroom, my feet reluctantly drag me back toward the party still in full swing in the ballroom, but a soft whimper stops me in my tracks. Tucked away in the recesses of the hallway are a couple of darkened alcoves, and I make my way toward one just beyond the restrooms. Cautiously peering around the corner, more than a little afraid to catch some couple in an illicit act, I see a figure pacing back and forth in front of one of the U-shaped sofas.

"Hey, are you okay?" I ask softly.

When he turns, I recognize Porter Hanson, right wing for the Heat, and one of the men who nearly had me swallowing my tongue earlier. His minty chocolate scent has lost its sweetness. It's now tinged with a slightly burnt edge that has flooded the space, making my senses go a little crazy.

His dark blond hair is mussed as if he's run his hands through it repeatedly. His tie and tuxedo jacket are laid out on the bench behind him, with half the buttons on the white dress shirt he's wearing unbuttoned. When his eyes meet mine, they're wide and glassy. *Something is wrong.*

His hand runs down the back of his neck as he swallows roughly.

"W-west. Hey. I'm fine. Just had to...uh...take a minute. Too many people, ya know?"

His rushed explanation might have made sense if I hadn't seen the man thirty minutes ago, surrounded by his teammates, looking like he just stepped off the cover of a magazine. Right now, he looks like he's coming off a bender.

"Hanson, you don't look so hot. Do you need me to get someone? Maybe the doc? I'm pretty sure I saw him—"

"No!" He grimaces, then collects himself and exhales harshly. "I mean...no, thank you. I'm okay, really."

Stepping further into the alcove, I see sweat beading along his forehead and his chest rising and falling rapidly. If I didn't know any better, I'd think he looks and smells like an Omega with a heat on the horizon, but that's silly. Hanson is a Beta.

*Unless... No. That's impossible.* If I remember correctly, he's already in his late twenties. Omegas usually present in their mid-to-late teens. Sure, there are exceptions, but none that would be quite as shocking as this.

I take another step closer, but he backs himself up against the bench, trying to stay as far away from me as possible. I'd think it was Barrett's hands-off talk doing its job if he didn't look seconds away from passing out.

"Hanson, you're a Beta, *right*?"

His fists clench at his sides as he nods. "Yup. Beta through and through. For twenty-eight years. Never been anything else."

He's rambling now, that terrified look making his big hazel eyes appear even larger.

Closing the distance between us, his scent hits me even harder. It's way too strong to be a Beta, which means he's hiding something. When I look up at his face, he's studiously avoiding my stare, and that's when another possibility hits me.

"It's okay. You can talk to me," I cajole. "Did your blockers wear off? Is that what happened?"

His shoulders slump as he shakes his head. "No. I've never taken blockers."

*If he's not coming off blockers, then that means he really is... Holy shit. A twenty-eight years old, first-time Omega. Talk about a fucking shock to the system.*

"Did your designation just come in?" I ask in a shocked whisper.

His eyes meet mine, then he nods, a broken sob escaping. "What the hell am I going to do?"

"Oh, Porter." I step into him—this man I barely know—and wrap my arms around his waist. His body sags into mine as he pulls me into his chest, holding on tightly. "It's going to be okay."

He chuckles, but the sound is not at all light or playful. It's self-deprecating.

"Fuck. I can see it now. Co-captain of the Phoenix Heat presents as an *Omega*. It's going to turn into a fucking media circus. My career is over."

My mind is racing. Being in his arms, surrounded by his sweetening scent, is playing tricks with my biology. There's this tug that I don't really understand, demanding I get closer. Everything inside me is pushing me toward this man with an urgency I can't begin to describe. That's when I feel a warm trickle of wetness between my thighs, but I ignore it. One—because he's a goddamn Omega, so what the actual *hell*? And two—because now is not the time to get horny. He's having a crisis for Christ's sake.

"Being an Omega isn't a death sentence, Porter. You're still the man who can snipe the puck right into the net, who the team counts on as we look toward the championship. Nothing about the game has changed. Just your designation."

When I pull back and stare up at him, he's looking at me with hope shining in his eyes.

"I'm pretty sure I'm going into heat, West. That's what this is, right?"

I nod, running my hands up and down his back in an effort to comfort him.

His eyes close with a ragged sigh. "What the fuck am I supposed to tell Coach? Or…fuck…the guys? I don't have a pack, and I've definitely never been with an Omega in heat. I don't know what the hell I'm doing!"

Worrying my bottom lip between my teeth, I consider the options. I'm an Omega, and I've lived my entire life as one. Porter Hanson doesn't have a clue what he's up against here. The heats, biology's demands, the way you lose autonomy over your body. It's a lot to handle when you're young and still malleable, but to have to figure this shit out as a grown ass adult…

*Fuck! Poor Hanson.*

His hand raises to my mouth, gently tugging my lip free. His calloused fingers brush along my skin, tracing the movement with heated eyes. When they finally meet mine, my breath catches. I'm not sure how it happens. One second, I'm comforting him, and the next, he has me pushed up against the wall, his lips crashing down on mine. The way the man kisses. Fuck. Me. It's the single best kiss I've ever had in my life.

His body surrounds me, warm and delightfully hard. A large palm lands on my back, pressing our bodies together until I can feel the evidence of his need trapped between us. His hips rock subtly, no doubt trying to gain the friction that can ease the pulsing ache he's experiencing. He whimpers softly, the sound both familiar and foreign at the same time.

We're in dangerous territory here. With his heat burying him under a lust-filled haze, we're running out of time. Not to mention we're in a very public place with the media sneaking around, just waiting to catch the next big story, and I'm not sure there's a bigger one than the lauded co-captain of the Phoenix Heat going *into* heat.

Fuck. He's right. I can see the headlines now.

When I pull back, he tries to follow my lips, but I have to be the strong one here. "Hanson, we need a timeout."

When he finally meets my eyes, his pupils are blown wide and his breathing is erratic. Dropping his forehead to mine, his whisper brushes against my swollen lips. "Shit. I'm so sorry. I... Fuck, I don't know what the hell came over me."

The distinct wetness between my thighs tells me I didn't mind one damn bit. In fact, I liked it, a helluva lot, despite knowing I damn well shouldn't. Omegas don't usually grow attachments to each other. We're meant for packs. For *Alphas*. Not for other Omegas. What is biology up to right now?

"It's not your fault. Your body is demanding release, and it's only going to get worse."

His eyes close, and he whimpers pitifully. "What am I going to do?"

Watching a man as strong and powerful as Porter Hanson come apart in front of you does strange things to your head, giving you insane ideas that typically would never see the light of day, but there is nothing typical about this situation.

"I..." Oh hell. Am I really going to offer this right now? Yes. Yes, I am because despite knowing I'm breaking my rules, and that I've only known Porter for all of an hour, my instincts are insisting that we can help him. And if a male Omega is anything like a female one, there's a simple way to do that. The words are leaving my mouth before I can talk myself out of them. "I can help ease the ache, at least temporarily, until we can get you out of here."

"Ease the ache?" he rasps.

"Mmmhmmm. But it will have to be quick."

"West, this isn't your problem—"

My finger lands on his kissable lips, silencing him. "I know. I want to help. Let me?"

Staring into my eyes, he finally nods, his breath brushing across my forehead.

"Undo your pants, and I'll take care of the rest."

He hesitates for only a second before he pushes off the wall with a rough exhale, hands shakily going to his pants. I drop to my knees in front of him, and a soft whimper slips from his lips as he stares down at me. I've never been with a *male* Omega before, or, hell, any Omega for that matter, but since I *am* one, surely I can figure it out. At the end of the day, he's still a man, and what man doesn't appreciate a good BJ now and again?

The second his button is undone and his zipper is down, his dick springs free, long and thick, precum generously dribbling down his length. My thighs clench as lust floods through my veins. Before I can think better of it, I raise my gloved hand, gripping him tightly.

I'm surprised when he's not the solid hardness I'm used to. There's more *give* to his girth than I expected. Intrigued, I squeeze tighter, watching more precum leak out. His moan has me licking my lips in anticipation. The need to taste him fires up my blood, and my tongue flicks out to lap at him before trailing along the veiny underside of his cock.

"Oh fuck. Please..." he begs.

When I look up, he's got his head thrown back and his fists once again clenched at his sides. I take pity on him. I've experienced the need and urgency that's rushing over him right now, and it can be downright painful. Wrapping my lips around him, I suck hard, letting my tongue play along the slit at his tip.

He groans, his hands moving to grip around my neck while his thumbs stroke my cheeks. He doesn't pull me down on his dick or thrust his hips. He's still got enough control that he's letting me take my time, but that's the exact opposite of what we need right now since someone could stumble across us any second.

My hand strokes up his length, and the throb of him against my tongue has a pleased hum brushing past my lips. My other hand grips his balls, and his hips buck, sending his cock deep into the back of my throat. I gag but recover quickly, playing my lips across his pillowy hardness.

"Fuck. Sorry. I just... I can't..."

Popping off of him, I lick my lips. "Shhh. Take what you need. Just be quiet in case anyone is close by."

He nods dutifully, and I eagerly dive back down. His grip on my face gets a little firmer before he begins to fuck my mouth, my lips suctioned around him and my cheeks hollowed out. His thrusts get faster, harder, and I force my throat muscles to relax to take as much of him as deep as possible.

"Fuck, West. Your mouth..." His voice is deeper, rougher with need. "I'm... Goddammit, I'm close."

He continues to pump in and out between my lips, my tongue swiping along his length until his legs begin to quiver and his breathing gets ragged. My fingers tighten around his balls, rolling them between my fingers, and he gasps.

"Oh. Oh god. I'm gonna come. I—"

He doesn't get to finish. He slams in deep, holding me down on his cock with my nose buried into the patch of hair at his base as he loses himself to pleasure. Thick spurts of cum rush down my throat, his cock pulsing between my lips.

"I can't... Ungh. It won't... Oh god. It won't stop. Fucckkk..." he cries.

My mouth is overflowing with more cum than I've ever experienced, and I'm urgently trying to swallow every single drop or we risk making a mess that will be really hard to explain. Cum and velvet don't really work well together. He tastes almost sweet and a little salty, and I'd be lying if I said his unique flavor wasn't making my desire spike off the charts.

Slowly, it starts to taper off, and he slides from my lips with a groan, allowing me a much needed breath of air.

"Holy fuck. I'm sorry. I—"

My hands squeeze his thighs as I try to catch my breath while one of his thumbs still strokes my cheek. "Don't be sorry. Lesson learned. Male Omegas have an endless supply of cum. Noted."

His rough burst of laughter makes me grin.

"Fuck. I really am an Omega." He offers his hand, and I let him help me to my feet. When I glance up, he's staring at me in awe. "West, I..."

Long seconds go by as I watch a multitude of emotions cross his face.

"What is it?"

"Fuck. I... Well, I was hoping you might... Um..."

"Spit it out, Hanson."

His eyes flash at my words, and I can see that was poor phrasing on my part, considering I've got a sex-starved Omega in front of me.

"You didn't spit. You swallowed me down like such a fucking good girl."

My pussy throbs, and I preen like the good little Omega he says I am. Swiping along my lower lip, he collects a drop of cum I must have missed and stares at it briefly. When his eyes lift to mine, there's barely banked lust in their depths. His scent deepens just before he pushes his thumb into my mouth. The move is dominant, so unlike a cuddly Beta or needy Omega, that I have to swallow down *my* whine. Instead, I dutifully swirl my tongue across the calloused pad, licking it clean, and his eyes damn near roll back in his head.

The energy between us is off the charts—nothing like I would've expected between two Omegas. There has never been anyone I was as immediately attracted to as I am with him, and I'm not sure what the hell to do about that.

"I need you. I can't explain it. I just..." He exhales harshly. "Stay with me tonight?"

My belly flips and my pussy gushes at his plea. "I'm not sure that's a good idea."

"I'm not either, but something is telling me not to let you walk away right now."

"Because you're in heat and need help?"

His hand slips around my waist, pulling me into his toned chest. "Because my soul is demanding things I can't voice right now, or I'd send you running in the opposite direction."

My breath catches as everything inside me screams for something I have no business wanting from this man. He's a fucking Omega, for starters, and a hockey player for the team my dad owns. Not to mention, he's not the only one wreaking havoc on my instincts. What would he say if I told him his Alpha friend Huxley nearly had me begging for a knot with just a simple touch? Or worse, that Nash Daniels makes my thighs slick…literally?

My mouth is opening before I can think through the ramifications of what I'm about to say. "You've got me for as long as you need me."

Relief flashes on his face before he drops his lips to mine in a softer, less frantic kiss. It's sweet, full of emotion neither of us is ready to look at too closely just yet.

Forcing myself to pull away, I step out of his hold. "We need to get you out of here."

He glances out toward the hallway. "If I go through there, I'll attract a lot of attention."

"Did you drive here?"

He shakes his head. "Huxley did."

"Why don't I go find him and let him know you're not feeling well? Then he can run and get the car so we can meet him around at the employee entrance."

"Okay. I've gotta tell Coach and your dad—"

"Leave that up to me."

He just nods, worry starting to filter back into his pretty eyes.

"Just relax, wait here, and I'll be right back."

"Okay."

I start to walk away, shaking out my shoulders and praying no one notices anything amiss. This is probably the most reckless, stupidly crazy thing I've ever done, but I'm practically bubbling with excitement.

"Hey, West?"

Pausing, I glance over my shoulder. "Yeah?"

His grin is a little lopsided as he tucks himself back into his pants. "Might want to take off those gloves."

I glance down, noticing the white stains splattered over my black-covered fingers.

"Fuck. That would've been embarrassing." Quickly, I peel off the offending garments and playfully toss them over to him.

He brings them up to his nose. "You know you reek of me, right?"

"Yeah. Not much I can do about that."

He grimaces. "Just...try to stay away from Matthews, okay?"

I bite back my laughter. "Definitely."

# 5

## WEST CARTER

Walking out of the alcove and down the hall, I plaster on my most polite smile and stride purposefully through the ballroom. Most people smile and steer clear as I navigate the crowd until I find a worried-looking Huxley McCarren standing at the bar alone.

*Thank fuck for small miracles.*

"Hey, McCarren," I call out softly.

He turns, eyes going wide when I get up close and personal, invading his bubble. His nostrils flare, and a flush spreads across his cheeks.

"West," he murmurs, his voice deep and low, making my pussy contract around nothing. The way he says my name is both a plea and a warning at the same time, and the effect is damn near as good as if he just swiped his tongue across my clit. I'm so fucking wet, my slick is dripping down my thighs at this point, and my perfume is pungent in the air around us. I swallow down a whimper, forcing myself to ignore the spicy black tea scent that's getting sharper the longer I stand close to him. "What can I do for you?"

*So much. So goddamn much.*

But, of course, I don't say that.

"There's a *situation* I need your help with."

"Situation? Does it involve Hanson? Because I can smell him all over you, except his scent is..." He swallows harshly. "Different."

"I'm sure he'll explain everything, but right now, I need you to grab your car and meet us around back at the employee entrance."

His brow furrows. "But—"

"No buts, McCarren. Your friend needs you."

He straightens his shoulders and takes another long draw of our combined scents. His eyes spark, fists clenching at his side. I'm not sure which Omega is sending the Alpha's pheromones into overdrive. Part of me wishes it was my scent that was driving him crazy. The other, smarter part knows it's better if it's Hanson.

"Is he okay?" His voice cracks, worry flashing on his face.

Realization hits. His interest *is* for Hanson. McCarren's got the hots for his best friend. I wonder if he has any idea.

"He's okay. Just *really* needs a ride home."

His shoulders relax, his full attention zeroing in on me. I bite my bottom lip to stop myself from asking for something I can't have.

*What the hell is wrong with me?*

He steps forward, leaving no more than a couple inches between us.

"It smells like Hanson isn't the only one who needs me." My brain short circuits when he leans forward, his nose trailing up my neck, careful to avoid touching my skin. "Tell me. What do you need, West?"

*I need you,* my instincts want me to scream, but I ruthlessly shove them back. This Alpha isn't mine. In fact, this situation just got a helluva lot more complicated. Omegas are possessive. We don't like to share. Hanson may think he wants me with him tonight, but what about when his Alpha is in close proximity to another Omega? Considering I know how close these two already are, I wouldn't be surprised if the new Omega is claimed before his heat is over. Where does that really leave me?

Regret whips through me fast and sharp.

Burying my misery deep down inside to be pulled out later with a pint of ice cream and a bottle—or maybe two—of wine, I ignore his question altogether. "I'll get Hanson out back. Don't be long."

He studies me, intense amber eyes searching for something he won't find. Disappointment flickers across his face, brows drawn tight and lips tense. Finally, he nods.

"Give me ten minutes, and I'll be out there."

Watching him turn and walk away, his plump ass stretching his black tuxedo pants tight, there's a hollowness in my belly. It's better this way, but it sure as hell doesn't feel like it.

Shaking off the feeling of loss, my eyes scan the room for my dad. I find him off to the side with Coach Michaels.

*Just the men I need to see. Perfect! Luck is in my favor.*

I skirt around the edge of the room, and Barrett catches my eye from the sideline. I give him a little finger wave, which has his eyes narrowing on me, but I don't have time for his protectiveness right now. Walking up to the pair, I plaster on my most innocent expression, stopping a little further away than I might normally in an effort to escape their keen noses.

"Sorry to interrupt, gentlemen."

Coach turns, smiling fondly. "Nonsense, West. You know your input is always welcome when your father and I get into one of our discussions."

"Oh no. Not another bet, I hope. If I remember correctly, the last one ended with one of you wearing a pink tutu to all league meetings for a week."

The two men laugh.

"You're such a breath of fresh air. We're really hoping your father can convince you to come on board full-time now that you've graduated. We could use someone like you to help put a new perspective on things."

One more reason I should be grateful that Hanson has McCarren. Working with the team and being forced to be around the two of them could get awkward really fast.

"We haven't had a chance to talk about it much, but I'm sure we'll get around to it while I'm in town." I glance around, making sure there isn't anyone else within earshot. "But I actually came over here for another reason."

"Oh, what is it, biscuit?" Dad asks.

"I just ran across Hanson in the hall, and he really isn't feeling well. McCarren is going to get him home safely. I told them I'd make sure you were aware of the situation."

Coach nods knowingly. "He's been off the last few days. Might be better for him to get some rest now, so he's ready for the game this week."

I nod, holding the rising misery back until I can get the hell out of here. Now, I have the perfect excuse to dip out early.

"I promised I'd stop and grab some comfort foods and other stuff to help him feel better in a jiffy and drop them off at their place on my way home. You know me, regular ol' mother hen when one of the players is sick."

Coach smiles warmly, but I notice my dad's eyebrow raise. He's not a fool. I haven't played doctor since I was six when all the guys humored my fleeting obsession to fix their boo boos.

"Anyways, I'll get out of your hair now. I'll make sure Hanson or McCarren reaches out and updates you on his condition."

"Thanks, West. It's been great seeing you tonight. We miss you around here."

"It's great to be back home for a visit." Not thinking, I lean over, kissing my dad's cheek. He freezes when he no doubt gets a hint of Porter's scent wafting off me, but thankfully he just gives me a pointed look which I dutifully ignore. "Bye, Daddy."

"Bye, biscuit."

I blow him a kiss just before I make a beeline for the hallway. Hanson is waiting for me when I round the corner, a look of relief crossing his face.

"McCarren should be out back any minute. You ready?" I ask, keeping my distance, which doesn't go unnoticed.

He nods, grabbing his tie and jacket, then steps closer. He's studying me intently, and I must do a shit job of hiding my growing despair. Or more than likely, my souring scent gives me away.

"What's wrong?"

"Nothing. C'mon. Let's get you to your friend."

Stepping out of the alcove, I head for the door to the stairwell at the end of the hall, hoping he follows me without saying anything more. Right now, my willpower is weak at best. Holding the door for him, I glance back and see Barrett glaring down the lengthy distance between us. Whatever he sees on my face has that fury shifting to a frown.

*Later,* I mouth.

He lifts his hand as if it were a phone, the recognizable symbol for *call me.*

I nod, then turn and let the heavy door slam shut behind me.

*Fuck. One more thing I'll have to deal with.*

Lifting up my dress so I don't trip and kill myself, I follow Hanson down the million stairs between us and the exit. We're silent the entire trip to the lower level, the access door to the back parking lot waiting for us at the bottom with a flickering *Exit* sign. Hanson steps out into the night, returning the favor by holding the door for me just as McCarren pulls up in a shiny black truck. He doesn't get out, just rolls down the window.

Hanson starts to head toward the vehicle, stopping when he realizes I'm not following him. He strides back over to me, his hand trailing down my arm until his fingers twine with mine.

"You're still coming with me, right?"

"Hanson, I—"

His arm snakes around my waist, drawing me into him. His scent has grown impossibly stronger, his minty chocolate making my mouth water.

"I need you."

"But you'll have McCarren."

His brow creases. "He's my friend. We're not—"

"He's an Alpha and is way more equipped to handle your heat."

He inhales deeply, his tongue coming out to lick across his plush lower lip. "That doesn't change anything. I still want *you*."

My grin is pitiful. "We're both Omegas. It doesn't work like that."

"You're an Omega?!" McCarren barks from beside us.

I didn't even hear him leave his truck.

"I—" Hanson runs his hand along the back of his neck before he pushes his shoulders back and faces his friend. "I am. My heat is starting, and West agreed to help me through it."

McCarren looks shell shocked, but I don't miss the way he adjusts his dick in his pants.

Neither does Hanson.

"If you would rather not have to deal with it, I can find a heat suite somewhere. I'm sure—"

"Fuck no. I'm taking you back to our apartment. We'll figure it out. Together. Just like we always do."

They stare at each other, making my heart pound with the intensity of the feelings these two obviously have for one another. I can't believe they haven't seen it before this moment.

"You should both go. I bought you at least a couple of days, so check in with Coach when you're ready to tell him what's going on."

Two sets of eyes land on me, and I fight the urge to squirm.

"You said I had you for as long as I needed you."

"And now you have McCarren so you *don't* need me."

"I don't want to put words into Hanson's mouth, but I'm pretty sure at this point we *both* need you."

A whine rushes out unexpectedly, and McCarren's nostrils flare at the same time Hanson steps into me.

"Please," he whispers.

"You guys don't get it. Omegas are possessive. We don't share. Ever. Not our Alphas and *definitely* not during our heats."

"You're assuming McCarren is mine and is going to participate in my heat."

My frustration flares as hope wars with the reality I'm facing. "And you're blind and stupid if you think he's not."

He turns to his friend. "Tell her it's not like that between us."

"I..." He takes a deep breath in and exhales, adjusting his junk again. Resolve tightens his features. "I don't think I can do that. Not with you over there smelling like my favorite ice cream, making my dick rock hard in my pants."

Hanson's eyes go wide.

"Told you so," I murmur smugly.

His eyes narrow when they turn back to me.

"McCarren?"

"Yeah, bro."

"You want West too, though, right?"

Amber eyes lock on mine. "I do."

"Then let's prove to her that I'm not at all bothered by seeing the two of you together."

"What?" the massive Alpha rasps.

"I want you to kiss West."

# 6

## HUXLEY McCARREN

Pretty sure my brain stutters. West's gorgeous blue eyes are wide, that plump bottom lip currently being tortured between her teeth. Her scent—the richness of sugar plums and cinnamon—has taken on a spicier edge.

"Kiss her?" My voice is hoarse, and my feet have taken a couple of steps to close the distance between us without even realizing it.

"I'm not sure—"

My best friend cuts her off. "What are you so scared of, West?"

Her eyes narrow, her throat bobbing as she swallows down her denial. "Fine. But don't say I didn't warn you."

Before I can process what's happening, she steps into me, her hands sliding up the lapels of my tux, tugging me into her. She's so small she has to lean up onto her tiptoes to reach me, but that doesn't stop her.

One second, her face is inching closer, then the next, her warm lips are pressing into mine.

Something inside me rears up, possessive and fierce, while my hands land on her narrow waist, fingers flexing as I struggle to hold myself back from mauling her the way I fucking want to. A purr rumbles forth, loud and strong, and her arms slip over my shoulders, holding on tight. With the first swipe of her tongue against mine, her taste floods my mouth, both savory and sweet. A whimper pulls her mouth from mine, and I catch the first hint of mint chocolate filling the air around us.

"Okay. This backfired," Porter rasps, stepping up to West's back with his calloused hands landing over mine so that we're holding her between us. "Seeing the two of you like this is doing the exact opposite of making me possessive. I'm rock fucking hard again."

West's forehead hits my shoulder, and my purr grows louder having the two Omegas damn near in my arms. I meet Porter's eyes, a world of unspoken words passing between us.

Tonight has been a whirlwind of revelations. My almost desperate need for the gorgeous Omega in front of me that had me damn near propositioning her in the ballroom. The surprise that the man who's been a constant in my life for longer than I can remember is also an Omega. The shock that his scent makes me want to bite him then turn right around and bite West too. It's like my brain is misfiring. An Alpha isn't supposed to want *two* Omegas, right? That's not how biology works. West said it herself.

But that doesn't change the fact that the longer we stand here like this, the more I have to tamp down the urge to claim them both.

"Hux?" Porter whines.

The plea is enough to have a low growl rushing out.

"Get in the truck. Let me talk with West for a minute, then I'll get us home."

His tongue comes out, licking his lower lip before he nods. "You two don't be long, okay?"

He drops a reverent kiss on the back of West's neck before he reluctantly removes himself from our little Alpha Omega Omega sandwich and walks over to the truck door with his fists clenched by his sides. Once he's in and I hear the door shut, I glance down at the spectacular woman in my arms.

"You okay, sweet thing?"

When she lifts her head, glossy eyes connecting with mine, I can't help but lift one of my large hands to cup the side of her face. Whether it's to soothe her or myself, I'm not sure. It just feels right.

"It's not supposed to be like this. I'm not supposed to want..." She swallows harshly.

"Not supposed to want *what*?" I hedge. I need her to say the words out loud so that I can convince her she's allowed to want us and not feel the slightest bit guilty for it because I'm trying to convince myself of the same thing.

"*This*. You. *Him*. The weird connection that's lit up in my soul like a beacon calling me home."

My purr is back, and I drop my forehead to hers. "Why not just give it a chance? See where it goes. No strings attached. Porter has no idea what he's doing, and I..." I take a deep breath and exhale slowly, needing a hit of her scent to ground me. "I need you. Not just to help us through his heat, but because I want to keep you close. You're not the only one feeling this *weird connection*."

She's studying me carefully. There are a million and one reasons why she should say no. Why she should head back inside, away from this crazy situation. From *me*. The guys explained her rules. She doesn't get involved with hockey players. Ever. But fuck, I hope she's brave enough to say fuck the rules and stay.

"You know this is going to end messily. Packs don't have two Omegas, and I've seen the way you look at him. There's already a deep bond between the two of you. I'd never want to come between that."

On the few occasions I let myself think about the kind of Omega I'd want, the image didn't even come close to measuring up to her. Beautiful, smart, and thoughtful. She's the perfect fucking package, and I refuse to let her talk me or herself out of this.

"But you're missing something."

Her brows furrow deeply as her eyes dart between mine.

"What's that?"

"You haven't seen the way I, no, the way *we* look at *you*."

She gasps, her body leaning into mine.

"McCarren—"

"Call me Huxley."

"Huxley..."

My name on her lips is like a jolt to my dick. I have the strongest urge to pick her up, throw her over my shoulder, and deal with the ramifications of that later, but I fight back those instincts, knowing the decision has to be hers.

Dammit. We haven't even known her more than a few hours, but my Alpha side doesn't give two fucks. He's already claimed her for himself.

And Porter too.

*Shit.* The man I've loved for years is an Omega, and we're about to discover an entirely new side to our relationship that I never would have anticipated. I was content with how things were, but now... Now, I see that those feelings were deeper than I ever could have guessed. My heart is hammering in my chest, and my dick is pressing hard against the zipper of my pants thanks to the new spark of interest shining brightly in my soul.

"Please, West. Give us a chance."

She glances over at the truck, finding Porter leaning out the open window. Dammit. I forgot I rolled it down.

"Hanson's right, West. Please? Just tonight. If it doesn't feel right, you can walk away, and we'll pretend this never happened."

"It's not that easy. You know that," she whispers, but it doesn't seem as forceful as it did before.

Porter's grin turns wicked. "What's hard about a night of filthy sex and debauchery? Other than our dicks, of course."

Her surprised laugh has me almost desperate to get her to make that sound again.

"Well, when you put it that way..." she teases.

"So you'll come home with us?" he asks, his voice just shy of a whine.

She turns back to me, a question in her bright eyes.

"I promise. No bite. No commitments." I let the smirk quirk up the corner of my lips. "Unless you want that, of course."

Am I coming on too strong? Maybe. But there's a fire in my blood, and these two Omegas are the spark that set me ablaze. I don't see myself wanting to give that up easily.

"Okay," she says hesitantly.

"Okay?"

A grin starts to light up her face as she nods.

"Fuck," I groan.

"Well, what the hell are you waiting for? Both of you in the car. Now."

"He's awfully demanding for an Omega," she murmurs.

"Something tells me he's going to throw the book out the window and make his own rules."

"Guess we'll just have to see."

She bounces up, dropping one more kiss on my lips, then pulls away and walks over to the truck. When she gets closer, she steps up to the open window, and Porter leans a little further out to reach her.

"Last chance."

"Get that tight ass in the car, hero."

"Hero, huh?"

"You sure saved my ass when I needed you most."

She gives him the same quick kiss, pulling away with a grin. Tugging the back door open, she glances over her shoulder, blue eyes landing on me. "You coming?"

"Oh, I will be."

She bites that damn lower lip again, and I growl into the night surrounding us. Her giggle mixes with Porter's deep chuckle, and the sound of their joint laughter sparks something fiercely possessive in my chest. I make it to the driver door, their combined scents rushing over me the second it's open, forcing me to fight back another growl. I'm turning into a fucking feral beast, but I need to focus, drive, and get us back to our place safely before I do something really fucking stupid like pull over on the side of the road and fuck them both senseless in the back seat.

# 1

## NASH DANIELS

The door slams shut behind me, and I drop my bag next to the sofa. We fucking lost. It wasn't a close game, either. It was a fucking *shutout*, and Coach blames me, says my head wasn't in it.

Yeah, no fucking shit. Because all I could fucking think about was West fucking Carter and the sweet luxuriousness of her goddamn scent. Even now, my dick is getting hard. I have to force back a growl or risk looking like a raving goddamn lunatic.

"Guess that means we're not celebrating at the club tonight?" Ziggy asks, walking out of his room with a pint of butter pecan ice cream and a spoon.

The snarl slips from my throat unbidden, but the Beta doesn't even flinch. Looking at his gray beanie covering his mop of messy blond hair and blue eyes that are innocently blank, my anger dissipates before it can gain steam.

"No. No celebration."

"Need a beer?" He dips his spoon into the container, then holds out a glob of partially melting goo that's nearly dripping off the edge. "Or a bite of ice cream?"

"A beer isn't going to cut it, and that shit looks nasty, bro."

"This is life, man. You're missing out."

I roll my eyes, striding into our ultra-modern kitchen with stark white glossy cabinets and opening the one designated for our liquor stash. It's not like either of us can fucking cook, so the entire high-end room with its top of the line appliances are lost on us.

The whiskey is calling my name, so I snatch the bottle along with a glass, carting both into the living room. The floor-to-ceiling windows show off the Chicago skyline, all lit up and gleaming while the rest of the world is dark. Dropping onto the sofa, the leather creaks under my ass, and I wonder, not for the first time, why we didn't splurge on comfort rather than aesthetics. Fuck knows no one ever comes here. I don't have any friends other than Zig because I refuse to let people in. Stubborn fucker just skirted all my roadblocks.

"Whiskey. Damn. Okay. That's the kind of night we're in for. Got it."

He rustles through the cabinet as I pour myself a drink, meeting me on the sofa and holding out a glass of his own.

"Might as well join you so we both can suffer tomorrow."

That's what I like about Ziggy. He has this insane ability to calm me down no matter what happens. His muted scent is like laundry fresh out of the dryer, and it soothes me every damn time. I tell myself I keep him around because he latched on to me like a burr in my ass when we were in college and I could never pry the fucker off. In truth, it's because he's one of the few people in my life I trust implicitly, and now I don't want to.

"Wanna talk about it?" he asks casually.

"If I say no?"

"Then I'll just ask again in a few minutes when you've thrown back a couple more drinks, then again a few more after that until you spill your guts. Either way, you'll tell me. How drunk you are when you finally do is up to you."

I snort, throw back the last of the whiskey in the glass, then pour myself another. It's not that I don't want to tell Ziggy. It's that my brain is still processing the fact that this woman has gotten so deep under my skin that it's starting to affect my game. It's something I was sure could never happen, but here I am. If *I* can't understand what's happening, how am I supposed to explain it to someone else? I try to get my thoughts in order, figuring that starting from the beginning where everything went to shit is probably as good a place as any.

"I met West Carter yesterday."

His head slowly turns toward me, his glass paused at his lips.

"And?"

"You know who she is, right?"

"Hockey's darling. Rich as sin. Gorgeous. Moved to Chicago to go to school." He takes a sip of his drink, staring at the wall as he thinks. "I've heard that she has this rule about hockey players. And that—"

"How the hell do you know all this shit?"

"You forget I'm a *professor* at the University of Chicago—where she was a student—bro. I've got my hand in *all* the gossip, and West Carter was *always* a source of gossip. Not because she's trouble or anything. Just because she's constantly in the news, with the media following her around like a pack of hungry wolves."

"Was she ever in one of your classes?"

"No, but she was in a friend of mine's. He said she was smart, a great student, and not as much of a socialite as the media would have you believe. He said she's actually really down to earth."

Well, that's not helping at all. If she was a total bitch, maybe I could talk myself down from this precarious ledge I seem to be balanced on. Hearing him extoll her virtues is doing the opposite.

"What did *you* think of her? By the look on your face right now, I'm pretty sure I could make some educated guesses."

"She's a rich, entitled brat."

"Your mouth says one thing. Your dick says another." He nods toward the tent in my sweats.

"I didn't say she wasn't hot as fuck." I roll my eyes, letting my mind replay our encounter for the millionth time, and something that feels a lot like grudging respect settles uncomfortably in my gut. "Did you know she can actually play hockey?"

He shakes his head. Glancing out the window, the lights blinking on in the distance lull me deeper into the memory—her skill, the plush lips, that cocky attitude—and fuck if those aren't just as tempting as her goddamn scent.

"She's impressive as fuck on the ice, smells like sin, and has a wicked mouth on her."

"You like her."

My gaze whips toward him. "I didn't say that. I told you she's a goddamn brat."

He rolls his eyes. "Which means she's a challenge and you like her. *A lot.*"

"Fuck no, bro. I don't have time for any girl, let alone one that has a huge warning sign flashing above her head. She's hands off."

"What do your instincts say about that?"

My fingers tighten around my glass of whiskey, nostrils flaring.

"Yeah. That's what I thought. So what are you going to do about it?"

"Nothing."

"Dude, look, I know the shit going on back home is fucking with your head, and that definitely puts a wrench into things, but biology wants what it wants. There's very little that can dissuade it from pushing you into the path destined for you. Keep that in mind when that stubborn streak you're so famous for rears up."

He tosses his whiskey back, holding out his glass. I swallow down the last of mine and pour refills for us both.

"I wouldn't be good for her. She's all pampered Omega, and I'm a surly Alpha. She's all sunshine, and I'm all-consuming darkness. I don't belong in her world any more than she belongs in mine. Biology got it wrong this time."

"Dude, biology never gets it wrong. We just fight against it. I could drone on about the numerous theories on bonds and the underlying root benefits of pack, or—"

"Fuck. Please don't. I've heard enough of that hippy dippy shit to last me until my dying breath."

One blond brow raises dramatically high. "All I'm saying is she doesn't have a pack yet, and from the rumors around campus, it wasn't for lack of trying. Men are intimidated by her and her celebrity. They can't handle the pressure. You could."

The moon is high in the sky tonight as I look over the city that's become my home. I left my family behind a long time ago—a dysfunctional pack of belligerent assholes who are constantly trying to milk me for money. Always telling me I'm not good enough and will never amount to anything. Siblings threatening to share my dirty secrets with the press if I don't pay to dig them out of their latest get-rich-quick scheme.

The idea of pack is something I'm utterly unfamiliar with. This idea that you love and support each other is as foreign as another language on my tongue, but there's a small part buried under all that trauma that is trying to push its way to the surface, and the lovely Omega is no doubt to blame. I can't be what she needs though. I'm too broken. Too dickish. She needs an Alpha who can coddle her and tell her she's pretty, not push her to her knees and tell her to be a good girl while she sucks their cock.

Fuck. That image has said cock throbbing in my sweats. She'd look so pretty staring up at me, lips swollen and pink, mascara running down her flushed cheeks from gagging on my dick. A whine leaving her lips when she begs for my knot. Her pussy drenched in her slick as I thrust in knot deep.

"If you're going to have a wet dream right out here in the open, at least give me the play by play so I can jack off to secondhand arousal."

My head drops back with a groan, and the image vanishes, replaced by a burning need in my gut that I've never experienced before.

"Just promise me this, bro." Zig sits forward, forearms resting on his knees with the glass hanging between them. "If you ever get another shot with her, don't blow it, okay? Be open to the possibilities biology has laid out before you."

Just like that, she's back, laid out on my bed, eager and wanting.

Maybe Zig is right. Maybe if we ever cross paths again, I could see what all the Omega hype is about. Give her one night. Rock her world and work her out of my system. Sounds like a brilliant plan to me. Biology doesn't dictate my life. I do. Because I'm Nash "The Beast" Daniels, and no fucking beauty is going to slay me. Not even West "Bright Eyes" Carter.

# 8

## PORTER HANSON

The gut-churning need is back—the blood in my veins a rising inferno that has a whine echoing around the empty room. A haze descends over my vision. The world around me is surrounded by halos of color that shift when the bathroom light hits them even though it's been dimmed as low as it can go.

*How the hell do Omegas deal with this shit? It's like a bad trip, but without the drugs to get you there.*

For the first time in my life, I feel completely out of control, and that's where I'm struggling the most. I'm not sure how I got from the car up to our apartment, and I only vaguely remember West getting me situated in the bath. A ragged exhale escapes as my hands grip the edges of the tub.

Porter Hanson, badass right wing and co-captain of the Phoenix Heat, is currently sitting chest deep in goddamn *bubbles*. Even now, a denial nearly bursts from my mouth, but then this warm fuzzy feeling explodes through my chest thanks to the care and attention West has been showering me with. I've never taken a bubble bath in my life, but I grudgingly admit it's now on my must-have heat list because this shit is highly underestimated.

My head drops back against the slight curve of the modern clawfoot tub, my body sinking lower to let the warm water ease tense muscles. The movement has the water sliding over my skin, which has become hyper sensitive. The heavy weight of my cock rests against my belly, familiar yet not. Unerringly, my hand slips around it, testing it in my grip. It's the same, but also different. Seemingly thicker, but also *softer* somehow. Even once it starts to harden in my fist, there's a certain plushness that's most definitely fucking new.

A groan echoes off the tiled walls, my fever spiking as my hips buck, searching for more. More what, I'm not sure. There's just this steadily increasing ache that's becoming downright painful. My hand tightens around my throbbing dick, and the movement of the water reminds me of the warm wetness of West's mouth as she gagged on me. My breath comes in rough pants, my body demanding things that I don't know how to interpret. This isn't simple need. This is lust on steroids, making me worse than a prepubescent boy willing to stick his dick in whatever hole is provided. I'm pretty sure I'd fuck any somewhat pliable surface right now if given half the chance.

I hear murmurs passing in the hall, West's sexy cadence mixing with Hux's deeper tones, and my mind shifts to my best friend. Tall, broad, and muscular. He's built like a lumberjack, rather than a hockey player, his beard long and full, with biceps that could swing an ax—or a goalie's stick—for hours without getting tired. The thought of him using that incredible strength with me has another whine revving up in my chest. Suddenly, I'm imagining West's mouth around my cock while Hux holds me in place and shoves his big dick in my ass.

"Holy fuck," I rasp. My hips thrust against my hand so hard that the bubbles have parted. The head of my cock pops up above the water, and that's all it takes.

The sight of the angry red of my shaft, thick precum dripping liberally from the tip, makes me come so hard it shoots up toward my chest. I continue to pump uncontrollably into my fist, and my body sinks back beneath the surface, cum continuing to pour out under the water as my release seems to go on forever. My balls become almost pained when the unending orgasm does nothing to cool the fervor inside me. If anything, it's like pouring gasoline on a fire.

I don't realize I'm whimpering, or that my grip on my cock has gotten so tight it's probably cutting off circulation, until I feel cool fingers brushing my hair out of my eyes.

"Shhh. I know. We're going to make it all better. Don't worry."

My eyes pop open, and West is staring down at me, her brows adorably furrowed. I should be embarrassed that she caught me jacking off in the tub. We barely know each other, after all, and in the course of a couple hours, she's already seen me come twice, but there's an understanding expression peering down at me.

"West—"

"I know, sugar. Let's get you out of there. The nest is ready."

Nest. Fuck. I have a goddamn nest. The way my heart beats loudly in my chest tells me part of me *really* likes the idea of that.

I stand, slowly, on shaky legs. She grabs a towel off the warmer beside the tub, and when I try to reach for it, she just tsks at me. Reaching up on tiptoes, she dries off my hair, my face, my neck and chest, then her hands dip lower. It's not at all sexual, but that doesn't stop my mind from sinking right the fuck into the gutter.

She's wearing a Heat t-shirt that's a couple sizes too big and a pair of boxers that are rolled up around her waist. They must be mine because she'd be swimming in Huxley's. The sight of her in my clothes is the sexiest thing I've ever seen.

*I need to be inside her. Now.*

Before she can guess my intentions, I rip the towel from her hand, tossing it off to the side of the bathroom as I step out of the tub. In the next second, she's in my arms, her long, powerful legs wrapping around my waist and delicate fingers sliding through my hair.

"I'm supposed to be taking care of you," she murmurs, her voice breathy.

"You're an Omega too, are you not?"

"I am, but—"

I drop my mouth to hers, kissing her until I hear the telltale whimper I'm already becoming intimately acquainted with. Only then do I pull back, just enough to look into her eyes.

"I'm not going to be a great Omega. I'm going to do this all wrong. Are you okay with that?"

"Hanson, there's no such thing as—"

"It's Porter, hero."

She smiles softly. "Porter, there's no right or wrong. I'm just enjoying taking care of you."

"Good. Because it's my turn to return the favor."

Heading for the door, which she thankfully left open, I head into what used to be an empty room we only used for storage. In the span of an hour, West and Hux transformed this space into a masculine-looking nest. Both of our mattresses are on the floor, covered in mismatched bedding. Every pillow we own is piled against the walls, and blankets that came from who the fuck knows where are stacked on one of the armchairs from the living room that is now set into the corner next to a small side table. The window has a dark sheet over it, blocking out the sun, but the lamp they added casts a warm glow on us as we walk in.

"Wow."

"I know it's not the best, but I figured—"

"It's perfect," I whisper.

Her eyes land on mine.

"You deserve more."

"I've got everything I deserve right here."

Her cheeks turn a pretty shade of pink, and her breath hitches.

"Where's Hux?" I manage to ask as I kneel on the mattress, laying us down so that I'm completely covering her small frame.

"I sent him out to grab a few things we may need. He said it was probably better if you and I, um..."

"Got things started?"

She nods, and the way she bites that lower lip makes me want to do filthy things to her. A snarl escapes, making her eyes go wide, and my dick nestles its weeping self into the soft apex of her thighs.

Staring down at her, I feel a moment's hesitation. "I know I begged you to be here, but you can still say no."

"Now, why would I do a stupid thing like that?"

Her smile makes her eyes sparkle in the dim light, and the need to have her becomes immeasurable.

"Hero..."

"Take me, Porter. Any way you want me."

She sits up just long enough to pull the t-shirt over her head and slide the boxers down her thick thighs, and I'm struck speechless. This woman is perfection. Round tits with pink pebbled nipples. Hips that flare just enough to form a perfect place for my hands to hold. A pussy that's so pink and wet I'm stroking my aching dick before I even realize it.

She spreads her legs wider to give me a better view, a wicked grin on her face.

"Let me help you feel better, sugar." She quirks her finger in a come here gesture, and I'm helpless but to obey.

My body settles on top of hers, skin on skin, and the breath rushes from my lungs.

"Fuck, you're so soft...*everywhere.*"

Her hands trail up my neck while her heels wrap around my back. "Just wait until you're inside me."

My hips roll back, the head of my dick finding her center. Her body immediately squeezes the tip as it pushes in and out of her wet heat, and I don't try to stifle my groan.

"Fuck."

"That's it. Give it to me, Porter. Don't be shy."

A growl rolls up my throat, rumbling my chest, and I thrust forward, slamming in balls deep. Her back bows off the bed, and she cries out, but it's muffled under the haze that's descended even more fully in my mind—this animalistic need to fuck burning in my blood.

My hips slam into her fast and hard, drawing little mewling noises from her lips as her heels dig into my ass. I'm chasing my release, desperate to stay lucid enough to make sure she gets hers, and her pussy tightens around me, trying to clamp down on my length, probably aching for a knot. A lucid thought breaks through the fog.

*What if this isn't enough for her? What if* I'm *not enough?*

"I'm... Fuck, I'm close, Porter."

Her words soothe the rising panic, and just like that, I feel like I can breathe again. Suddenly, I can think of nothing but this fierce longing for her to come, to lock around my thick Omega cock to see just what can happen when two Omegas come together.

"Touch yourself for me, hero. Fucking come for me," I command.

My eyes track the movement of her hand. It slips between us, her fingertips skimming over her clit with rough strokes. My eyes are glued to the spot where we're connected, my balls aching with the overwhelming need for release, but I continue to plunge into her wet heat, sucking back the whine in my throat.

"Oh, fuck, Porter. So. Good. I—"

I feel it then—her body tightening around me to lock me in place. I swell inside her, this incredible pressure making it almost impossible to pull out. My body drops to hers as I instinctually rut into her, my release barreling through me. My forehead drops to her shoulder, her fingers digging into my hair and gripping so tightly I moan. The rhythmic squeezing of my dick feels fucking fantastic, but underneath it all is a steady demand for more.

"That's it, sugar," she murmurs, her voice hoarse. "You feel so goddamn good. Use me. Fuck me. I'm... I think I might—"

My body refuses to stop moving. Her pheromones mix with mine, creating an intoxicating combination that I can't begin to describe. The spicy cinnamon mixing with my chocolate-tinged scent is just adding fuel to the fire boiling inside me. Her pussy tightens around me further, a strangled moan rushing out of me as I grind my dick into her.

I'm still coming when she peaks again, gasping for breath. It's not until it slowly begins to taper off that I realize I'm practically pushing her into the mattress with my weight.

"Shit!" I try to push myself up but barely have any strength left in my muscles. "I'm sorry. I—"

"Don't move yet. You feel—" Her hips rock, forcing another strangled groan from my chest. "So good, Porter. I had no idea."

Lifting up, I stare down into her eyes that have darkened into a pretty seafoam blue. All of my insecurities rush forward again when she glances up at me.

"Not as good as a knot."

Those pretty eyes narrow. "I wouldn't know, actually. Omegas don't always need a knot or a lock, Porter. We can get off just fine without them. Unless this wasn't good for you?"

"Are you kidding? This was, hands down, the best sex of my life."

The corner of her lips curves up in a smug smirk. "Oh just you wait, sugar. When we get that Alpha in here for you, you won't even be able to speak coherently."

My entire being goes still. This intense need to reassure her floods through me, demanding I make her understand something I'm not sure *I* fully understand yet, though I've already begun to come to terms with my sudden feelings where she's concerned.

"You know you're enough, right? I'd be okay with anything that happens or doesn't happen with Hux and me because I've got you here by my side."

It's the truth, I realize. She's everything I've ever dreamed of having. Of course, Hux joining whatever this is between us would be the cherry on top of our little Omega sundae. I just have to figure out a way to ensure they're both willing to stay when this is all over. If I get my way, they'll be as invested in each other as they are me. Or is that being too presumptuous here, with my heat frying my brain cells?

She studies me carefully, her lower lip being abused by her teeth. Bending down, I suck her lip into my mouth, right along with her gasp. Her hips roll against mine, making my dick slide through the mixture of her slick and my release, and we mewl in unison. Her back bows, breasts pressing into my chest, and I'm hard all over again.

She somehow manages to catch me off guard, pushing her hips up and effectively rolling us over until she's straddling my waist, poised above me, looking like a goddess descended to earth to give me orgasms. Or at least that's what my heat-baked brain thinks.

"I'm going to ride this weeping Omega cock now, sugar. You okay with that?"

Without waiting for a reply, she begins to fuck me senseless. One second, she's rocking on top of me, holding her glorious fucking tits. The next, her hands are planted on my chest and mine on her hips as I roughly thrust into her from below.

"West..."

Her knowing smile has a whine bursting from my lips. "You need to come again, sugar?"

I nod, my eyes squeezing shut tightly, more than a little desperate.

"Eyes on me, Porter."

Immediately, they snap open, connecting with hers.

"Please," I cry, my fingertips digging into her hips.

She doesn't complain, just leans down until her nose is trailing up my throat. I tilt it back instinctively, opening myself up to her even though I know she's only an Omega.

"Bite me. Please, West. I... I need you to bite me."

"Sure, sugar. I'll bite you real good." Her tongue slides up my sweat-drenched skin. "But only if you bite me too."

"Oh fuck." My dick *really* likes the thought of that. Possessiveness rears up at the thought of claiming her. Making her mine is suddenly the sole focus of my entire being, which is something I've never experienced. Not even with Hux. "Okay."

My head lifts, lips kissing along her shoulder, my dick still impaling her pretty pussy.

"You ready, Porter? Ready to be mine?"

My heart sings even though logically I know that her bite won't connect us the way an Alpha's would. Omegas don't get to have that power in a relationship.

"I'm yours, West. Have been since the moment I saw you."

She hums. "And I'm yours, Porter. For as long as you'll have me."

She says it so softly that I start to confess that I want her forever, but then I feel her teeth grazing my neck, and the words die on my lips as all blood rushes to my dick. She bites into my throat, an almost purr breaking through the haze. Without thought, I bite down on her shoulder until the copper tang of her blood bursts on my tongue, and we groan in unison as we come with a ferocity that has the world narrowing to a pinpoint around me until all I can feel is her.

West Carter is fucking *mine*.

# 9

## WEST CARTER

In the deepest recesses of my soul, the faintest hint of shock, then confusion, and finally heartwarming joy burst into existence. For a moment, I'm too overwhelmed by the most intense orgasm of my life to realize that something inside me is different. *Changed.* It isn't until the euphoria starts to ebb that I pay closer attention to that added bit of *something* now residing inside me.

"West?" Porter's voice is full of awe and something else I can't quite place.

Lifting my head, a lock of hair falls into my face, but his hand is there to tenderly tuck it behind my ear.

"Yeah?"

He's studying me with eager yet cautious eyes, and wonder gently bubbles up inside me. Which seems...out of place.

"Do you feel it?" he whispers reverently.

"Feel what?"

His brows knit in confusion. "I thought... Well, for a second I could've sworn..."

Panic begins to rise up, swift and fierce, along with the smallest niggle of fluttering disappointment that most definitely is not my own.

"Porter..." My voice is hoarse, my rising anxiety sending my nerves into a tailspin.

We're both Omegas. Omegas can't form pack bonds. *Right?* I would've known that, *surely*. I mean, I've been an Omega practically my entire life. *Someone* would have warned me. My dad would have covered that in one of the awkward sex talks we had when I hit my teen years... Wouldn't he?

"Shhh," he soothes. "I'm sure it's just a...a fluke. It can't be *permanent?*"

It's not a statement, but a question. My brain frantically tries to process *exactly* what it is that I'm feeling, working through all the possible explanations, but I only come up with one.

*Holy. Motherfucking. Omega. Fuckery.*

"We're bonded," I rasp, eyes widening.

He swallows harshly, his Adam's apple bobbing. "I was too scared to say that word. Didn't want to send you running."

I blink. My chest tightens as the ramifications of what we inadvertently did come into full focus.

"We're *pack*, Porter!"

"It...um... It appears that way, yes," he murmurs.

With his dick still firmly rooted inside me, I search within myself, finding the burgeoning connection sparking to life between us. It's soft and pliable, bending to my will as I attempt to reach out to it in my mind. The rush of panic starts to ease once the overwhelming warmth of the bond begins to spread through me. At least until the realization of what I just forced him into hits me like a sledgehammer.

My eyes lock onto the bite mark still swollen and red on his throat.

"Oh my god, Porter. I'm... I'm so sorry! I... I didn't know. I didn't mean to... How in the hell did this even..." I try to pull away, but he just tugs me back down. "I've always been an Omega and didn't even fucking know this was a possibility. I... I'm not the one in the throes of a heat. I should've been more careful and—"

A thick finger lands across my lips.

"This isn't solely on you, West. I begged for it, and if I'm honest..." His eyes shift to a spot just above my head, avoiding my gaze, and the silence draws out as the seconds tick by.

"Porter?" When he doesn't respond, I pull that dude move I've only ever seen in movies, gripping his chin and tilting his face down until we're eye to eye. "I always want you to be honest with me, even if it hurts, okay? I'm a big girl. I can take it."

My belly flips as the words spew from my mouth. If he's regretting what happened, the reality of being tied to me for eternity, I'll face it head on. No matter what he says, it's my fault. He's in heat, so of-fucking-course he's going to beg for a bite, but I've been an Omega since my early teens. I should know better. Although nothing could've prepared me for *this*—two Omegas fucking *bonding* each other.

"Hey. Don't do that. I don't regret it." He pulls me down until the tips of our noses touch, his eyes staring longingly into mine. "I'm... I'm really fucking happy, actually. Now I don't have to convince you of forever because we already have it. I just..."

His eyes close, nose scrunching up as the first trickles of sincerity and excitement start to make their way to me in the bond. He's purposely pushing his feelings, one by one, through our new connection, and I'm fucking blown away by what he's experiencing right now.

My heart is pounding rapidly in my chest, but the longer I sit here and look down at my Omega—fuck, that sounds weird—calm begins to seep into me. Sure, we barely know each other, and fuck knows this wasn't planned, but there's this sort of *rightness* about it all too.

The sound of the front door opening and closing has our eyes widening. Porter sits up, the slide of his dick inside me making my walls clench tight around him. His groan brings a completely inappropriate smile to my face considering the situation we're facing.

"Fuck, hero, you're so fucking warm and wet, squeezing your Omega's dick so damn good."

Him vocally reinforcing my earlier thought has me preening on the inside. *I* just claimed the pretty new Omega. Though if I called him pretty out loud, I'm not at all sure he'd appreciate it. Unable to stop myself, I lean forward and swipe my tongue across my mark on his throat. He groans, his hips rolling beneath me.

"Again," he begs. "Fuck, please do it again."

So I do, feeling his lips pressing against his mark on my shoulder. There's an answering tug in my pussy at the first lick against the soreness there. His need mixes with mine until we're wrapped around each other tightly, our hips grinding together while we tend the bites that have drawn us into this mess. Through the bond, I'm getting hits of Porter's heat, a sort of foggy halo tainting the edge of my consciousness, but I push through it, determined to stay as clear headed as possible.

"Porter," I murmur against his skin, "do we tell Huxley?"

"Tell Huxley *what*?"

Our heads snap up, and we turn to stare at the large man taking up most of the doorway. His hair is starting to pull free from the tight knot at the top of his head, and his dress shirt is unbuttoned down to his chest, showing off a spattering of chest hair that has me licking my lips. A brown paper bag dangles from his gigantic hand.

For long minutes, no one speaks, then Huxley clears his throat. "Sorry. I...uh... I tried to knock. No one answered, so I figured I'd just drop this stuff off and...*go*?"

Porter and I share a meaningful look, but I don't need that to know just how much my Omega wants his best friend. I can feel it inside me, coiling around my own need for the giant man whose cheeks have turned the slightest bit pink.

"You want him to go, hero?" Porter asks, his voice low and sensual.

"No. Do you?"

Porter shakes his head. "But you should know that Hux and I have no secrets between us."

One brow quirks up as a smirk spreads across my lips. I lean forward, whispering in his ear, "Except that you're both attracted to each other."

It's Porter's turn to blush as he inhales deeply and lets the air out in a rough sigh.

"Except that," he whispers back.

When I turn to Huxley, his nostrils are flared—our combined scents no doubt pungent in the small room—and his fist is clenching around the top of the bag while the other grips the doorjamb so tightly I'm surprised he hasn't dented the wood.

"Tell me to go, and I... I will, I swear." His voice is gruff, the bulge behind the zipper of his dress pants telling me just how much that statement would cost him if he were forced to walk away.

"Join us, Hux. She doesn't bite."

I snort. "Actually, I do."

The completely ironic comment breaks through what was left of my panic, though nerves still simmer in my belly when I think of the big man beside us.

Porter's smile grows wide, his eyes meeting mine. "Yeah. I take that back. She bites, but you'll like it."

Huxley's eyes flash, the muscles in his jaw clenching as he continues to hold on tightly to that impressive control of his. I want to see what will happen when he finally gives in to it instead.

"Come here, big guy." I hold out my hand, palm up.

His arm falls to his side when he straightens and closes the distance between us. He's so fucking tall, I have to bend my head back to stare up at him from his best friend's lap.

"Fuck, you two look..." Hux groans, his fingers tangling in mine.

"Like yours?" Porter whispers.

Huxley's growl is quick and fierce. There's this flash of doubt in the back of my mind. What if he wants Porter and not me? What if I've read the entire situation wrong? I've tied myself to the man he so obviously wants. We're a package deal now. There's no me without him, and if Huxley doesn't accept that... With that thought, my stomach drops to the floor.

"Huxley..." I swallow harshly. "There's something you need to know."

Tearing his eyes off Porter, his searing look turns to me. For a long second, I almost chicken out, but then Porter's arms tighten around me. With our fingers still interlinked, I draw Huxley's hand up and brush against the mark—*my* mark—on his best friend's neck. Porter whimpers, and Huxley's fiery eyes return to me, unerringly finding the mark on my opposite shoulder.

"So things got a bit *kinky*?" His free hand drops to rub the large bulge in his pants.

"You could say it was that and so much more. We somehow...um... That is, Porter and I—"

Porter cuts me off after Huxley's brows furrow deeply. "What West is trying and failing to tell you is that we claimed each other."

"You mean, like, figuratively claimed each other, right?" Hux asks.

"We're bonded, Hux," I murmur gently. "We don't know how it happened."

His eyes widen, and his hand drops from Porter's throat like it might burn him. He doesn't speak, just stares at the marks blankly. I wish I knew what he's thinking right now because I can sense his rapid emotional retreat.

"So you're...what? Pack?" he manages to choke out.

Porter begins to whine at the look of devastation flashing across Hux's face despite his valiant effort to keep it locked up tight.

"Huxley..." I begin, but the big man shakes his head, running a hand down the back of his neck, and my heart starts to break.

"Are you sure you want me here? I don't want to be a third wheel in your new bond."

"You're not going anywhere, Hux. West may be mine, but so are you," Porter asserts, then his voice softens. "That is...if you want to be."

*Silence.*

Porter's grip on my hip tightens, and I can feel his rising panic.

Huxley drops to his knees next to Porter. There's this stillness in the room as the two men stare at each other. I'm the one that should feel like a third wheel for observing this intimate moment that's been a long time coming, if I had to guess, but I don't. Not one single fucking bit. Instead, I feel proud that they're finally getting their moment and even a hint of smugness that I may have helped make it happen in a roundabout way.

Huxley's hand returns to his best friend's neck, long fingers wrapping around the back while his thumb strokes over the mark. When his lips part, I hold my breath.

"And you are mine," he grunts before he leans forward to drop a tentative kiss on Porter's mouth.

Surprise and lust and a myriad of other emotions whip through me so fast, I can't bite back the moan quickly enough. It's like that first press of their lips together sets up a chain reaction, and the kiss goes from timid to incendiary in the blink of an eye. The sight of the two men together, losing themselves in each other for the first time, has my breath hitching in my throat. My eyes scrunch tight against the carousel of feelings that started off so slight but is gaining strength with each passing minute. I let it all wash over me, let my body just *feel*. It's goddamn *glorious*, the single most erotic thing I've ever experienced, and it's not even happening to me. I'm more than a little shocked to admit I'm damn near on the verge of coming, my pussy fluttering around Porter's cock. I'm so lost to the sensations that I don't realize they've gone quiet.

"Open your eyes, sweet thing," Huxley whispers in my ear.

I obey, my heavy-lidded gaze meeting Porter's. He murmurs against my lips, "Don't think we forgot about you."

"As if we could ever do that." Huxley's hand slips behind my neck.

I gasp, every nerve ending in my body begging for more as the weight of their stares heats my blood.

"And what about you, West. Are you mine too?" Hux asks against my lips.

"Yes. Yours," I say mindlessly, needing them more with each passing second.

His lips touch mine, and I'm lost in him. In both of them. Porter kisses his mark, tending to it as his best friend renders me speechless.

He finally pulls back, and I'm high off his rich, spicy scent mixing with Porter's sweetness.

"You don't want to miss this," Porter murmurs in my ear, drawing me back to the present and the large man in front of us.

Hux is getting to his feet, pulling his shirt out of his pants. He starts to undo the remaining buttons, and need flares hot in my belly with each inch of exposed skin. His dress shirt falls off his shoulders, and I get my first glimpse of his broad and muscular chest covered in dark hair that makes my fingers itch to touch him. Then his hands go to the belt of his pants, and something about the sound of the leather slipping through the belt loops makes my pussy strangle Porter's hard cock inside me. My Omega's head falls back with a groan, and I roll my hips as my need spikes. Or maybe it's Porter's. Who am I kidding? It's probably both of ours.

Huxley grins before he unzips the black dress slacks and pushes them down his thick, powerful legs, and those aren't the only things that are thick and powerful. My mouth goes dry at the massively full length of him, so hard and ready that I can already see the slight swell of his knot at his base. I may joke with my friends about finding a hot Alpha to knot me all night long, but the reality is that I've never experienced one, and I'm suddenly a little... Not scared, exactly. Maybe a little intimidated?

Sexy amber eyes meet mine, and we're stuck in this moment, neither of us sure who should make the next move.

"What are you waiting for, Hux? She needs you, and I want to watch every filthy second of it."

A loud rumbling purr echoes through the space as Huxley once again kneels beside us. "I'm getting to it. Patience."

Porter pouts dramatically. "Says the Alpha who isn't fighting back his heat."

I set my own needs aside, which is damn hard with an Alpha staring me down. "But this is supposed to be about you."

Porter snorts. "If you think this isn't about me, you're out of your damn mind. You swallowing me down while my best friend fucks and knots you until you scream... *Shit*. Sounds like goddamn Heaven to me."

Hux turns to me with a knowing look. "I got all the stuff you asked me to pick up."

Something passes between the two of us—a secret of what's to come for our wicked Omega. One that only we know. "Thanks, Huxley."

He smirks, and the butterflies in my belly take flight. The man is so incredibly hot that I'm surprised I haven't spontaneously combusted.

"Call me Hux. With what's about to happen here, it feels weird hearing my full name leave those swollen lips of yours."

The reminder that we barely know each other should douse the growing lust swimming in my veins, but it doesn't. If anything, it only fans the flames hotter. The heat of his body envelops me from behind, and then I'm sandwiched in between my Omega and my Alpha.

And that's just what they are. *Mine*.

The Alpha that stares at his best friend like he'd jump in front of a moving train for him. The Omega that has taken hold of my heart and refuses to let go. These men I couldn't have anticipated are making me want to keep them with a ferocity that is unexpected to say the least.

With impressive strength, Hux's arm wraps around my waist and lifts me off my Omega, who spreads his legs so I can kneel between them. Porter drops back onto the bed just as the Alpha's fingertips guide my face over my shoulder to where he's waiting. His kiss is fierce and possessive and over much too quickly. When he pulls back, his thumb swipes across my swollen lower lip.

"Be a good girl and present for your Alpha while you suck your Omega's dick."

His massive palm lands between my shoulder blades, pressing down until my face meets Porter's throbbing, needy length. Hands tangle in my hair, guiding my mouth to him.

"Open up, hero. I need my Omega to choke on my cock."

His fat head presses between my lips, stopping any further questions, just as I feel the brush of fingers through my drenched slit. Maybe I should be embarrassed—and a teensy part of me definitely is—but there's an underlying sense of elation when the first fat finger slides into me, immediately followed by two. Hux is stretching me wide, preparing me for that monster dick of his while I slurp down our Omega's thick desire.

*Holy fucking shit.*

# 10

## HUXLEY McCARREN

I'm not sure what's more surreal. The memory of my first kiss with Porter—the man I've admired my entire life—or that my fingers are pumping into the scorching drenched heat of West fucking Carter.

She's so goddamn perfect I can't wrap my brain around my reality. This isn't some really lucid dream where I wake up choking my dick with my hand.

Porter's eyes meet mine over West's shoulder, the same shoulder where his bite mark taunts me, full of promises for what will come in time. I want it all, anything he's willing to give me, and if that includes the beautiful Omega between us, I eagerly accept.

They're fucking bonded, and at first I felt like I'd been sucker punched. If they had each other, what did they need me for? Then my best friend looked me straight in the eyes and announced I was his.

Mind. Fucking. Blown.

Pretty damn Alpha-like for an Omega, I've gotta say. But I like this new blend of the man in front of me. The one who's got the Alpha bite but the Omega's need and a newfound sort of bravery to tell me that he wants me.

Now, the woman between us is swallowing him down while I prepare to fuck her like I've wanted to since the moment I laid eyes on her. How the hell is this real life?

"God, yes. Suck my cock, baby." Porter groans, his eyes still locked with mine. The desire staring back at me has a growl working itself up my throat. "Hear that, West? Hear how badly our Alpha wants to fuck you? How desperate he is to thrust that heavy knot of his in that sopping little cunt?"

He's rewarded when she whines around his dick, taking him deeper, and his fingers fist in her hair, his head falling back onto the pillows with a pained look he can't hide. His heat is present but somehow not dragging him under. At least not yet. The thought of what will happen when it does sends a rush of excitement through me, my dick aching for relief.

"Fucking hell. You two really are going to kill me," I mutter, pulling my fingers from West's body to stroke my dick while I watch the mix of her slick and Porter's cum drip out of her and run down her thighs. It shouldn't be hot. It shouldn't make me damn near come hands free, but *fuck me*. I feel like I'm ready to detonate. My brain is misfiring from the fucking perfection of their combined scents and the sight of the two of them together.

"But what a fucking way to go," Porter moans, fucking up into West's mouth as she takes him all the way to his base. "Fuck her, Hux. Show our girl just how much you want her."

*Best goddamn idea I've heard all day.*

Lining myself up, the swollen head of my cock presses into the tightest fucking pussy I've ever felt. She immediately clenches down on me so fucking hard I can't go any further.

"Relax, sweet thing," I coax, lightly trailing my fingers down her spine.

She mewls like a kitten and bows her back which juts her ass even higher in the air. My Alpha instincts go crazy. The immediate need to sink deep into her, letting my knot fit into that slot inside her pretty little Omega pussy so she can lock around me, becomes a soul-deep ache. I need to claim her just like Porter did, biting into her soft skin until I feel the burst of her blood on my tongue.

My thoughts are animalistic. Aggressive. Damn near feral. And completely unlike me.

I hesitate, meeting Porter's gaze. He must see what I'm struggling to hold back, recognizing the short leash I have on my control, and when he smirks up at me, I know I'm fucked because he's not going to help me. He's going to push me over the edge, which isn't surprising, honestly. This is the norm for us. Me holding my leash and Porter pushing me to lose my grip.

"Tell your Alpha how much you want him, hero. Tell him how badly that sweet pussy wants to gush all over his cock."

He roughly pulls her head back, her mouth popping off his dick. Her groan has my fingers digging into her hips, holding myself back, but when she whines, her swollen lips parting, I know I'm fighting a losing battle. She smells like sugar and cinnamon, her rich plum taking a back seat to the overwhelming sweetness she's giving off right now.

"Please, Hux. Fuck me. Hard. Fast. I need..." She whimpers. "I fucking need you, Alpha."

My growl is immediate and fierce. What little hold I had on my control vanishes with her plea. I'm slamming forward before I can stop myself, filling her up so fucking full that she screams. Part of me knows I should stop, make sure she's okay, but the feral Alpha inside is demanding more, demanding that we claim our Omega, while our greedy side plots to claim the other one too. One Alpha with two Omegas? That's unheard of. But fuck if I'm willing to give either of them up after this.

Pulling out, I plunge back in and watch the swell of my knot stretch her tiny hole.

"You okay, hero?" Porter asks, his voice hoarse with need that he's struggling to deny.

"I've never been more okay in my life," she gasps out.

His chest rumbles with something that sounds like a purr. "Such a good fucking girl for us, West, taking his dick like a perfect little slut." She groans loud and deep. "Now back to me, baby. Time to satisfy your Omega while your Alpha takes what's his."

Porter has always been a dirty talker. We've shared more than a couple of girls between us, and his mouth has always fueled the fire inside me. That fire has become an inferno where West is concerned. His strong hands guide her back to his dick that's dripping so much liquid the bed beneath them is soaked. He doesn't take it easy. Doesn't go slow. He thrusts into her mouth hard, making her gag, chasing his ecstasy the same way I'm already barreling toward mine with each thrust of my hips.

"Fuck. Just like that, hero. Shit, I'm... I'm gonna fucking come. Swallow every single goddamn drop. You hear me?" Porter growls.

West hums around him, and her pussy contracts around me, making me hiss.

"She's got a stranglehold on my dick. Hurry the fuck up, bro."

Porter loses the battle with his control, a ragged whine bursting free. He roughly pumps down her throat once, twice, then he's coming with the sexiest moan I've ever heard in my entire fucking life. He holds her down on his dick, her nose nestled into the hair at his base, and I watch with rapt fascination as her throat bobs with each swallow of his cum.

A pained cry splits through the hypnotizing sight, and my eyes dart up to find Porter's lips parted and strain etched across his face. He's still coming, his hands wrapped around West's head as she fucking takes everything he gives her. I don't even realize I'm growling until one of his hands falls limply to the mattress, the other stroking the back of West's neck as she pops off his cock, gasping for air.

"Son of a bitch," I ground out, so turned on that my vision is starting to go a little hazy.

His minty chocolate scent has sweetened with his release, combining with the spicy cinnamon of West's perfume, and my mouth is watering.

She glances over her shoulder, pink hair plastered on her sweat-drenched face.

"Your turn, Alpha. Knot me."

"Fuck. West, I—"

I want to tell her I'm not sure that's a good idea, that I'm pretty sure I'm going into a rut, but she doesn't give me a chance.

"Please, Hux?" she whines.

Fuck it. I might be a nice guy, but I'm not a goddamn saint. I pull my hips back, my tip barely notched into her wetness before her body tries to clamp down on me to keep me in place.

"Hold on, sweet thing. This might sting."

Slamming forward, my knot meets the resistance of her pussy, and it's like time slows. Her body struggles to relax, to take my knot the way Omegas are meant to, but it's larger than a gentle swell now. Not quite full blown, but damn close. Her head drops to Porter's thigh as he strokes her hair, whispering how she's such a good girl for taking my knot and how fucking pretty she looks, flushed and sweaty after swallowing his cum.

Leaning over her back, my mouth latches on to Porter's mark on her shoulder, sucking and licking it until her body finally gives and my knot slips into her tight little hole. There's this blinding hot bite of pleasure, her pussy locking around me and squeezing my knot until I feel like it might explode. My teeth skim over the mark, and I bite down as my orgasm rolls through me. Not hard enough to break the skin—I have barely enough control to hold myself back from going too far—but just enough that she screams my name. My Alpha side roars with triumph.

In the rush of elation, my vision narrows, and I can feel my knot swelling further as I grind into her from behind, losing myself to a rut for the first time in my life.

# 11

## PORTER HANSON

Is it wrong of me to be thankful West took one for the team and rode out Huxley's rut with him? He fucked her senseless for hours while she made sure I was taken care of as well. Her hand. Her mouth. Her breasts. I've come so many times I can't believe I'm still fucking hard.

Maybe a typical Omega would be upset about it all—their Alpha's knot deep in another Omega—but I find I'm just...*not*. They needed this time to grow the connection simmering between them. Hux and I, we're solid. Where we go from here will no doubt be easier than what he and West will face while they get to know each other. My only hope is that they'll want to keep each other as much as I want to keep the both of them once this heat is over.

That fun little quirk of biology is still battering at me, threatening to pull me under its tow despite all of the sex and orgasms. It's this burn in my gut that's demanding things there are no words for. I'm not sure I'm ready to throw my ass in the air to be fucked by my best friend when we've barely managed our first kiss—even if the fantasy in my head is on a constant playback reel.

Beside me, a sleepy Hux rolls onto his back, stretching his large body with a groan. When his eyes slowly open, blinking up at the ceiling, his hand drops to rub down his junk. I lick my lips, trying to keep the looming lust at bay because the man deserves a little rest, but when his head falls to the side and his big brown eyes meet mine, I can't stop the smirk that twists my lips.

"How ya feelin', *big guy*?"

He grimaces slightly before scanning the room, no doubt searching for West.

"She's in the bathroom *washing off the copious amounts of ick* we dirtied her up with." At his raised brows, I chuckle. "Her words. Not mine."

"Fuck. Is she..." He runs both hands down his face. "Is she okay? I can't believe I—"

"Fucked her like a wild animal?"

He curses. My best friend is a lot of things, but he's not an asshat. He's a good guy who always makes sure the women he's with are taken care of. Not that there have been many, mind you, but West isn't just any woman either. She's *special*. We both realize that.

The need to reassure him pushes to the forefront of my hazy mind. "Bro, she's fine. Sore, maybe a little tired, but otherwise smiling and happy and most of all *satisfied*."

A blush spreads across his cheeks, and the fire that I've managed to keep on a low simmer flares higher.

He sighs. "I just rutted West Carter. Is this real life?"

"As real as an Omega's heat, brother."

He turns back to me, his gaze serious. "And you? How are *you* doing considering I stole your heat toy for myself?"

My laugh is sudden and genuine. "Wonder what West would think if I called her my heat toy from now on."

His huge fist pounds into my shoulder, causing me to laugh harder. "Don't you fucking dare, bro."

"What are you gonna do about it if I do?"

"Depends."

"On what?" I murmur. His lids drop to half mast, and the need inside me rises to dangerous levels.

"Whether you meant what you said earlier, that it wasn't just the heat talking."

"About you being mine?"

He nods slowly, eyes locked on me like a predator just waiting for his prey to make the wrong move. I could blame the heat for these sudden intense feelings for my best friend, but that would be a lie. It's more the catalyst that's thrust my innermost desires—the ones I wasn't consciously aware I was harboring—out into the open, and I can't really say I'm all that upset about the end result.

"I meant every fucking word."

His nostrils flare, and he hesitates for only a moment before he leans over and places one of his massive paws in the middle of my back, tugging me toward him. Our naked bodies press together, and my dick comes to rest on top of the monster he keeps between his legs. He's still sporting a semi, but the moment our bodies collide, he grows thick and hard against my belly. Yet another reason I'm a little hesitant to take that next step. Dude's gonna break me in two with that thing, though my body doesn't seem to give two fucks about that. My dick is already leaking from the thought of him filling me up.

"Then I have ways of keeping that sinful fucking mouth shut."

A whimper skims up my throat and past my lips, the sound needy and desperate. And then he's there, swallowing it down as his mouth crashes into mine.

*Mouth shut indeed.*

Lust explodes in my veins, a desperate frenzy demanding attention as he fucks my mouth with his tongue. It's messy and uncoordinated as we learn this side of each other. He's different in so many ways. Where West has this softness I want to lead and control, Hux is solid and aggressive and unforgiving. He *consumes* me. He's all Alpha, and I find the budding Omega in me submitting to his command.

I don't even realize my hips are rolling, sending my dick sliding along the length of his, seeking friction. When his hand dips between us, long fingers wrapping around both of our cocks as I grind against him, it feels fucking amazing. There's so much wetness leaking from my tip we don't even need lube, our bodies becoming slick with my growing desire.

"Fuck, Hux. *Please.*"

He hums against my lips. "What does my dirty talking Omega need? Tell your Alpha."

"*Shit.* I need to come. Fucking please. *Please* make me come."

His hand squeezes around our dicks tighter, his hips bucking into his fist. We're sliding against each other, my slight softness to his exquisite hardness, and I groan, tilting my head, inadvertently offering my throat.

His mouth lands on West's mark, licking and sucking lightly. It's like a lightning strike. My hips thrust harder, my breath a ragged pant in my chest. When his other hand wraps around my balls, rolling them between strong fingers, I moan, my hand snaking up his neck to fist harshly in his hair.

He drags his teeth over my mark which just sends me into a frenzy.

"Bite me, Alpha. Fuck me. Please. I fucking need you."

He growls. "Not gonna bite you yet, but you're mine regardless. You hear me?" he barks into my ear.

"Yes. Yours. Fucking *hell*, Hux."

"Come, Porter. Come all over my fucking hand."

My balls draw up tight as he grips them, my release exploding out of me at his command, coating Huxley's hand and our stomachs. There's so much fucking cum because my dick just keeps pumping with each wave of my orgasm.

"Oh god," I groan, my dick still hard and aching for more. My skin feels like it's stretched too tight, my body oversensitized and needy. I can't stop the desperate grind into Hux's grip.

"You need more, baby?"

"Yes. I need—"

The click of the lock sounds moments before the door opens, shining light into the dim room. West stands in the doorway, wrapped in a fluffy white towel, wet hair dripping water down the curve of her breasts.

"I see you started the next round without me," she purrs.

Hux clears his throat. "I'm pretty sure the heat is in full swing now. He's burning up."

"Is that right, sugar? What do you need? Tell us, and we'll help you."

"Hero, get that pretty pussy over here and strangle my dick." The words come out in a growl, so different from how I was with Huxley mere minutes ago. When I look at my best friend, he's studying me intently. "I need you too, Hux."

"I'm here. We both are."

"Mmhmm," West hums, walking closer as I roll onto my back and stroke my cum-covered cock. She pulls the towel off and hands it over to Hux. "You can use this to clean up a little. Not sure I'd be too thorough since we're all about to get messy again."

He's staring at her perfect body the same way I am—with fierce longing in his gaze despite the fact that we're both sporting the evidence of our recent releases. He takes the towel, cleaning off his stomach and hand before tossing it away when he's finished. West twists her wet hair into some kind of knot, then picks up the bag Huxley brought in, sifting through it until she pulls out a package from inside.

"I've got a surprise for you, sugar."

"What is it?" I ask, and this small part of me is thrilled that she has something for me.

"A lock."

My eyes widen even as my dick jumps in my hand.

"A what?" I rasp.

"Male Omegas are made for female Alphas. Since we don't have one of those handy, this is the next best thing." She pulls out a blue rubber ring that looks a lot like a normal cock ring...until she pulls out the little remote, handing it to Hux. "You're in control, Alpha. Do your worst."

She steps over me, kneeling to straddle my legs with the ring in one hand and my cock gripped in the other. I'm slick, fluid liberally dribbling down my length. Her elegant, cool fingers slide up my length, stroking me hard and slow. My chest is rapidly rising and falling in uneven breaths, my heat damn near suffocating me. Watching her jack me off is incredibly erotic. Maybe more so because Hux is watching us both. She uses the wetness she gathered to coat the toy, and it slides over my swollen head and down my shaft with ease, fitting tightly around the base.

"This doesn't seem like such a big dea—" The rest of my sentence is cut off when West, who had shifted to be poised above my dick—drops onto my length until I'm balls deep. Her body attempts to clamp down on me, but instead, she tightens around the rubber ring. There's no time to breathe, no time to react, before Hux flicks the toy on. Its vibrations are so intense I feel fire racing up my spine.

West gasps, her eyes going glassy before her head falls back. The sight of her lost to the same ecstasy taking over my body forces a growl from my throat, and my hands clamp onto her hips as I roughly buck up into her warm pussy. It's fan-fucking-tastic, and when my orgasm hits, I come with a loud whine, warmth spilling into her while the lock tightens even more around my dick.

The sounds that are being pulled from my throat are raw and guttural, mimicking the rhythm of my hips' punishing thrusts.

"This feels... It's almost like a...like a knot. Oh my god!"

She cries out, and my eyes flash open. Huxley is leaning over me, lips fastened around one of her nipples, suckling her hard as her fingers tangle in his hair, holding him to her breast.

"Goddammit," I groan.

The haze returns to my vision as my heat overtakes me. With the ring still locked on me tightly, I'm stuck in a perpetual loop of pleasure. I'm writhing beneath West, mumbling and mostly incoherent thanks to the lust bulldozing through me. Words leave my mouth before I can fully think them through.

"Fuck me, Alpha. Knot me."

Hux pops off West's nipple, hair messy and lips swollen.

"Porter—"

My whine is loud, giving voice to the piercing ache in my chest, and I shrink back at my Alpha's unspoken denial. All logic has left the building. My grip on West becomes bruising.

"Shhh, sugar. We've got you."

When my eyes connect with hers, my gaze turns watery.

*Fuck. Me.* I've never felt anything close to the tsunami inside me right now. Desire battles against every rational instinct I have.

"He needs you," West murmurs softly, turning to Hux.

I watch their silent interaction, still grinding against West's sopping cunt, my body moving on autopilot. Hux's hand brushes a hair off my face, studying me intently. Whatever he sees there has him straightening, shoulders wide and full, then taking a deep breath. His scent grows sharper, and another whine builds on my tongue.

"Flip her over," he commands with a full Alpha bark that makes me jump to do his bidding.

In seconds, West is flat on her back with a squeal of surprise. My hips pummel into her, the new position allowing me to hit deeper into her tightness. Hux hits a button on the remote, and the vibrations grow even more intense. West whimpers beneath me, and my mouth drops to hers as I swallow it down. Fingers brush against the spot where our bodies are joined, the shock forcing me to suck in a ragged breath of air.

"You want my cock, Porter? Want me to knot this tight little virgin hole?"

It's my turn to whimper as I nod, my forehead dropping to West's.

"Need you to say the words, baby. Tell me what you need."

I gulp, preparing to beg for what my body is telling me it so eagerly wants. "Fuck me, Hux. Hard."

His slick finger rims my hole, and I tense.

"Eyes on me, sugar." West kisses my lips, her impossibly sweet scent distracting me from what my best friend is doing behind me.

At the first fiery press of his finger into my ass, I flinch.

"Feel that, sugar? Feel your Alpha preparing your ass for his cock?"

Her words have my hips bucking involuntarily, his finger slipping out and then deeper into me, except this time, the pain is replaced by a sliver of pleasure. My groan is obscene.

"Mmhmm. Feels good, right?" West murmurs against my lips.

My body relaxes as Hux pumps the finger in and out, circling around the tight ring of muscle. When he pulls it out and replaces it with two, I gasp. They slide in deep, past the knuckle, and curl slightly, skimming along my upper wall, hitting a spot that has a ridiculously embarrassing sound rushing out.

"He's so fucking tight," Hux says, plunging those two fingers in and out, over and over until I'm fucking back against his hand with West's warmth hugging my dick snugly.

His fingers disappear, and the whine that echoes through the room is deep and gut wrenching.

"One more, baby. Gotta stretch you out for my dick, then I'll fuck you so good."

The tight ring of muscle fights against the three fingers demanding entrance into my asshole as I grit my teeth. When a rough hand runs along my spine, up into my hair, and tugs lightly, my back bows and my body gives just enough that Hux can push three thick digits into me. There's a pinch of pain, but it's like my body welcomes it—welcomes the demand of my Alpha behind me because it knows it's finally going to get the release we so desperately need.

"Look at you taking your Alpha's fingers so good, sugar."

"*Our*," I choke out. "Our Alpha's fingers..."

West just hums against my lips, and I kiss her fiercely. Hux pulls his hand back, and something soft and thick prods my ass, replacing his fingers. I lose myself to West's mouth, the squeezing of her pussy around my cock, and the slow press of Hux's dick into my ass.

"Breathe, baby," Hux croons softly. "Look at this sexy ass taking my dick."

His words have a part of me preening, and warmth fills my chest at the thought of pleasing my Alpha. No, not just my Alpha. Hux, my best friend, the one who knows me better than anyone else. Taking this step will cement the ties between us in a new way that can't be broken or loosened, and the thrill of that has me breathless all over again.

Then the vibrations in the ring shift, the rhythm switching to two long strokes followed by three rapid ones, then starting all over again. My body can't process all of the sensations. I'm drowning under the lust inundating my soul.

"Oh fuck. Oh god. Please," I beg, my voice a barely there rasp. "Fuck me, Alpha. Make me yours."

His growl is the only warning I get before he slams the rest of the way in.

I call out his name, my body going taut as my dick sinks deeper into West. The lock tightens to the point of pain when her body clamps down around me. Hux pulls out and slams in again, the stretch of him inside me fucking perfect even with the bite of stinging pain. His hand is still in my hair, fingers tightening and pulling my head back. Our bodies are pounding together, skin slapping against skin, creating the most erotic sound I've ever heard.

"Knot him, Alpha. Fucking claim your Omega," West groans, her voice sounding far away in my mind.

"Is our pretty little Omega right, baby? You need my knot?"

"Goddammit, yes. Fill my ass, Alpha. Give me your knot. Bite me. Claim me. Fucking *please*."

The rumble of Hux's growl is the spark my heat was waiting for. That and the fat knot that slams into my hole, making me scream. My orgasm hits me like a freight train, every muscle in my body seizing as Hux grinds into my ass and West's pussy fastens around me, the lock damn near cutting off circulation to my dick.

I don't even care. I lose myself under the wave of my heat, not bothering to come up for air.

## 12

### WEST CARTER

My phone rings, and I cringe, seeing Barrett's picture pop up on the screen. It's the one I took when I was eighteen and conned him into going to prom with me. Or maybe it was the other way around considering he cockblocked me all night. He pretended not to notice the spiked punch I kept sneaking, so the details are a little murky.

I've got five voicemails and at least twenty texts that I've ignored over the last two and a half days, but now it's time to face the firing squad.

"Hey, B. What's up?" I chirp sweetly.

He growls loudly enough that I have to pull the phone away from my ear. "West Carter, if you don't tell me where you are and what you're doing right now, so help me God, I will put out an APB on your ass."

"I'm sorry. I've just been super busy, catching up with old friends and—"

"Don't bullshit me, Carter. The only friends you still talk to live in Chicago near you. If you're where I think you are, those boys are going to end up with their faces on missing persons fliers."

Hux walks out of the makeshift nest, shorts hanging low on his hips, chest completely bare, and I get so distracted I forget to warn him to be quiet. One muscular arm wraps around me, tugging me into his side as he nuzzles into my hair.

"You hungry, sweet thing?" he murmurs seductively.

Barrett's growl echoes through the speaker.

"They're dead men walking, Carter. Tell them to watch their fucking backs because they won't see me coming until it's too late."

Hux's head whips up, eyes wide. "Matthews?" he mouths.

I nod, and his forehead hits my shoulder with a groan.

"Barrett, I'm a grown ass woman. You do not get to dictate who I can and can't sleep with."

I realize my mistake too late.

"You're *fucking* McCarren?" he snarls.

My hackles rise. Bitch-mode activated. "And Hanson too. There's been some kinky three-way action happening the last couple of days."

Rub salt right in that wound. Though I suppose it's also better to get it all out now than risk drawing his ire later. It'll give him time to come to terms with the idea that I'm bonded to his teammate.

A string of curse words fly across the line, and Hux grimaces.

He whispers, "I'm gonna go warn Porter."

Kissing my temple, he retreats, and warmth rushes through me as I watch him walk away.

"Barrett," I say softly, vulnerability entering my voice unexpectedly.

He goes silent on the other end. Suddenly, I have all these emotions hitting me square in the chest as my current reality rears up and forces me to face it.

"What is it, sugar plum? Despite being super pissed off at those asshat teammates of mine, I'm not mad at you. *Never* at you. You can tell me anything."

There's the best friend I so fiercely need right now. I walk toward the floor-to-ceiling windows of Hux and Porter's lavish apartment, looking out over the Valley. I search inside myself, find Porter's flash of worry, and do my best to push calm through our bond. He responds with something warm and fuzzy that I don't want to analyze too closely while dealing with a stormy Alpha on the other end of the line.

"I need to tell you something, and I don't want you to freak out, okay?"

Another round of muttered curses hits my ears, and I roll my eyes.

"If either of them hurt you, they'll be deader than dead, you feel me?"

I snort. "You can't be deader than dead."

"Wanna bet?"

My smile is real and full even though my eyes are watery. "Porter is an Omega, Barrett. His designation came in at the charity event, and he went into heat. I... Well, I offered to help him out. One thing led to another, and, um, we sort of bondedeachother."

I say that last bit as one long word, trying to spit it out as quickly as possible. Rip that Band-Aid *right* off.

"I'm sorry. It sounded like you just said you bonded Porter, who is now suddenly an Omega. You took biology classes, West. You know that's not possible."

"And yet here we are," I say simply.

He's silent on the other end of the line, so I pull the phone back to make sure we didn't get disconnected.

"Barrett?" I whisper, my voice cracking.

"Fuck. Are you... Shit. How do you feel about that? Being bonded to another Omega? One that's a fucking *hockey* player?"

"I'm..." The bond fills with support, Porter shoring me up on the other end. "Is it weird that I'm happy? Like...*really* happy?"

Barrett heaves a resigned sigh. "It's not weird, West. If you're happy, then I'll come to terms eventually. But fuck. Why's it gotta be my co-captain? And how the fuck is Hanson an Omega?"

"I have no idea. He was surprised and a little lost. His heat was coming on, and he had no clue what to do. And before you say anything about the heat influencing anything, even before I found him in that hall—a hot mess, mind you—there was this *spark* in my soul when I first met him. I..."

"Tell me."

"I feel like I've found my people, Barrett. My *pack*. Remember all those awkward talks we used to have about boys and packs when you nominated yourself as my sidekick? You always said I'd know when it was right and not to settle. I'm not settling, B. My soul feels like it's finally found its home."

Another long sigh. "First of all, I'm not your sidekick. If anything, you're *my* sidekick. Second, I'm happy for you, kid, truly, but what about McCarren? Where does he fit into this little triangle of yours?"

"We're not... I mean, he didn't bite me..." My eyes dart to the bedroom door that Hux shut behind him, hope making my chest tight. "But I want him to," I whisper.

"And you're okay with seeing your Alpha with another Omega...assuming that's going to be a thing? I've fucking seen the way Hux looks at him."

"Trust me. It won't be an issue."

He says the one thing I've been trying to avoid thinking about. "You need to talk to your dad, sugar plum. He needs to be aware of this situation, and the team's PR and media managers will need to be looped in so they can get a head start on the sensational fury this is about to kickstart."

"What if he doesn't approve, B?"

"Little late for that now, isn't it?"

He's right. Bonds can't be undone, and like I told him earlier, I'm a grown woman. I make my own decisions. To be fair, I'm not sure why I'm worried. Dad has always supported me, even when he knew I was making bad choices. Part of growing up is learning from your mistakes, and he was always there to pick me up after the particularly hard ones.

"Yeah. It is. I'll call him after this. Maybe see if he'll meet me for lunch."

"You know I can make Porter disappear if you decide this isn't truly what you want, right? Poof. New Omega...*gone.*"

I chuckle, my worry fading with each passing second. "Don't touch my Omega, B."

"Look at you. Almost as possessive as an Alpha."

My grin is wide. "Who knows. Maybe my dad imparted some sort of latent Alpha gene which made all of this possible?"

"You are the most *Omega* Omega I've ever met. You like to be pampered despite your incessant need for independence. You love the attention even if you complain about it. You even subconsciously latched on to all of us older Alphas for support when you were struggling...because that's what Omegas do. If anything, it's all Porter's fault."

I roll my eyes. "Of course you'd think that."

"Just know I'm here if you need me. For anything, any time, okay, West?"

"Thanks, B."

"This doesn't mean those jackasses aren't going to catch heat from me and the guys. Better prepare them now, sugar plum." I groan, and he chuckles. "Take care of yourself and those boys. They're gonna need it."

He hangs up, and I stare out at the barely rising sun. I'm not sure how long I stand there, processing the messy emotions flicking through my brain, but the scent of mint chocolate chip ice cream suddenly surrounds me, swiftly followed by strong arms that wrap around me from behind.

Tender lips kiss my shoulder, right on top of his mark, and I relax back against his chest.

"You okay?" Porter asks.

I nod.

"Hux told me Matthews is super pissed. Do we need to enter witness protection?"

My laugh is loud and free, my mind settling once my Omega wraps me up in his embrace.

"He's slowly coming around to the idea, but you both should be prepared for all kinds of fuckery when you head to the rink later."

He groans playfully, but I can feel his grin against my skin.

"You're worth it."

Those simple words have my heart pounding in my chest. It's been hours since his heat broke, so I know this isn't some lust-driven declaration. It's real, making this new reality sit more calmly in my soul.

Turning in his arms, mine wrap around his back, my chin resting on his solid chest.

"You're worth it too, but B was right about one thing. I need to talk to my dad. The team needs to be prepared for the fallout of both your designation shift and our bonding."

"I'm not worried about what anyone thinks but you and Hux. Do you regret this? *Us*? I can't help but feel like it's my fault for dragging you here and taking away any choice you had in the matter."

His pretty hazel eyes remain locked on mine, his gaze serious, but I can feel the guilt and worry he's trying to hide from me.

"I don't regret a thing, Porter. You're mine now."

"And you're mine."

His kiss is soft, sweet, and romantic, lacking all of that dominant energy he gives off in the bedroom. Maybe Barrett was right. Maybe Porter is the one with the latent Alpha gene. Not that it matters to me either way.

"Where's Hux?"

"Probably wearing out the carpet in the bedroom." His eyes sparkle with silent laughter. "He wanted to give us a second alone after your call."

"You two talk at all? About where you want this to go from here?"

"A little. But I think it's pretty obvious where we stand with things now."

"You going to ask him to claim you?" I'm holding my breath, a flurry of nerves catching flight inside me.

"Eventually." The corner of his lips quirks up. "Are you?"

I don't know this man, but my soul seems to recognize him, making honesty the only possible answer here.

"I want him to. Are you okay with that?"

"Are you kidding? I wish he'd bite us right here, right now. I want to start this new life with both of you with nothing in between us."

There's a flash of a memory—dark hair and piercing blue eyes—immediately followed by guilt at the thought.

"What is it, hero?" he murmurs softly.

My phone rings, the song blaring through the quiet that has encompassed us. Glancing down at the screen, I see my dad's picture staring up at me.

"I need to take this. You okay if I slip out for a quick lunch if he can swing it? We need to get a handle on things ASAP."

His eyes narrow at my redirection, but he nods. "Go talk with your dad. He'll figure it all out and make sure we're all okay. You know that, right?"

I nod, feeling his warm lips press against mine before he pulls away.

"We'll see you at the game tonight?"

"Wouldn't miss it."

He pulls me in, hugging me tightly.

On the professional side of things, I have all the faith in the world that Maxim Carter will handle things quickly and efficiently, and we'll weather the oncoming storm as best as we can. On the personal side, well, I just hope Daddy isn't disappointed that his little girl bonded his co-captain and wants to bond his goalie too.

# 13

## WEST CARTER

The elevator dings just before the elegant lobby of Porter and Huxley's apartment building comes into view. The concierge sees my approach as I make my way toward the front door, lost in thought. There's a brief pause when he spares me a glance.

I know what he sees. A woman in a pair of too large sweats, rolled at the waist, and a Phoenix Heat t-shirt that's tied into a little knot to appear at least a teensy bit fashionable. I'm totally going to make Sports Grunge the new *in* thing. It's definitely a far cry from the ballgown I arrived in a few days ago, but considering I hadn't exactly planned for the days-long sleepover, this was the best I could do.

Wonder if he's seen this sort of scene play out often? One of the many puck bunnies shuffling out the door after a night with the guys. My good mood sours at the thought. I really know so little about them, though maybe that's a good thing. If they were bunny chasers, surely I'd have heard of their conquests by now. There's a flash of warmth through the bond, and it does exactly what he probably meant it to—draw me out of my wayward thoughts.

I clear my throat, and the concierge scurries to open the heavy glass door. Stepping out into the sunny Arizona morning, the dry desert air soothes me in a way that only it can. It's been too long since I've been back here, and my heart pangs at the wistful hint of longing that strikes right at its core. I love Chicago—the city, the hustle and bustle, the food—but I miss home. Even more now that I've got a future just waiting for me to fully grasp it.

Looking up, I find my dad's sleek black Lincoln Town Car waiting at the curb. Hopefully, he told the driver to take me by the house before meeting him at the quaint bistro we both love. As much as I love having the guys' scents surrounding me, this look isn't exactly what the media is used to seeing me in.

I haven't taken more than two or three steps before a camera and mic are thrust into my face.

"West, are you the Omega rumored to have left the charity ball with Porter Hanson?"

"Ms. Carter, rumor has it there's a love triangle occurring between an unspecified Omega, Porter Hanson, and Huxley McCarren. Is that true, and are you that Omega?"

"West, it seems like you've gotten cozy with a couple of the Phoenix Heat players. How is your father going to feel about that?"

"West, are you wearing Porter Hanson's clothes?"

A growl sneaks out. I'm being inundated with questions, and a possessive, protective side of me is rising to the forefront. The vultures have laid in wait, hoping that a newsworthy story would pop up, and I just dropped one into their goddamn laps.

"Are you sleeping with your father's players, West?"

"Who's better in bed?"

"Is Porter getting preferential treatment on the team because of his involvement with you?'

The questions devolve into a smear campaign against Porter, and my stomach pitches.

Luckily, my dad's security detail—AKA a large, bald man that looks a lot like Mr. Clean, but with more tattoos—comes to the rescue. He steps through the throng of reporters that seems to be growing by the second, gently guiding me through their persistent shouts for answers until he opens the rear door, and I slip inside. Falling to the leather seat, my head drops back as my heart tries to pummel its way out of my chest.

"I had assumed we were having a casual lunch, but I didn't think it would be quite *this* casual. It's a new look for you, biscuit."

I suck in a ragged breath at the sound of his voice. Reinforcing my bravery, I let my head fall to the side, eyeing my dad. He's taking in my choice of outfit with an amused expression crinkling the lines beside his eyes. He's in a full three-piece suit, looking put together and professional. Everything I am currently not.

"I didn't realize you were coming along for the ride."

"And miss the priceless opportunity for my daughter to explain why she's being picked up at my players' apartment building, apparently wearing their clothes, after being MIA for close to three days? Not a chance."

I groan, his chuckle making me feel like a kid caught with her hand in the cookie jar. It's always so easy between us. Ever since Mom died, it's been him and me against the world. Long trips away with the team, him and the guys helping me with my schoolwork. It's always been us two. Now, that's all about to change because of one impulsive moment that I wouldn't take back even if I could. I'm bonded to one of his players, and I'm about to set off a shit storm no one saw coming.

I'm also smart enough to know this is only the beginning. When the news catches wind of Porter's change, well... It hurts my soul to think of the most private part of his life plastered across headlines and the memes that will no doubt crop up. The Phoenix Heat are so hot they sent their new Omega co-captain *into heat*. My heart hurts already.

"Dad, I..." My voice breaks. "I'm sorry."

His weathered hand drops to the leather, his steady fingers wrapping around mine.

"There's nothing to be sorry for, darling. You're a grown woman. I try very hard not to think too deeply about what or *who* you may be doing."

"Gross, Dad," I groan.

He just laughs, the sound deep and familiar, but not even that can lighten the dark clouds rolling over me.

"You don't understand."

"Then explain it to me. Whatever it is, we'll face it together." His eyes narrow. "Unless TJ needs to turn this car around right now so I can storm that apartment and knock some heads together."

I grin even as the first tear falls. "Porter's an Omega, Dad."

His bushy brows raise dramatically high. "That...is not what I expected."

"His designation came in during the charity ball, and he went into heat. That's why he wasn't feeling well."

He blows out a deep breath. "Okay. I'll have to get the media team on it before—"

"There's more."

He studies me intently, then nods. "Okay. Hit me with it."

"We're bonded, Daddy. We're not sure how it happened." Another tear falls.

He silently assesses me for a moment until he gives up, one arm tugging me into his side as my head falls to his shoulder.

"And are you okay with that?" he asks gruffly.

"Yes," I answer without hesitation. "It feels...*right*. Like one of the missing pieces in my heart has slid into place."

"That's how it was with your mother. Just this instant sort of connection that I've never experienced with another soul."

"I miss her."

"Me too, biscuit. Me too." His sigh nearly breaks my heart. "So where does McCarren fall into all this? I'd imagine, with Hanson's Omega designation making itself known, the Alpha had to be going a little crazy with two Omegas under the same roof, especially with one of them in heat."

"Him and Porter are practically a sure bet. It's just a matter of when at this point."

"Hmmm," he hums. "And what about the two of you?"

"Would you be surprised if I told you that I want a bond with him too?"

Pushing my head back, I glance up at my daddy's strong jaw, lightly covered with a salt and pepper beard that quirks slightly with his grin.

"At this point, not much would surprise me, no."

"What do I do, Daddy? Two Omegas bonding? Sharing an Alpha? That's not normal, right?"

"What's *normal*, really, West? A construct that society shoves down our throats? You don't have to be like everyone else. Just be the strong, independent, and determined young woman you are. That's all I want for you."

Staring up at the one constant in my life, my soul settles. The final piece of acceptance has fallen into place, and having the full support of the one parent I have left just reaffirms my belief that I'm doing the right thing. To be honest, I'm astounded he's taking this so damn well.

"You really don't care that I bonded Porter, or that I want to bond Huxley? What will this mean for the team? How are you being so calm about this?"

He tsks at me. "Give me a little credit here. You act like I don't know you at all. I could tell something was going on at the charity event when you walked up smelling like Hanson's mint chocolate. Didn't take much to figure out that *something* involved the three of you when you all went radio silent at the same time." I sigh, and he hugs me tighter. "Look, don't worry about the team. I've got the media reps on standby. We'll handle any controversy."

I grimace lightly. "I'm sorry."

His head lays on top of mine. "Don't be. I just want you happy, and if those boys can help with that, then I'm all for it. Just no more surprises, okay? This old man wants peace and quiet...and a few grandkids."

Why—at that thought—my mind whips to Nash, I can't fucking fathom. The rugged Alpha with an attitude problem is brash and arrogant, not to mention he plays for a rival team. I shouldn't be attracted to him at all, but even though I try to deny it, I still get all giddy at the thought of the short moment we shared. Maybe it was just a fluke. Maybe my emotions simply latched on to his potent Alpha pheromones and that's all it was. Omega biology at work.

Porter peeks into the bond with a curiosity that is warranted considering I'm sure I'm blasting him with a healthy dose of lust on his end. I basically blow him a kiss—or at least the emotional equivalent of one through the bond.

"Your silence is not reassuring, biscuit."

Snapping out of my memories, I don't mention the six-four center of the Chicago Storm that has my brain all kinds of messed up. Because I absolutely don't want Nash Daniels. Nope. No way. Not at all.

My grin is a little lopsided when I look up at my dad. "I'll try to keep all future surprises to a minimum. Promise."

His snort tells me he doesn't believe a word of that. I'm not sure that I do either.

# 14

## NASH DANIELS

The crowd of piranhas gathering by the back entrance of the arena is loud and frenzied, but thank fuck they're focused on someone else. Wonder what one of my dipshit teammates did this time to ignite a media fury? The smirk is curving my lips before I can think better of it.

*Dumbasses.*

This is why I stick to my fucking self and keep my head down. I'm here to play hockey—the game my contract agrees to pay me good fucking money for. Why fuck that all up just to get shitfaced one night or to knot everything that moves? I swear to Christ I'm surrounded by a bunch of numbnuts.

"What the hell? Touch me again, and I'll sic the team's lawyers on you guys."

The voice has me stopping in my tracks.

The throng of reporters parts enough that I catch a glimpse of pink hair and long legs. West is attempting to move past them toward the door, but they're roughly shoving mics in her face, cameras crowding her in order to get the best shots. One of the crew gets jostled from the back, tripping and smashing into her, nearly sending her body toppling to the ground before she rights herself. Her loud whine pierces the air, and I see red. Before I even know what I'm doing, I'm storming forward, pushing bodies and equipment out of the way while people shout and curse and threaten to sue me. They can fuck right off. The woman my instincts have gone psycho for is trapped in the melee, and the Alpha inside me is demanding I get her the hell out of there. *Now.*

When I finally reach her, she's holding her arm and scowling at the guy who got knocked into her. The growl rumbles free before I can curb it. At the sound, the entire group freezes then takes a wary step back.

Fuck. What can I say? Sometimes it pays to be the asshole.

I feel fucking feral right now, wanting to rip every motherfucker's head off. It's not rational. It's one hundred percent primal. As if sensing the danger, the group holds its collective breath to avoid catching my attention. I level the jackasses with a steely glare before turning back to West. Her eyes are wide, that plump lower lip caught between her teeth and her scent sharp and bitter. Reaching up, I tug her lip free because I'm the only one that gets to torture it, and she gasps. The need to touch her is so strong that I allow my hand to cup her jaw, my fingers sliding through the silky perfection of her hair.

"You okay, bright eyes?" I manage without a hint of the snarl that wants to break free.

"Y-yes. Thank you." Her pretty lips part, and I ignore the insane urge to kiss them. "What are you doing here, Daniels?"

I grin, a real one that feels as foreign as the drumming in my chest. "Guess you missed the memo. My team is in town for the game tonight."

Her eyes go wide, and I use her surprise to curl my fingers around the back of her neck, her skin soft and warm. I try to center myself against the raging storm inside, but it doesn't work. Shooting one more look over the crowd, I curse my damn instincts. These fuckers are rabid for any hint of a story, and I may have just fucking given them one.

*Son of a bitch! Who's the numbnuts now?*

Doesn't stop my mouth though. The unrelenting fury inside spews out, aimed at the jackasses that thought it was okay to come at my girl.

My *girl? Ah, hell.*

"I catch any of you treating a player, staff, fan, or *any* fucking one like that again, and I'll handle it personally. You get me?" Everyone nods, the scent of fear thick in the air. "And this better not end up in the news or on social media, or you'll face consequences you aren't prepared for."

Another round of nods, not a single mic or camera in the air. Doesn't mean they aren't recording though. Fucking sharks.

When I glance over at West, she's staring up at me with glassy blue eyes that make my heart flip. "C'mon. Let's get you inside."

As if I've done this shit a million times before, my hand lands on her lower back, purposefully guiding her toward the player entrance. She doesn't say a word, just follows my lead, and an unexpected purr builds in my chest, but I keep that shit on lockdown because what the actual *fuck*? I'm pretty goddamn certain I've never purred in my life, but why am I not surprised that this woman would drag that out of me?

The longer the silence draws out between us, the more time I have to analyze what the hell I just did and more importantly, the reason I did it. My irritation flares, and I struggle to push back the rising fear of what could've happened if I hadn't been here.

"What the hell were you thinking?" I mutter, shoving my bag toward the keypad and waiting for the green light.

"They're not usually that pushy," she murmurs softly.

The click of the lock sounds, and I hustle her into the dimly lit hall. I should walk away now. She's inside. She's safe. But I can't. It's like my body is moving on autopilot, pushing her back against the wall before I can stop myself.

"That was fucking reckless, and I don't like it."

*Son of a fucking bitch. Shut your mouth, Daniels. Shut. Your. Motherfucking. Mouth.*

Her brows draw together, creating these adorable little ridges above her nose. I nearly roll my eyes at myself.

"What the hell do you mean?"

"Don't you have security or some shit? You shouldn't be walking back here alone."

My hand plants itself on the cement wall beside her head, and I realize just how small she is without skates on. Delicate but strong. Slender but curvy. Temptation and danger wrapped up in one all-too-alluring package. My dick stretches against the soft fabric of my sweats, desperately trying to get closer to the pretty Omega it insists is ours.

*Down, boy!*

It doesn't listen.

Her eyes narrow dangerously. "This is always how I enter the arena. Have my own badge, in fact. Not that *any* of that is your concern, by the way."

"I'm making it my concern."

With her anger comes a tart tang to her scent, along with something else that slithers through her thick plum and cinnamon decadence. It smells like some sort of spiced tea which seems somehow familiar. I'm leaning in, my nose trailing up her throat without a single thought of how inappropriate that is. I hear and ignore her rough inhale.

My growl slips out, low and deep, at the scent of another Alpha on her.

*Who. The fuck. Scent marked her?*

My Alpha is going fucking berzerk, and I'm struggling to rein him in.

"Nash?" she whispers, and I realize my nose is burrowed into her hair, picking up added hints of minty chocolate.

As I pull back, her hair falls over her shoulder, and I catch sight of the fresh bite mark.

"Who claimed you?" I demand, trying—and failing—to keep the snarl out of my voice this time.

She straightens, which puts us nose to nose, the fire in her eyes burning off the last hints of fear from just moments ago. Her lips curve in a full smile, so beautiful I damn near rub at my chest, worried I'm having a heart attack or some shit.

"That's none of your damn business," she responds sweetly.

"Bullshit. With you, bright eyes, everything is my business."

There's a flash of something across her face before a growl echoes down the hall. Huxley McCarren and Porter Hanson are walking toward us with twin looks of rage.

"Step the fuck away from her right now, Daniels," McCarren barks.

*Challenge fucking accepted.*

I smirk. "And if I don't?"

"I'll call stadium security then report you to the Center For Omega Care for fucking with a bonded Omega," Porter snaps once they stop a few feet away.

"Like I give a fuck about the CFOC. Your threats need some fucking work, Hanson," I taunt.

McCarren takes a step toward us, but Hanson holds him back.

"West, baby, you okay?" Hanson asks.

"Yeah, sugar. I'm fine."

The endearments have my inner Alpha roaring inside, demanding I show these two just who the top Alpha is around here. Not just because she's an Omega, but because she almost got hurt, or worse, without someone around to watch out for her.

"But she almost wasn't, no thanks to the two of you. The media was out for blood and nearly got hers." Their worried expressions do nothing to calm the tempest inside me. "Luckily, I was there to get her the hell away from all of them."

"Guys, I'm fine. Really," West says, which has anger replacing the worry on both men's faces once again.

"Doesn't explain why you're all up in her fucking face, bro," Hanson growls. "She's fucking mine."

My laugh is loud and instantaneous. "You're a fucking Beta, Hanson. You can't claim any fucking body."

He and McCarren share a loaded look that has me glancing down at West, who's gnawing on her lower lip. Hunger blooms bright in my gut, along with a sense of impending doom that has me swallowing harshly.

"Is he right? Are you his, bright eyes?" I whisper, like a fucking fool.

I don't want to admit that my emotions are on a goddamn roller coaster, which is making me feel like I'm gonna fucking puke. That reaction is usually reserved for phone calls from my family and visits to the dentist.

"I am," she whispers back.

Her eyes are staring into mine, and I wish like hell I could read her thoughts because she's still not moving out from under me. That's gotta mean fucking something, right?

"Back. Off. *Now*," McCarren growls again.

Reluctantly, I push off the wall even though separating myself from her is one of the hardest things I've ever had to do. But I still don't get it. A Beta can't bond an Omega, but now that there's more distance between West and I, Hanson's overly rich mint chocolate scent becomes clearer and more potent. My eyes slowly widen until I probably look like a goddamn cartoon.

"You're a fucking *Omega*?"

He grimaces, running a hand down the back of his neck before he meets my eyes. "Yeah, and I'd appreciate it if you could keep your fucking voice down. It hasn't been announced publicly yet."

I'm still processing the news that the co-captain of the Phoenix Heat is suddenly a goddamn Omega when another thought hits me. "Then there's no goddamn way you bonded her."

West finally moves, slipping past me to sidle up next to Hanson. Her hand reaches for his and grips it tightly. My jaw muscles are working overtime as I struggle to keep my instincts in check when what they really want to do is pull her right back to us.

*Mine*, the Alpha inside my head growls.

West's voice is soft when she replies, "We're not sure how it happened, but it doesn't change the fact that it *did*."

My glare shifts to McCarren. "Then what the hell is your problem? You're not even fucking bonded to her."

"Yet," is all McCarren says.

West gasps as McCarren steps up behind the two bonded Omegas, a possessive glare aimed my way.

*Oh. So it's fucking like that, is it?* Greedy fucking bastard. If he's making a play for Hanson, then why the hell does he need West too?

My blood pressure is through the goddamn roof. I need to get out of here, right now, or I risk doing something really fucking stupid like sinking my teeth into her before the other Alpha can. Fisting my hands at my side to avoid grabbing her, I stalk forward, not giving a single fuck about McCarren's growl. Bending until I'm at eye level, I stare into the sea of her sparkling eyes and have to force back the urge to throw her over my shoulder and cart her off to somewhere private.

"When you're ready for a real Alpha, bright eyes, you know where to find me."

Her swift intake of breath, followed by two snarls, is all I hear before I grab my bag and stomp off down the hall toward the locker room. I need to get my head back on straight, though I'm pretty sure that's a lost fucking cause at this point. She's invaded my senses, and there's no getting her out. The small issue of her bond with Hanson is a problem for another day. Right now, I need to prepare to face them on the ice. I'll take my frustrations out on them there.

# 15

## HUXLEY McCARREN

His scent—a rich blend of vanilla and clove and cardamom, like an expensive spiced rum—is burning my nostrils, hanging heavy in the air around us. I try to ignore the fact that West smells like him, but I fail.

Gripping her waist, I spin her into my arms and lift her off her feet to pull her in close. A surprised gasp rushes out, but I'm already nuzzling into her temple and along her jaw, a purr rattling in my chest before I hear Porter's soft chuckle beside us.

"Way to go all caveman, bro."

I grunt, not quite willing to let her go yet even though it's a possessive asshole move. My Alpha side is demanding we replace Daniels' scent with our own to make her smell like pack. If I'm honest, I'm half ready to bite her and accept the repercussions because I saw the intent on the other Alpha's face. He wants what's ours.

Soft fingers thread through my hair, digging into my scalp against the tight knot on the top of my head. I groan, damn near suffocating West in my need to get closer.

"I'm okay, big guy. He didn't do anything."

"He wanted to," I rumble deeply.

"But he didn't." She gently tugs on my hair, forcing my eyes to meet hers. "He really did save my ass out there. The reporters were in a feeding frenzy, and the one from channel twelve got shoved into me hard. It could've gotten nasty."

"We shouldn't have left you alone," I murmur, watching her lips curve into a sexy smirk.

"I'm a big girl, Hux. I've managed on my own just fine for all these years."

"But now you don't have to."

Her heart is pounding in her chest, her scent taking on a sweet edge as she stares down at me. In a short amount of time, this woman wormed her way into my heart, and there's no changing that. Porter has the same feelings plastered all over his handsome face.

"He's right, hero. You're our responsibility now. We really should've anticipated this, considering..."

He trails off, but we're all thinking the same thing. With the news catching wind of West's involvement with us, they're being more aggressive—stalking our home, the team's headquarters, and now the arena. We had assumed she'd be safe and would come to the arena with her father to watch our game tonight. If we had known they were going to part ways, we wouldn't have headed here early to meet with the Heat's PR team.

Was I relieved we arrived way before the rest of the team due to the urgent meeting with management? I'm a little ashamed to admit I was. Neither Porter nor I are looking forward to that inevitable confrontation with Barrett and the others. We're on track to reach the playoffs, and the last thing we need is inner turmoil. But for her, we'll deal with whatever comes our way because we're pack. Or at least, we will be once I work up the courage to claim them both.

It's not that I'm hesitant. They're mine, and I don't want to rush it. I want to enjoy the burn of need and the desperation that fuels those moments leading up to the bond. Need to make sure they each know I want them individually, and not just because they're already bonded to each other. With Porter, that shit will be a lot simpler since we've got a lifetime of history, but with West, that connection is still new and exciting, and I don't want to taint it.

This is all new, for all of us, but somehow it feels settled and incredibly strong. With the chaos of Porter's heat and the media, we've barely had a chance to talk about logistics. Chicago is West's home. She has a life here—friends, a condo, interests outside of hockey. There's so much we still have to learn about her, but how are we supposed to do that with two thousand miles separating us? It was hard enough leaving her to come to the arena, and look at what happened when we did. I can't imagine leaving her to fly halfway across the country.

"You know this is going to get worse before it gets better, right?" Her voice cracks, bringing me back to the present and making my heart twinge. "Maybe we should consider taking a step back until everything dies down."

My growl echoes down the empty corridor just as Porter forcefully snatches her out of my arms, setting her on her feet and bracketing her face with his strong hands.

His forehead drops to hers. "Don't you even think about it, hero. We're stronger together."

Their combined scents have soured slightly with the weight of the media scrutiny bearing down on all of us. I want to reassure them both, tell them we have nothing to worry about, it will all be fine, but I know I can't make that promise. How does an Alpha protect his pack from prying eyes that will eagerly put our lives on blast for the entertainment of others, with no regards to our feelings or the truth?

"Porter, you know as well as I do how this works. They'll latch on and not let go until a bigger story comes along. If we just wait them out, we can get back to working through all of this *quietly*, without their constant judgment hovering around us."

"I don't give a damn what the media or anyone else has to say about what's happened between us or what they'll think when they discover the truth about my designation. I've come to terms with it, and they'll have to do the same. You helped me through all of that, hero, and I'm not letting you back away from this just to give me an easy out."

Her sigh is full of unspoken words, and I wish I had the bond to help me fill in the gaps.

"You don't know what it's like, Porter, to have every minute of your life scrutinized. That's what's going to happen. They'll dig and dig and come up with some scrap they uncovered from decades ago then twist it to fit their narrative. It will be invasive and cruel and painful, and I..." Her voice is barely a whisper, broken and full of hurt she can't hide. "I don't want that for you."

I've never considered what it must have been like for her, with the media following her every move since she was just a little girl. From the outside, it's easy to forget the woman we're so enamored with was once a sad little girl who had lost her mother. They took away her ability to grieve in private. Thinking about that makes my heart hurt all over again.

"Look, we'll figure this out, you two. No need to—"

"Fuck. There you three are," Matthews calls down the hall, looking frazzled. "Carter's looking for all of you. The media has somehow caught wind of Porter's designation shift, and they're getting ballsy. Some of the news channels are doing stupid shit in order to be the first to break the story. Two reporters were just arrested for attempting to gain access to the arena by pretending to be part of the team's staff."

West pulls out of Porter's arms, whispering a soft, "See what I mean? This is just the beginning."

"We'll be okay, hero. Promise."

She stands tall and exhales a deep breath. "How bad is it, B?"

He grimaces, sparing a glance at my best friend. "You've become a big fucking meme, Hanson. #SlickOnTheIce is trending all over social media. Coach wants to see you two, and your dad would like to have a word before the game, West."

Porter curses, running a hand through his hair. There's a flash of something across West's face, a steely look that has me narrowing my eyes.

"Hey," I say softly. She turns to me, anger flooding her cheeks with a pretty pink. "We're grown men. We can handle it."

"But you shouldn't have to. I've dragged you into this mess because the media can't leave me the hell alone." She shakes her head, stepping over to Matthews. "Take me to Dad, B."

"West, wait," Porter calls out nervously as they start to walk away.

She turns, her face a shuttered mask that's completely unlike the open, smiling girl we've become so enamored with. He races toward her, tugging her into his arms.

"We'll be okay. Don't worry."

"You're right. We will. I'll make sure of it." Sliding her hand along Porter's jaw, she leans forward and kisses him slow and sweet. When she pulls back, her eyes study his intently. "Trust me?"

"Always," he murmurs.

She drops a kiss on his nose, then turns to me. "And you, big guy? Do you trust me?"

Closing the distance between us, I grip her chin, watching heat flare in those pretty blues.

"I do, but do you trust us?"

"I do." My purr echoes down the mostly empty hallway before that steely look reappears in her eyes. "But it's not a matter of trust, Hux. It's a matter of making this right. That's what I plan to do."

I've opened my mouth to tell her that we can do that together when her lips crash into mine. Her intensely rich flavor sweetens, like a sugar plum ripening on my tongue. She pulls away, stepping back and starting to walk down the hall. Matthews sends us a telling look—we're still not off the hook.

"Find Coach," he says before he follows West.

We stand there, watching them leave. My instincts are rioting over the fact that our girl just walked off with another Alpha. Even though the relationship between them isn't remotely romantic, biology doesn't give a damn.

"What do we do?" Porter asks softly.

"We do what she asked. We trust her."

"Why do I get the feeling she's about to do something really fucking stupid?"

West turns the corner and disappears from sight, and I can physically feel every muscle in my body going taut as the need to keep her close fights against the logical side of my brain that insists she's in good hands with Matthews.

"Because she probably will, but it doesn't matter. It won't change anything. When this is all over, she's gonna fucking be mine." When I turn to him, closing the distance between us, my hand grips behind his neck. With only a few inches on him, we're pretty damn close to being eye to eye. "And you too. You hear me?"

I feel his breath rush out against my lips, his body sagging into me. "Yes, Alpha."

Fuck, what those words do to me. I never would have anticipated this. Him. *Them*. But I've found my pack, and I will do whatever it takes to make sure it's safe.

When my lips touch his, he sighs, and I sip from him in a way that has my dick thickening in my pants. I know we don't have time, but I need his taste to gentle the furious Alpha inside. I've got one of my Omegas with me. Now, we just need to make sure the other doesn't slip through our grasp because as much as Porter fulfills me, I truly believe that without West to complete our connection, there will always be something missing in our bond.

When we come up for air, we share a meaningful look, and I know that we're on the same page.

"C'mon. Let's find Coach and figure this shit out."

"And West?"

"She's here, and there's no way in hell any one of us will let anything happen to her inside these walls. We'll figure out the rest after the game."

# 16

## WEST CARTER

Bad ideas are becoming my specialty. One particularly awful notion keeps playing on repeat in my brain, and I'm trying to talk myself out of it while I face down the only other people in the world who mean anything to me. Lucky for me, they're on my phone screen and not here in person.

"Are you out of your goddamn mind?" Cadence snaps.

One of my best friends is staring at me with something resembling horrified shock, and the other with a silently assessing glare.

"I assure you, I'm completely lucid."

"Obviously the fuck not if you went and bonded yourself to an *Omega*. What the actual fuck, West? Leave it to you to give biology the middle finger."

Tamping down my rising anxiety, I shrug. "It happened. There's nothing I can do about it now, not that I would."

"I told you to fuck one specific hockey player. *One.* Never did the words *go have a fucking threesome with two hockey players* leave my mouth. And then you have the audacity to get yourself packed up? For fuck's sake, West," Elliott mutters.

"Wait. Which hockey player?" Cadence asks, brow creased in confusion.

I ignore her and roll my eyes at Elle. "Oh, I'm sorry. Next time, you should really spell it out for me so I don't fuck up the details, Elle."

Her head cocks to the side. "Well? How was it?"

My head tilts at the abrupt change of subject. "The threesome?"

She shakes her head. "The knot. And the rut. I've had a threesome."

My mouth drops open, then slams closed.

Cadence jumps in, knowing I'm on the verge of a mental breakdown. "Now is not the time to sit here and discuss your random lays, Elliott. We've got some serious shit happening, and we need to help her figure out what to do about it."

Elle just crosses her arms over her chest, continuing to stare me down while my skin damn near crawls under her scrutiny.

I throw my hands in the air. "What do you even want from me right now?"

"I want to know how a normally level-headed, intelligent woman gets herself into this situation to begin with." Her lips quirk up. "I'm also *very* curious about the knotting."

"Oh, for fuck's sake. West, listen to me." Cadence rolls her steely gray eyes. "What did your dad suggest? Did he offer any solutions? He's usually *great* with this sort of thing."

My sigh hits soul deep. "He told me he'd handle it. That the media will get tired of the story eventually and it will all die down."

Cadence nods. "Sounds completely logical to me."

I snort. "When was the last time a professional hockey player turned Omega on a dime, shacked up with his longtime friend that plays on the same team in a novel-worthy bi-awakening moment, then bonded the daughter of the owner of said team who the media happens to be obsessed with?"

Silence.

Because the girls know this isn't a simple story. This is a multi-faceted one that has the potential to reach beyond the sports world and right into mainstream media. This isn't going away soon despite what my optimistic father might believe. It's going to be the tsunami of all news stories, with devastating consequences.

"She's right," Elle finally offers helpfully. "Word is already spreading like wildfire around PackChat. I wouldn't be surprised if the *Chicago Daily News* picks up on this and the whole equality factor."

My eyes narrow. "Please tell me you didn't tell your editor about this. All I need is him coercing you into using our friendship to get the inside scoop for your paper."

"As if I would. My boss knows where I stand as far as you're concerned."

Partially mollified, I turn to Cadence. "Have you heard anything from Crew or Cohen?"

She grimaces. "Not yet, but I'm sure it's only a matter of time. You know how TheOmegasGuide feels about this subject, and Bexley and Arden *adore* you, so when they hear you're involved with this, they're going to reach out. I need to know what you want me to tell them."

I glance out over the ice. The arena nearly filled to capacity for tonight's game. People with hot dogs and hockey jerseys, completely oblivious to the catastrophe brewing around them, sit, laughing and talking in their seats. I'm tucked away in the privacy of the owner's box suite, with a lavish spread of food along the side of the room. Personally, I just keep eyeing the wine and wondering how pissed off Daddy would be if I got shitfaced so I didn't have to deal with any of this...including the two men who are going to be super pissed off when they realize I meant what I said. I will literally do anything to protect them from the shit storm I've brought down on them. All I need is to take the heat off by giving the press something else to focus their attention on. Surely I can make that happen, right?

"West, you're starting to worry me," Cadence murmurs. "Do we need to catch a flight out there?"

Shaking my head, I look back at my best friend. "No. I'll be heading home after this. The guys are leaving for a string of away games."

"Then what do you want me to tell Bex?"

"I think this is something TheOmegasGuide could really use to promote true equality amongst designations. Proof that an Omega can hold a prime position within a professional sports organization and still perform his role just as well as a Beta or Alpha can."

"But?" Cadence hedges.

"Right now, it's all hitting just a little too close to home. I need to wait for the official statement to see how Porter and the PR team are planning to present his new designation to the press. Not to mention make sure he's on board with being the poster child for Omegas in professional sports. Because you know that's what this is going to be focused on. Whether he can play the game and maintain a level head without his hormones getting in the way."

"Do you think he can?" Elle asks.

I picture Porter with his dark blond hair and serious hazel eyes. He's not really full Omega when we're together, especially outside of his heat. He's strong and steady, sure of himself and who he is—even with the wrench that this has thrown into his career. It's what makes him a great player and an even better co-captain. Then there's how he is with Huxley. He's more submissive, softer even, though the man is one solid wall of muscle. Can he pack that away? Ignore the inherent draw of other Alphas on the ice and not let the pheromones get to his head? There's only one way to know.

The announcer's voice sounds through the large opening facing the rink, drawing me out of my head as the sound of skates on the ice pulls me forward.

"I think he'll excel at it, and we're about to find out."

The lights dim, and I'm walking forward. One hand grips the metal railing while the other one holds my phone. The background music gets the crowd on their feet as the voice over the loudspeaker welcomes the fans to the game and begins to announce the starting lineup. The spotlight jumps to the front of the tunnel as the music kicks up and the beat gets heavier. The fans go wild when the first player appears. Barrett rushes out, followed by Porter, Nixon, Flint, Rafferty, and finally Hux, until the entire starting lineup is on the ice. The crowd is on their feet for the home team, and I swear my heart is pounding in sync with the heavy bass throughout the arena.

The lights come up, and the Chicago Storm appear at the opening of the tunnel—Nash's familiar form barreling onto the ice. The energy in the arena is palpable for the player everyone loves to hate, sounding off with both the slight smattering of cheers and a chorus of boos from the crowd. A small spark of an idea begins to form as my body reacts to the one man I have no business wanting. Doesn't mean my instincts agree.

Both teams make their way toward the bench, and for a brief second, I swear each of the guys makes eye contact, leaving me breathless.

"Well, here we go. Let's see what your guy can do."

"My guy?" I ask absently, my mind flipping between Porter, Hux, and yes, Nash.

Memories of that moment in the hall when he crowded me against the wall play on repeat. He's so big, so...*raw*. But I... Hell, I *like* it. Maybe Elle was right after all. I bet he's a beast in bed.

Elle growls, drawing me out of my naughty daydreams. Her chin is jutted out, her incredulous expression telling me I need to pay closer fucking attention before I look like the lunatic I swore I was not.

"Porter Hanson. Phoenix Heat co-captain. New Omega. Your fucking *bond*mate."

"Oh. Right."

"Who'd you think we were talking about?" Cadence asks. "Huxley McCarren?"

Nerves threaten to close off my throat as I feel a blush flooding my cheeks.

"Yup," I chirp, a little too quickly. "Wasn't sure which one of them you meant."

Elle's eyes narrow. "You're thinking of *him*, aren't you?"

"Thinking of who?" Cadence asks innocently.

"I'm certainly the hell not."

I am. I totally fucking am. What the hell is wrong with me?

Cadence's gaze darts between the two of us, trying to figure shit out.

"You little hockey slut. You're still into him!" Elle declares, a knowing smirk tilting her full wine-colored lips.

"Who? She's still into *who*?" Cadence demands.

We have about ten more seconds before Cadence threatens some ridiculous form of retaliation. She hates secrets more than either of us do, for valid reasons.

My eyes narrow on Elle in warning. Her smirk ratchets up a notch.

"Nash Daniels."

Cadence's eyes go wide. "No fucking way!"

"Oh, yes way. Ask her about their moment on the ice before she left for Arizona."

My head drops back on a groan. These are my best friends, but even they have their tolerance limits for my bullshit. This latest news will definitely exceed that.

"And today," I mutter under my breath.

"I'm sorry. It sounded like you just said *today*. Are you leaving your two best friends, the ones who have been by your side since we were in shitty *diapers*, in the dark?" Elle shoots Cadence a smug grin. "She's holding out on us. What's the penalty for keeping secrets—*important ones*—from your besties?"

Cadence smiles. "The Sin Bin. One night, of our choosing, where the accused must supply wine and ice cream and divulge *in full descriptive detail* a play by play of an encounter of our choosing."

Elle's fist pumps in the air. "Fuck yes! Alpha knotting rut here we come!"

I laugh because how the fuck can I not? These fucking girls are psychos, but I love the hell out of them for it.

"Now spill. Nash Daniels. How the fuck does he play into this whole thing?"

Sighing, I fill Cadence in on our ice encounter, followed by today's save outside the arena.

"You mean to tell me you're bonded to an Omega and have two fucking Alphas ready to sink their teeth into you?" Elle murmurs in awe. "It's been a goddamn *week*, West."

I shrug. "I've been busy, okay? Don't judge."

"What are you going to do?" Cadence whispers. "There's no way Hanson and McCarren will even consider letting Daniels into what you're forming with them."

Barrett and Daniels skate up toward the referee for the face-off. Even from here, I can see the disdain the two men have for each other. When I find Porter, his eyes are locked onto Daniels, and Hux is in the crease just in front of the goal, hitting his stick against the ice.

The puck drops, and Barrett wins the face-off, skating around Nash and passing the puck to Porter, who flies down the ice. Players are on him, forcing him around the goal, but he doesn't ease up. He passes it over to Flint Campbell, who hits it right back as Porter circles around the Storm's left defenseman and swings the stick, sending the puck sailing past the Storm's goalie's attempt at the block and right into the net.

The crowd's collective gasp of surprise is heard over the announcer's voice as the Heat take the lead. I glance up at the TV installed on the overhang and read the text overlaid on the screen. The sports reporters' accounts of the developing story regarding Porter's designation are already starting to shift. One play, and he's already proving the naysayers wrong.

Pride rears up inside. My Omega just proved his designation doesn't mean shit when it comes to his abilities, but will it be enough?

Back down at the ice, Nash and Porter are shouting at each other, but I can't hear over the din of the crowd. That spark from earlier gains momentum. It's a horrible idea. *Awful*. But kinda brilliant too. It might just be enough to draw some of the heat off Porter and McCarren, at least where I'm concerned. They'll still talk about his designation, no doubt, but with the way he's playing tonight, they won't have much fuel for their fire there. Maybe Cadence can pull in Bex and Arden to really sway public opinion.

My plan is both brilliant and really, really stupid. I just have to hope that the guys really do trust me, or I'm dooming our pack before we can even get started.

"I recognize that look in your eye, West," Elle murmurs. "I really hope you know what you're doing."

"So do I, Elle. So do I."

*Spoiler alert: I don't.*

# 11

## WEST CARTER

It's the second intermission, so I need to make my move. With my eye on the sportscast throughout the first two periods, it was evident the media's focus definitely wasn't on the game. They were here for the story—a Beta-turned-Omega who had fallen for the team owner's daughter. Like our relationship was some sort of midafternoon soap opera.

With the Storm leading by one, I could see the frustration on my guys' faces as they headed off the ice for the locker rooms. As much as they'd deny it, the stress of the media hype is getting to them, and their game is suffering for it.

Porter nudges me in the bond, curious pokes to see if I'm okay. He's worrying...about *me*. Doesn't he understand I'm accustomed to the scrutiny? And sure, maybe they are too, to some extent, but nothing at this level. This is the kind that digs deep, finding your biggest insecurity and feeding off it. I know all too well how detrimental it can be, and that deep well of fierce protectiveness inside me is why I'm willing to do just about anything to keep the media from tainting the two men who've swept into my life like a tornado.

Taking a deep breath, I push back my love and support and pray that's enough to block out the nerves that are swirling into a toxic combo in my gut.

*Wait. Love?* I can't really *love* him yet, right? It's too soon for that, *isn't it*? Of course, what do I know of love? Is that what would send a typically levelheaded girl off to do something absolutely batshit crazy?

Fuck. Yup. Pretty sure this is love, alright.

If I think about it hard enough, I can remember my mom and dad and the love they shared. I remember being almost jealous of it as a little girl who thought the world revolved around her—as most three-year-olds do. They were always in each other's embrace, with me tugging on pant legs to be included. Daddy would lift me up and place me between them. There's never been a time in my life when I've felt more secure than that. Until now.

My belly takes a nosedive. The guys aren't the only ones who are going to flip the fuck out at my latest antics. Poor Daddy's gonna have a heart attack.

Heading out into the mass of people funneling through the arena looking for food, alcohol, and other gimmicky things they can get their hands on for way too much money, my plan, if you can even call it that, stutters in my brain. *Make a scene with Nash.* What does that look like? Well, I haven't gotten that far.

I could always call out his name from above the tunnel. Maybe throw a little wave. Add a wink for good measure. Let the media infer what they will.

*Okay. I can work with this. Let's make this Plan B because surely I can do better.*

If I *really* wanted to make a splash across the headlines, I could flash him as the team walks back through the tunnel toward the ice. Maybe get a two-fer, and not only shock the media but shock Nash so badly it throws him off his game.

*Meh. That's too desperate for my tastes. I'm not exactly ashamed of my body, but knowing my dad is here tonight, it's also not something I really want him to see either. Let's keep this as Plan C.*

What if I sparked an argument between the two of us somehow? That wouldn't be hard considering the tension that surrounds us any time we're in the same bubble.

*Potential. I like it. Plan A. Simple and less possibility of fallout after the fact.*

I'm so lost in this godawful plan as I make my way toward the player tunnel that I'm barely paying attention to my surroundings. Turning the corner, I run straight into a solid wall of muscle. Strong hands grip my biceps to steady me, and when my stunned gaze trails up, up, up, it finally lands on a pair of icy blue eyes that are staring down at me with genuine concern. The man has a square scruff-covered jaw, a thin straight nose, and plush lips that I can't help but stare at. He's attractive in a boy-next-door kind of way, if the boy next door was a hottie with broad shoulders and long, lean legs.

"Shit, sorry. You okay?" he asks. The scent of laundry fresh out of the dryer envelops me. Immediately, my nerves begin to calm, and I get the strangest urge to throw myself into his arms and ask for a hug. "Hey, wait a minute. You're West Carter."

Shaking my head to clear the Beta fog I've fallen into, I clear my throat. "I am, and you are...?"

His hands slowly slide down my arms, leaving tingles in their wake when he pulls back and shoves them into his back pockets. I fight back the disappointment that slithers through me.

"Ziggy Marshall. I'm a professor at the University of Chicago. That's actually how I recognized you. And from the news, of course."

My blush is immediate. Last thing I need is him recognizing me from the news.

*Redirect, stat.*

"You're a long way from home, Ziggy Marshall. What brings you to Arizona?"

"My roommate is on the Chicago Storm, and I occasionally get perks like free tickets to away games if I can swing the time off."

"Wow! That's really awesome." I smile, thinking of how sweet it is that his roommate gives him this opportunity. I've traveled with the team before, and they're some of the best memories of my life. "I'm...um...so sorry for not paying attention to where I was going. I should let you get back to the game."

One side of his lips quirks up, revealing an oddly adorable dimple under his scruff. "I'm in no rush. Just went to see if they had any of the new Heat jerseys in stock. Wanted to buy one so I could watch Nash flip out when he sees me wearing it."

My eyes snap up to his. "Wait. Your roommate is Nash Daniels?"

"Yesss..." he hedges. "Please don't hit me. I know he can be an asshat, but I promise he's a good guy."

The snort escapes before I can stop it. "I'm not going to hit you, but I *am* questioning your choice in friends."

"He may be rough around the edges, but Nash is fiercely loyal and protective of those he cares about." His grin widens. "And you've managed to gain his respect, even if he wouldn't come right out and admit that. Plus, he was right about one thing. You're way hotter in person."

The butterflies in my belly take flight at the inadvertent admission, but also maybe a little because this sexy man with the five o'clock shadow and yellow beanie is staring at me like an adorable puppy dog who wants to lick my face. I kind of want to burrow into that broad chest and let him.

"So, he..." I clear my throat again. "He's...um...*mentioned* me?"

That easy going expression turns wicked, and I practically melt when he takes a step closer.

"What if I told you he had?"

I lick my bottom lip and match his playful grin. "Would it be wrong if I was flattered?"

"Not at all," he murmurs.

The world around us has become completely unimportant, and I find myself locked in a staring contest with a Beta I've never met before. There's a warm and fuzzy feeling bubbling up inside and maybe a hint of panic that it's happening at all. What is wrong with me? Is my biological response malfunctioning, turning any red-blooded male into an impossible-to-resist pack magnet? It's not helping that he's the roommate of the Alpha that drives me a little crazy.

"I should really go..." I whisper, under some sort of spell the longer I stay here with him.

"Where were you headed?"

"Um..."

What the hell do I say to that? *Oh, you know, I was just on my way to create a scene with your friend to get the media's attention off my bonded Omega by giving them something else to concentrate on?*

"I was just making my way down to the ice. Really wanted to support the team up close and give them a morale boost. That's all."

*Fuck, I'm a shit liar.*

"Sure it has nothing to do with getting closer to a certain six-four, raven-haired center?" He wags his eyebrows.

I can feel the embarrassment heating my cheeks. "What? No. Of course, not."

His head cocks to the side. "Hmmm. You sure? You're pretty deep in Chicago Storm fan territory."

Glancing around, I realize he's right. I'm directly above the Storm's bench.

I sigh. "You honestly wouldn't believe me if I told you what I was going to do."

"Hmmm. Well, maybe I can help."

"Help?"

One eyebrow rises to his beanie. "You think I haven't seen the media frenzy involving you and Hanson? The reporters don't seem to want to talk about anything else."

My mouth opens and closes. I've got nothing.

His head tilts playfully. "You know, word around campus was that you were something of a savior and protector of the underdog. Wanna know what I think?"

"What?" I whisper, drawn to him when he lowers his voice and leans in.

"I think you're getting ready to do something risky in order to protect him."

"If that was the case, which it most definitely is *not*, mind you, how would you be able to help in this scenario?"

Without saying a word, he grips the neck of the jersey he's wearing and pulls it over his head in that inherently male way that females find sexy as sin. The simple black tee underneath proves the dude is way more ripped than the jersey gave him credit for, and I have to force my mouth to close or look silly with drool dribbling out. When he holds the shirt out to me, I stare down at it, admiring the way his forearms tense under the slight weight.

*Fuck. Seriously. What's wrong with me?*

"What am I supposed to do with that?"

"I dunno? Maybe *wear it?*"

"What?"

"Don't you think the media will go a little nutso to discover why you, West Carter, are wearing the rival team's apparel?"

*Shit! He's right. This is brilliant, and I don't even have to face Nash. Score!*

"Are you sure?" I deny the urge to raise it to my nose to take a good whiff.

"Oh, I'm damned sure. And I may want to see the look on Nash's face when he realizes that West Fucking Carter is wearing the Storm jersey he got me. He's going to go ape shit."

I fail to fight off my grin. He's just so laidback and easy to talk to. To hell with it. If I'm gonna do this, might as well go big, right? I slip it over my head, covering my white Phoenix Heat shirt. Sacrilegious? Maybe. But what about my plan isn't?

He leans in, rolling up the sleeves, which damn near has us nose to nose.

"I like this way more than I expected I would."

"Like what?"

"You in my clothes."

He winks. I blush.

"Come on, pretty girl. We've got a media storm to stir up."

He grips my hand in his much larger one and tugs me through the throng of people to the stairs leading down to the seats that run alongside the Chicago Storm bench.

"Where are we going?" I ask.

"My seat. Front row, right next to the bench." He turns to me with that smirk he does so well. "Perfect for what you need, am I right? It's like it was meant to be."

Air rushes into my lungs when he gives me a pointed look.

Now, here's the thing. I'm a woman, and an Omega at that. I completely understand things like biology and instincts, but this, what's happened to me over the course of barely a week? This shit ain't natural. Part of me wonders if it's all some elaborate joke or maybe a delusion. Did I have an accident? Is this all a hallucination brought on by a head injury?

There's got to be a rational explanation for a young woman, without a single potential pack in sight, to suddenly have men falling into her lap. Pity I don't mean that literally because my hungry vagina is chomping at the bit to, well, chomp on somebody's bit. My biological response doesn't give a damn that Ziggy is a Beta. It simply wants what it wants, and I'm helpless to this new fierce pull.

Ziggy drags me down to the front row, guiding me to the seat closest to the door that leads directly into the Chicago Storm's box. My nerves skyrocket.

He takes the seat next to me and drops into it. His hand grabs mine, and something about that simple connection soothes my frayed edges, giving me a level of peace I acutely need right now. We're surrounded by fans, none seeming to notice me as my eyes skim along the crowd, anxiously waiting for the teams to return to the ice. I startle when a warm hand skims along my jaw before strong fingers wrap around the back of my neck.

"West," Ziggy murmurs.

I swivel in my seat, coming face to face with the Beta who's slowly turning me inside out, and swallow harshly.

"Kiss cam," are the only words he gets out before his soft lips brush mine.

I mewl like a kitten, and instantaneous heat unfurls inside when he makes a rough sound in the back of his throat. Suddenly, the simple kiss turns into something that's not simple at all.

I barely hear the roar of the crowd or the sound of metal skidding across the ice. Almost miss the harsh banging on the plexiglass. What I don't miss at all is the Alpha snarl that has goosebumps breaking across my skin and a whine brushing past my lips that Ziggy consumes without hesitation.

One minute, I'm kissing the captivating Beta. The next, I'm roughly yanked from his grasp, spun around, and finding myself facing off with a furious Nash Daniels.

"You are not going to wear my fucking name on your back then put your goddamn lips on someone else. You're mine, West. The sooner you realize that, the better off we'll both fucking be," he growls in my face.

I'm not afraid. Quite the opposite, in fact. The heat Ziggy stirred in my blood spikes hotter and higher.

I'm pretty sure I'm not breathing when his lips smash into mine, fierce and undeniably possessive. His Alpha pheromones rush over me, making me feel a little dizzy, and two padded hands land on my back, pulling me into him until the thick metal bar of the railing is the only thing separating us.

My fists tangle in the back of his jersey, and I'm lost.

Too lost to even notice the crowd…or the kiss cam broadcasting the entire scene on the jumbo screen above the center of the ice—and probably national television too.

*Fuck. Mission accomplished?*

## 18

### WEST CARTER

I'm forced back to reality when a strong arm snakes around my waist and pulls me back into a warm, hard chest. Nash's growl is loud and fierce.

"Think you've caught everyone's attention, pretty girl. Best get you outta here before those boys of yours hit the ice and lose their minds," Ziggy whispers in my ear.

"Hands. Off," Nash snarls.

Coach Tomlinson appears just behind Nash. "Daniels, get your ass back on the bench *now*, or you'll be warming it for the rest of the game."

Nash's teeth grind together as he fights against his instincts. Slowly, his hands pull back, releasing me into Zig's hold.

"Stay with her. Don't let her out of your sight, but keep your hands and your goddamn lips to yourself," he barks to Ziggy, a hint of his Alpha power in his words, then those startling blue eyes meet mine. "We're hashing this out before I leave tonight. Don't run off, bright eyes. I don't want to be forced to come hunt you down."

He returns to the bench just as the Phoenix Heat skate out of the tunnel. They file into the box, but Porter pauses just before jumping the pony wall. Our eyes meet across the ice from where I'm standing, and his possessive stare and strained jaw aren't the only indications he knows what just went down. He's a livewire in the bond, too many emotions to even begin to wade through them all.

*Mine*, Porter mouths before he's forced to climb into the box. McCarren's too far away, already skating toward the goal box, but I have no doubt I'm going to have a shit ton of explaining to do.

"Time to go." Ziggy threads his fingers through mine, tugging me up the stairs and out into the main thoroughfare which is significantly less crowded than it was earlier now that fans have made their way back to their seats. "Which way is your suite?"

I take a deep breath, hold it in, then exhale as I try to wade through the jumbled mess of my mind.

"This way," I murmur, tugging him around the arena and through the door that leads into the box suite. We have a direct line of sight across the ice and down into the players' benches.

I pause in the center of the room, staring at nothing.

"You okay?" Ziggy asks softly, coming up beside me, our hands still intertwined.

In his eyes, I find a steadiness that breaks through some of the Alpha pheromone fog that's making it hard to think straight.

"I'm not sure," I answer honestly.

He nods, looking out as the announcer begins to recap the score, followed by the sound of the buzzer indicating the start of the third period.

"You've landed yourself in a very sticky situation, pretty girl."

"What do I do, Zig?" I whisper. "I'm bonded to a new Omega, his Alpha best friend has made it clear he wants us both, and I've got a pissed off Alpha, who also happens to be their enemy, making my heart feel funny. This can't end well."

Ziggy's calming presence helps bolster me when I feel the first tear slip through my defenses. I'm not sad. I'm not angry. I'm simply overwhelmed and confused.

"I think you're forgetting that you're an Omega, West. One who knows who she is and what she wants." When he glances down at me, there's something sparkling in his eyes that makes my belly flip. "I have no doubt you can bring these boys to heel. It won't be easy, but I'm thinking it'll be worth it."

"And you?" The words rush right past my lips before I can stop them.

The dimple digs deep into his cheek when he smiles down at me. "I'm already there."

With a squeeze of my hand, he strides forward until he finds one of the plush chairs lining the bar at the front of the suite. There's a large TV above us and a perfect view of the ice. He situates himself on the tall chair and lifts me into his lap. "Now c'mon. Let's watch the guys fight it out on the ice. It's gonna be an intense race to the finish."

I settle into the lap of the Beta who has so effortlessly taken control. Where the others all come with a certain demand for time and attention, Ziggy seems to just exist in my space, never pushing for anything and giving me more than I can begin to calculate.

Minutes tick by without a single score between the teams as Barrett and Nash fight each other for control every play. Then Porter gets the puck, moving it around the ice with that fluid grace he's known for. When he slaps his stick forward, the puck flies right through the Storm's goalie's legs, and the horn sounds. The game is tied, but that's not what has my attention.

Porter and Nash are shouting at each other, words we can't hear, then Nash throws his gloves off and charges at Porter. My Omega doesn't stand down, throwing a swing at Nash. They land a couple of good hits before the referees finally break them apart, sending them both to the penalty box.

The suite door slams open, and I jump in Ziggy's lap. My father comes storming toward us.

"What in the hell were you thinking, West?" he growls. I can count on one hand the number of times he's been truly angry with me, and this is one of them. "And who the hell is *he*?"

Ziggy stands, setting me on my feet as he faces my enraged father. "Ziggy Marshall, Mr. Carter. I'm a big fan."

Daddy's eyes narrow. "And you're in on this mess my daughter's concocted, Ziggy Marshall?"

"I am," he responds confidently. "She was going to do it alone, and I figured she'd be safer with someone by her side."

My dad blinks, and I suck my lips between my teeth to stop a smile from appearing on my face. Now is not the time. When Daddy looks back down at me, his scowl has softened slightly, but his disapproval is still plain on his face.

"Biscuit, what are you doing?"

I shrug, feigning nonchalance I'm most definitely not feeling. "Drawing attention off the guys. Giving them a little room to breathe while the media focuses on me."

"And Nash Daniels was your best option?" he barks. "Could you have picked a more divisive player?"

"I—"

"Pretty sure he's going to be fighting for her right alongside the other two, sir. He's got it bad."

Poor Daddy. His eyes are so wide I'm a little worried they may get stuck that way.

"Let me get this straight. Nash *'The Beast'* Daniels is interested in *my* daughter?"

I pray Ziggy knows what he's doing because right now, we're on very shaky ground.

"He is."

Daddy runs his hands down his face before he straightens his shoulders and levels me with a look.

"I sure as hell hope you know what you're doing, biscuit. I realize you've been looking for a pack, but establishing your own is going to take a lot of work, especially with the men you've chosen." He turns to Ziggy. "Where do you fall into this whole thing?"

"Wherever she'll have me, sir."

The poor butterflies in my belly have to be exhausted at this point.

Daddy considers him carefully. "Where are you from, Ziggy?"

"Chicago, sir. I'm a professor at the University of Chicago. Nash Daniels is my roommate."

My dad nods absently. "You're both going to have your hands full. I hope you know what you're doing." He strides forward, pulling me into a big hug. "I love you, biscuit. Be careful, you hear me?"

"I will, Daddy."

"I'll make sure she's taken care of, sir," Ziggy adds behind me.

Daddy stalks back out of the room muttering, "Time to go handle the press."

For a few moments, Ziggy and I stand there in silence. My thoughts are all over the place, and my heart is a chaotic jumble of emotions, but I can't help but voice the one thing that keeps pushing to the forefront.

"Did you mean it?" I ask softly.

I can feel his stare but can't quite bring myself to look at him. Then his fingers grip my chin and force my eyes to meet his.

"I don't say anything I don't mean, West."

I swallow down my whimper. "It's going to be messy."

That damn dimple appears again. "I like getting messy. Something tells me it will be a whole helluva lot more fun with you involved."

My cheeks heat, and I bite down on my bottom lip.

My dad was right. Hands full indeed. And probably mouth and other holes too.

# 19

## PORTER HANSON

The score is tied, and we're in overtime. Matthews, Campbell, and I are on the ice with Hux back at the goal. The first team to score, wins, and I plan to make sure that's us.

Staring across the center line, Nash Daniels is focused on Matthews with a glare so intense I can practically feel it from here. After seeing that kiss splashed across the screens in the tunnel, my emotions are in turmoil. West is all over the place in the bond, and all I want to do is find her and hold her so we can both find our balance again. Then we'll talk about whatever the hell that was…right along with where the fuck mystery dude came from.

The ref skates over, whistle in his mouth, prepared to drop the puck.

"You fucking touched West. She's hands off, Daniels," Barrett growls.

A smug smirk appears on the asshole's face. "You staking a claim too, Matthews? You sure your boys are willing to share?"

"She's ours," I growl.

Daniels' smile grows wider. "We'll see about that, now won't we?"

"Enough!" the ref barks, dropping the puck as the whistle blows.

Barrett wins the face-off, speeding around a growling Daniels toward the far end of the rink. Flint's locked up with the Storm's defenseman, but I skate a circle around the other, confusing him enough that he loses track of where I'm at. Barrett takes the opening, sending the puck speeding across the ice and right into my stick. I shoot for the goal...and miss.

*Goddammit. I need this fucking game to be over.*

The right wing for the Storm makes a push for the goal, but Hux is ready, blocking his slapshot. The game's still fucking tied. Time to end this. Hux drops the puck and passes it off to Campbell, who hurries to the other end of the rink. He passes it off to Matthews just as Daniels knocks me into the glass. Angry blue eyes collide with mine.

"She's fucking mine, Hanson. Better come to terms with that. Nothing will stop me. Not even her bonded Omega. You get me?"

He pushes off me before I can respond, and fury ignites in my blood, swift and fierce. West is mine. We're a package deal, and I'm not sure I'd ever be able to accept an Alpha who truly doesn't give a shit about my Omega. He's probably only concerned with her image and who her daddy is, not the special woman Hux and I are just barely starting to get to know. She deserves more than a prick like Nash Daniels.

"Hanson," Matthews snaps, and I shake off my anger to find Campbell in possession of the puck.

He swings behind the Storm's goal, the defensemen on his tail. I see it then, the perfect opening. I catch his eye, and he swiftly passes the puck to Matthews, who shoots it off to me. I make it right in front of the goal, the Storm's goalie still focused on Matthews, just as the puck connects with my stick. He doesn't even see me coming. With a quick strike against the puck, it goes sailing between the goalie's pads and the edge of the net.

The horn blares, and the lights flash.

*Hell yeah! We just fucking won! One step closer to the playoffs, baby.*

The team skates onto the ice as I catch Daniels' eyes over the chaos. He's smiling wider now. Then it hits me.

Holy shit. He fucking played me. With the Heat winning the game, there will be press interviews and shit. He'll get to head right to the locker room, change, and get the hell out of here. Except that's not his plan. He's making a run for West, and I just gave him the perfect fucking opportunity.

*Son of a bitch.*

I search the bond, finding West's excitement lighting up between us. Fuck, she's something. I'm not sure what the hell is going on between her and Daniels, but I need to get to the bottom of it soon.

"Great game, Hanson," Coach congratulates, patting me on the back. "You just proved that designation doesn't matter. Hockey doesn't discriminate. Way to fucking go!"

"Thanks, Coach. I'm not sure I'm ready to face the press yet. Any chance Matthews could speak for the team tonight?"

There's a knowing gleam in Coach's eye. "You got it. Those nosy fuckers don't deserve the chance to take cheap shots at you after a game like that. I'll have Matthews handle it so you can get out of here."

I nod, grateful for a coach who gets it, and that he's close with the Carters. He knows exactly why I'm so eager to get out of here.

Hux skates up, gloved hand pressing against mine, and pulls me in for a hug as he pats my head with the other. It's nothing different than we would do after any other win, but it suddenly means so much more. Being in his arms now is better than any post-game celebration we've ever attended.

"Nice goal, bro."

"Nice save."

He taps our helmets together. "Now, it's time for a different kind of save. Ready to get our girl?"

I nod. "Let's get cleaned up and go find her."

We make our way toward the tunnel with the rest of the team, heading into the locker room to undress, shower as quickly as we can, and get our suits on. The team requires players to dress professionally going to and from the game, and we rock that shit. Hux and I have entire collections of high-end suits that we've grown rather fond of.

I pull the navy pinstripe jacket over my white button down and gray tie, grabbing my bag just as Matthews and Campbell walk into the room, still in their gear. Rather than heading for the showers, they head straight for me and Hux.

"I told you she was fucking hands off, Hanson," Matthews growls. "Now, you've dragged her into this mess."

I knew it was too easy. We avoided this earlier because the talk with Coach dragged right up until game time. By the time we got to the locker room, most of the guys were already heading out for pregame warm ups. They couldn't corner us when we had a game to win, but now is a different story. Hux steps up to my side as a fully suited up Brooks flanks Campbell and now Sorensen. They're a wall of pissed off muscle looking for any excuse to hand us our asses.

How do I want to play this? Like the hard ass, or like the man who's only just discovering what it means to be in love? It's then I know exactly what to say.

"I love her. I'm sorry for the way our bond happened, but neither of us would take it back now."

Saying it out loud for the first time makes my gut pitch. The word doesn't seem fitting enough for what exists between us—basically two strangers. On the other hand, it perfectly sums up what I feel, so I straighten my shoulders, owning it.

Campbell and Sorensen go wide eyed. Brooks is still glaring with his massive arms crossed over his chest, but Matthews doesn't seem the slightest bit surprised. Thank fuck West soothed the worst of his anger over the phone.

"You're lucky she said damn near the same thing to me, or I'd be smashing your face in right now. As it stands, I've got a hands off order because I can't punch a helpless fucking Omega, now can I?"

I can hear the gentle ribbing in his tone even if it doesn't appear on his granite face.

"Helpless? Didn't seem all that helpless when I was slamming the winning goal into the net."

"You're lucky you did damn good out there tonight," Brooks mutters. "If we lost, I was going to stuff you in a locker and let the cleaning crew find you."

"This mean we can't rough him up?" Campbell asks with a pout.

Matthews sighs. "West kinda likes the guy, so no."

"Dammit," Sorensen grumbles playfully.

"And the two of you..." Matthews motions between me and Hux.

"All but bonded," Huxley proudly declares, earning a round of nods like they're not surprised by that either.

*Fuckers. Just want to give us shit when all we want to do is find our fucking girl.*

Brooks glances between me and my Alpha. "But what the hell was that with Daniels and the other guy?"

Matthews drags a hand over his sweat-damp hair with a sigh. "She's protecting them. Or thinks she is. Why the hell she'd pick that asshole, I have no idea."

"They've got some sort of history. We found them together at the entrance before the game. He's made it clear he thinks she's his."

"Over my dead fucking body," Hux growls.

Matthews shares a look with Brooks. "Look, you're both our brothers, so I'm gonna be straight with you. When I faced off with Daniels after that kiss, he was damn near feral, and West wasn't exactly trying to push him away. If it were up to me, I'd have her steer clear of all of you fuckers, but since that isn't possible anymore, then I'm fully in West's corner. Whatever she wants, she has my backing, and I'll see to it that any and all parties know that when it comes to her, I don't play around. You hurt her, you pay. Brother or not. It's as simple as that."

A round of grunts meet that statement, the others agreeing with our captain.

"We'd never hurt her."

He meets my narrow-eyed stare head on. "Maybe not intentionally, no, but if you force her to choose, it could hurt her far worse than you may realize. Consider that carefully before you go making demands. She's loyal, and that means she'll honor your bond above all else despite what her heart says."

Huxley and I share a look. We noticed her closeness with Daniels earlier. The scent of her perfume was so damn strong it was impossible to miss. There's attraction—there's no denying that. But does it go deeper? And how does the mystery guy play into all this?

Hux straightens. "I hope like hell she's not seriously considering Daniels for a mate, but if she is, then we'll work through it. She's already bonded to Hanson, and I have every intention of making us pack. I won't take advantage of the trust she's already given both of us."

Matthews steps forward, slapping me on the shoulder. "Good luck, brothers. I sure as hell hope you know what you've gotten yourselves into with that one. She's going to keep you on your toes."

I grin because I can feel her in the bond, full of anxious energy. "She already is, bro. She already is."

"And I don't want to hear shit about what y'all do behind closed doors, ya feel me? She's like my little sister, and that shit makes me want to gag."

The other guys chuckle.

Brooks shakes his head. "Tell her no more crazy stunts for a while. We could use some goddamn peace around here."

"Yeah. I'll get right on that."

# 20

## ZIGGY MARSHALL

Her hand is small in mine, and the juxtaposition of our sizes is doing weird things in my brain.

I had a few plans for this last-minute trip. Watch some hockey. Eat some bad-for-me food. Find a way to irritate Nash, just because he's so damn fun to rile up. Not once was *kiss West Carter* on that list. And there definitely wasn't any sign of metaphorically throwing myself at her feet and praying she decides to keep me.

I totally got sucked into the Omegaverse. Question is, do I even want to find my way out?

We're walking along the mostly empty halls, heading for the Phoenix Heat's locker room. The game is over, Porter Hanson having won the game by a well-played shot. I've gotta give it to the man—Omega or not, the dude can play a decent game of hockey.

Of course, I won't say that in front of Nash or risk getting my teeth knocked out.

Thoughts of my roommate and his claim on the woman walking quietly beside me bounce around in my head. From the outside looking in, there's no way these guys will ever be able to set aside their differences and make this work. As the man on the inside, able to see past their public personas, I think these men need each other. Sure, there are bound to be growing pains and some heated exchanges as they try to work around their love of the same woman, but something tells me it'll be worth it. I'll get to watch this pack form from the ground up, and I'm not sure I've ever been more excited about anything in my life...except maybe the idea that I might get to be a part of it. For the first time, I feel like I fit in. Like I belong with a growing pack where everyone is learning and growing and coming together to form something great. I can be useful in a way that most established packs don't necessarily need. I can be the neutral force that helps West bind everyone together, but more importantly, I can be West's support when the others are being dickheads.

"You're quiet," she murmurs, shooting me a hesitant glance.

"As one is when their entire world is shifting right before their eyes."

She blinks a couple of times, the corner of those plush lips quirking up. "Touché."

"I'm a little in awe of you, to be honest." I squeeze her hand a little tighter, overcome with an insane need to draw her into me and keep her close. I refrain, barely.

"In awe of me? Psssh. I'm in awe of *you*. Stepping right into the middle of the battlefield, only a kiss for a weapon and no shield in sight. You're a brave man, Ziggy Marshall."

I grin. "Brave or incredibly overconfident?"

"Probably a little of both to be fair."

I chuckle lightly even as my heart pounds fiercely in my chest. "And here you are, walking hand in hand with a guy you only met a little over an hour ago, and you call *me* brave."

"Guess we're two peas in a pod then, aren't we?"

Never in my life could I have anticipated the thrill of being compared to a green mushy vegetable that I usually despise, but I'll be damned if I'm not.

"That we are, pretty girl."

We're close to the Heat's locker room, so I know my time with her is coming to an end...at least for now. I can't help but want to leave her with a little memory of me to carry with her until I can see her again.

Stopping abruptly, I tug her into my arms, loving the little gasp of surprise that rushes through her lips. One hand snakes around her back while the other cups the side of her gorgeous face. Her eyes are sparkling, her cheeks are flushed, and I've never seen anything more beautiful.

"When will I see you?"

Her pink tongue tentatively brushes along her bottom lip, and I can feel my rock hard dick weeping in my jeans.

"The guys leave for a string of away games tomorrow night. I'll be heading back to Chicago, sooo..."

"How do I find you?"

Her head tilts playfully. "You seem like a pretty intelligent man, Ziggy Marshall. If you want to find me, you will."

A slight growl bursts free right before my lips touch hers. It's slow and sweet, her flavor on my tongue carrying hints of sugar plum and cinnamon, and I'm suddenly starving for her. But that will have to wait. Now is not the time, and this isn't the place.

"I'll find you, pretty girl. And when I do, I think I'll deserve a reward."

"A reward, huh? Have anything specific in mind?"

"So many things."

Her smile is so bright, it could light up the entire Chicago skyline. That incredible shine is probably why I don't catch a hint of the two angry hockey players until it's almost too late.

"Who the fuck *is* this dude?" a voice growls down the empty hall.

We jerk apart, but I don't let her get far. My fingers tangle with hers, needing that last connection to get me through the next couple of days.

"Guys, this is, um... This is Ziggy Marshall. He's a professor at my old college."

"You kiss all of your professors, hero?" Hanson snaps.

Her hand squeezes mine. "About that—"

"It was my fault. The kiss cam focused on us, and I just went along with it. That wasn't part of her plan."

Two angry stares turn my way. I can sense McCarren's Alpha pheromones filling the air around us, a heavy presence that tells me I need to tread carefully. Hanson's scent is sweeter, minty with a hint of bitter chocolate, but just because he's an Omega doesn't mean he can't beat my ass if I so much as twitch wrong. But I've lived with Nash for years, so there are few things that can intimidate me. It's almost as if dealing with the other Alpha's notorious mood swings has been preparing me for this moment, learning to defuse situations exactly like this where I'm facing off with an angry Alpha and unpredictable Omega.

"Doesn't explain why we just caught you kissing our girl...*again*," McCarren growls.

"Guys, let me explain—" West starts.

At the same time I say, "Look, I know I should've come to you both first, but—"

"Come to us first for what?" Hanson's hands are fisted at his sides, clenching and unclenching as if he's holding himself back from launching at me.

I run my free hand down the back of my neck as I try to put into words what I want. It all seems so impossible when I realize the woman I want to declare myself to has known me for barely over sixty minutes. Doesn't change my mind though. I want West Carter more than I want to irritate Nash, and the ferocity of that truth nearly bowls me over.

"I want to be part of your pack."

No one says a word. West's grip on my hand is so tight, her nails are digging into my skin, but that just keeps me grounded.

"West?" Hanson asks softly.

There's this moment of panic, my gut churning as all these thoughts flood through me. What will I do if she doesn't want me? Will I be able to move on from this? My heart is going to be decimated if I read this entire situation wrong and she walks away. What if—

"I want him too," she says confidently, and my heart stutters.

She's choosing me. *Me*—the man who rarely gets picked for anything. All of the men before us who passed this woman up have no idea what they're missing out on, but I do, and I may send each of them thank you cards for their stupidity.

"Do you even *know* him?" McCarren asks softly.

"I know enough." She glances at me for a brief moment. Our eyes connect, and the truth there nearly has my heart bursting from the level of sincerity shining back at me. "But there's something else you need to know."

Hanson's hands go to the top of his head, threading through his long hair. The white cuff of his dress shirt peeks out from the navy pinstripe sleeve.

"This is about Daniels, isn't it?"

She nods, swallowing harshly.

"He's my roommate," I jump in, saving her from at least that portion of the explanation.

McCarren growls, but he cuts the sound off as if it was an accident.

"Look, I know it seems a little too coincidental, but I swear to Christ I had no intention of getting involved. Then, when I did, well... There was no letting go."

Hanson and McCarren share a look, one loaded with things I can't interpret.

McCarren is the first to meet my eyes. "We understand all too well how that happens. West is an incredible woman."

"She is," I agree.

"But where does that leave Daniels?" Hanson asks.

"He wants her. Badly. Even though he tries to talk himself out of it."

Hanson looks over at his Omega, concern and deep affection apparent in the way his hazel eyes take her in. "And what about you, West? Do you want him too? Because I'm going to be honest. I'm not sure I ever see that working."

"I don't know," West whispers. "There's something there. I won't deny that. But we're kind of like oil and water, and I'm not sure I'm willing to risk what we all have together just to test the waters with Nash."

McCarren's hand lands on his pal's shoulder as they share another look. "Nothing you do will ever risk what's building between us. It's just that what we've got is still so new that the threat of our rival coming in like a wrecking ball has us on edge. But we're also smart enough to understand that we bulldozed into your life much the same way, barely a week ago. We're willing to fully support you and what you need if you're willing to be patient with us when we act like possessive fools."

She nods, biting her bottom lip between her teeth. Turning into her, my thumb wrestles it free.

"None of that, now," I rasp softly.

When I look back at the guys, their stances have relaxed. They're once again silently communicating in the way only old friends can.

Then Hanson's eyes clash with mine. "We're leaving for a couple weeks. Three away games in a row. You're in Chicago?"

"I am."

McCarren crosses his massive arms over his broad chest. "Can we trust you to keep an eye on her while we're gone? We'd feel better not leaving her alone."

"Guys, I've lived on my own for years. I don't need a babysitter."

"My first babysitting gig. I can get down with that." She laughs, and my heart pounds louder in my chest. I grin down at her. "We've got a bet going. If I can find her, I get a reward. Now, I'll have added incentive, considering I don't want her left alone either."

Her cheeks flush a pretty pink again, and I fall...hard. No way this should be happening this fast, but it is. There's no stopping it. Even when my brain tries to tell me that there are only rare reports of first-sniff scent attraction so quickly followed by intense devotion, my instincts simply tell it to shut the hell up. Look at Porter and Hux. Look at Nash. The reports are wrong.

"You can call me Hux," McCarren says, stepping forward and holding out his hand.

I shake it, his entire fist engulfing mine. The man is a giant.

"Porter." Hanson steps forward, hand out.

"Most people call me Zig," I murmur.

I'm overcome despite myself. It's not every day one goes from being mostly alone to forming a pack. I was only partially kidding when I told West my life was changing right before my eyes, but I now understand just how true that really is.

"We should get going, sweet thing," Hux says, reaching for West's hand.

She nods before glancing back at me with a questioning look.

"Go. I'll see you soon, pretty girl."

Her hand slips free from mine, and it takes an enormous amount of self-control to keep from reaching out for her again.

"Bye, Zig." She blows me a kiss.

Like a weirdo, I pretend to catch it and bring it to my lips just before the guys flank her and walk toward the exit. No sooner does the door slam shut behind them than there's a shout from the far end of the hall.

"Zig!"

Nash comes running toward me wearing a gray suit with a gray vest and black dress shirt. His shiny black dress shoes clack against the cement with each long stride he takes.

"Where is she?" he growls, bright blue eyes flashing with desperation.

My hands slide into my back pockets, wondering how I should play this. If I stall, it will give them time to get away without a scene. If I don't—

He grabs me by my biceps, brows furrowed as he growls under his breath.

"Where. Is. She?" he demands.

Now is apparently not the time to fuck around with my slightly feral Alpha friend. I know he won't intentionally hurt me, but biology is riding him hard right now, and the level of emotion he's showing is concerning. Releasing a harsh breath, I tip my head toward the door.

"She just left with Hanson and McCarren."

Before I can stop him, he's charging for the exit.

"Shit!" I curse, rushing after him. "Nash, wait!"

He's the athlete, not me. I'm not used to fucking running, and sure, my abs have gone MIA which is proof of that, but West didn't really seem to mind.

He bursts through the doors with me on his tail. Pausing, he scans the lot until he catches sight of West climbing into the back of a black SUV. He's sprinting toward them while I'm barely catching my breath. By the time he makes it to the vehicle, the door is shut and McCarren is starting to slowly pull from the parking spot.

"Open this goddamn door, McCarren!" Nash pounds on the glass, West's shocked face barely visible in the dim light shining from the parking lot lamp overhead. "You're mine, bright eyes. Don't leave with these jackasses."

The car continues to slowly pull forward, Nash following it every step of the way as West's delicate palm connects with the window.

"West!" he growls, the sound catching slightly at the end as he places his larger palm over hers atop the glass. "Please!"

The SUV pulls ahead, and Nash is forced to step back or risk getting run over. His arms fall to his sides, his chest heaving, and I stand there, unsure what to do. This is not the Nash Daniels I'm used to, and definitely not what the public is familiar with. This man is on the verge of going feral, breaking at the sight of his Omega driving away from him.

His head drops, and I know I need to do something. He's my friend, my roommate, and that's our pack right there. Where we go from here will make all the difference in how things change for us.

"Hey, you okay?" I ask softly, stepping up and gently placing my hand on his shoulder.

He whips around, eyes glassy and fury written in every line of his face.

"Do I look okay to you, Zig? She fucking left me."

"Hanson's her Omega, Nash. What did you expect?"

His eyes close before he takes a few deep breaths and slowly exhales.

"I don't know. I just..." He runs a hand over his hair. "I need to see her, Zig. My chest is tight, and my heart feels like it's going to explode. That kiss... seeing her with my name on her back... Fuck!"

"I know, brother. Trust me. I do. She's heading back to Chicago tomorrow, and the guys will be on the road. We'll find her, okay?"

His eyes snap up to mine. "How the fuck do you know all of this?"

My face scrunches up as I take a surreptitious step back. Dude's punches hurt like hell.

"How would you feel if, hypothetically, I said I wanted her too?"

He snarls, nearly foaming at the mouth. I take another step back and prepare to run, knowing damn well he can catch me. Not a runner, remember?

"What the fuck do you mean, Zig?"

"Remember that hippy dippy shit about bonds and packs you didn't want to hear the other night? Well, I'm living proof that biology gets what it wants, and it apparently wants all of us to be pack."

"All of us?" he asks menacingly.

I nod hesitantly. "Me, you, West, Porter, and Hux."

"You're on a first name goddamn basis with them now?" he shouts. "You fucking kissed her a nanosecond ago. Now, you're...what? In *love* with her?"

I shrug casually. "Maybe? I don't know yet. I'm still working through my feelings. I'm sure the same could be said about you."

He growls, the sound blasting into the night around us.

"I can't deal with this right now." He runs his hands down his face before he continues barely above a whisper. "I need her, Zig."

"Me too, brother. Me too."

I slap him on his shoulder and guide him back toward the building as the door opens. Coach Tomlinson pokes his head out.

"There you two are. Where the hell have you been? We're waiting on the bus that will take us to the airport. Get your asses back inside so we're ready to go as soon as it arrives."

"C'mon. We'll get back to Chicago, then we'll find West and figure all of this out, okay?"

"Fuck. Okay," he answers reluctantly.

As we head inside, my mind automatically starts calculating how I'm going to find her, where I'll start, and what reward I want when I do. A number of enticing images come to mind, and I find I'm not at all surprised when Nash is suddenly included in the various options.

The more the merrier is about to be my new damn motto.

## 21

### WEST CARTER

The car stops, and Porter opens the door, lifting me out before I can protest. The entire ride, we were all lost in thought as Hux navigated the busy Arizona streets. Seeing Nash so desperate to reach me really fucked with my head *and* my heart.

"Hey," Porter whispers in my ear. "We figured we'd stay at our place tonight since we're hitting the road and won't see you for a couple weeks. Unless you really want us to take you home?"

I shake my head, nuzzling along his jaw, needing his scent to steady me.

"I want to be here with you guys tonight."

Hux rounds the car, catching my eye. "You never have to ask that. You're always welcome here with us."

Porter carries me through the parking garage toward the elevator, with Hux following closely behind us. He hits the button for their apartment, and the elevator begins to move.

"We haven't talked about logistics," I murmur.

Porter's nose brushes against mine. "Logistics of what, hero?"

"You both live here in Arizona. I have an apartment in Chicago. We're not going to want to be so far apart all the time. Not counting when you all have to travel during the season, of course."

When I glance up, I see him eyeing Huxley intently.

The elevator dings, breaking their silent communication as we enter the foyer. In seconds, the door is unlocked, and their scents rush over me the moment we step inside. They're familiar, comforting, but more importantly, they smell like *home*.

Porter sets me on my feet, his eyes dropping to the jersey I'm still wearing.

"Before we dive into that, I need to get you the hell out of his jersey. You smell like *him*."

Hux chuckles, heading toward his room. "I'm going to take this shit off, then we can all talk."

Porter ignores him, too focused on getting the offending garment off me. He grabs the hem and lifts it over my head, but before he can toss it aside, I snatch it from him. That's when I see Daniels stitched onto the back.

*Fuck. I had no idea.*

"This is Ziggy's." I narrow my eyes but let a slight grin tilt my lips. "Don't want you to get any crazy ideas like stealing it to burn it or something."

"How'd you know what I was going to do?" he jokes, shrugging off his jacket.

I roll my eyes while carefully folding it then set it on one of the barstools lining the breakfast bar so I remember to grab it before I go. When I turn back, Porter's eyes connect with mine. A little bit of hurt filters through the bond, and I sigh.

"I didn't know it had his name on the back. Ziggy lent it to me with the goal being catching the media's attention. All I wanted to do was take the heat off of you guys. No way could I have predicted everything that would happen after."

"We know why you did it, hero. Fuck, I even admire you for it. But we're grown ass men who can take care of ourselves."

One brow raises high. "And like you told me earlier today, we've got each other now, so you shouldn't have to."

His shoulders drop with his sigh, but I see the smile he's fighting.

"Smart *and* beautiful. That's why you're so damn impossible to resist."

I step into him. "Flattery will get you everywhere."

Hux strides into the room and scoops me up. He's in a loose pair of sweats and a gray sleeveless workout tee that shows off his ginormous muscles and the tattoos lining his arms. I really try not to drool. The man is big, sexy, and soon to be all mine. Well, Porter's too, but he's already proven he's willing to share.

Porter opens his mouth, but Hux cuts him off. "Nope. You got time with her in the car. It's my turn." He carries me over to the sofa and drops down with me in his lap. "Go get changed, brother. It's time for that talk."

Porter mutters something about pushy friends all the way down the hall, and I watch him go with my grin growing wide. When I glance up at my gentle giant, he's staring down at me with this undecipherable look on his face.

"What is it, Hux?"

"You know I want to claim you, right, baby?"

My breath catches even though he's already made it clear where he stands. "I know, big guy, and I'm ready when you are."

He shakes his head. "But you deserve to be courted. Presents and pampering. Date nights. All the things that would traditionally happen when an Alpha finds his Omega."

My hand trails down his bearded jaw. "You going to court Porter?"

His deep brown brows furrow. "I don't—"

"Because he's your Omega too, Hux."

His thumb is brushing along my bare side, just under my t-shirt that has ridden up slightly. "But with you, it's different. I kinda feel like I've been courting Porter my entire life."

"He's not wrong, West," Porter adds, coming back into the room. He's wearing a black shirt and awkwardly hopping into gray basketball shorts, but it's the fuzzy socks that catch my attention.

"Hold up. What's with those?"

Hux laughs. "He's always worn those damn things when we're at home. I rib him all the time for his love of fuzzy socks and blankets."

"Huh. So you've actually been a closet Omega your entire life."

Porter snorts. "I suppose when you consider the current situation...yes, yes, I have."

He sits down beside us, pulling me out of Huxley's lap to sit sandwiched between them. My head falls to his shoulder, and his rests against mine. Hux threads our fingers together as he spreads his other arm along the back of the sofa behind us both.

"Don't change the subject," Porter demands. "I don't need to be courted. Looking back on it, Hux is right. We have tons of memories and moments together that have solidified what exists between us. You, on the other hand, deserve to be wooed."

I chuckle. "Wooed, huh?"

He nods exaggeratedly. "Yup. Candle-lit dinners. Bubble baths. *Ahem*!" He gives me a pointed look, and I remember the bath I set up for him when his heat was starting. "But more importantly, we should be creating memories that we can look back on years from now and remember how special this time was for all of us."

I swallow, my eyes going glassy as I take in the sincerity staring back at me. How many times did I long for a pack to step in and do exactly this? Court me. Take me to fancy plays and expensive restaurants. Buy me presents. Not because I needed any of that, but because that's what little Omegas are raised to expect from their potential Alphas. My dad was so great at that—spoiling my mom—that I sort of equated that with love. As an adult, I see how skewed that idea was. He loved her, so he spoiled her. He didn't spoil her to earn her love.

Now here I am with two men I want to make my own, who aren't even officially pack, but I don't care about presents or dinners. I could give two shits about being pampered. I just want someone to love me for who I am and not how they can benefit from being with me. Someone who can handle the intense media pressure. Someone who—

"Hey, we didn't mean to make you cry." Hux wraps his arm around my waist as he cuddles into Porter and me.

"It's not that. I just..." I shift, leaning my back into Porter so I can cup Huxley's face with my hands. "I don't need any of that stuff. I just need you. Period. End of story. I want to be yours, and I want to see what the future holds for us."

His purr is loud as he leans in, dropping a reverent kiss on my lips.

"How the hell did we get so lucky?" he murmurs against my mouth.

"You're welcome," Porter quips behind me, nuzzling into my neck, marking me with his scent.

Hux and I break apart with a chuckle.

"He's so modest." I glance over my shoulder, finding Porter with a goofy grin.

"Well, I'm an Omega so…"

He kisses me, warm lips pressing into mine. In the bond, he's happiness and peace and all these things that I never would've expected.

"As am I. And if you don't need to be courted, then I don't either. Just accept me for who I am, and I promise to do the same."

"That's a given, sweet thing." Hux brushes a hair out of my eye, tucking it behind my ear.

"Look, just let Hux do the Alpha thing to calm his anxiety, and let me spoil you too, just because I can, and we'll all be happy."

"I'm not going to say no to spending time with you all, and if that includes some of those things, then I won't complain, but do *not* go crazy, okay? We have bigger fish to fry. Like figuring out our living situation."

Hux grips my chin. "I know what I'd prefer when it comes to our living arrangements, but what do *you* want, sweet thing?"

I stare at the ceiling, trying to get my thoughts in order, which is becoming increasingly difficult with their scents distracting me.

"I love Chicago. My friends are still there, and I've made a great life there," I begin, pushing through when Porter's anxiety spikes in the bond. I grip his hand at the same time I take Huxley's. "But it was always going to be temporary. I was always heading back to Arizona, which makes this next part all the more complicated."

"We're big boys, hero. You can be honest with us. We can discuss this like rational, mature adults and work through it together. I promise."

I take a deep breath and exhale. "Ziggy's a professor at the university. I'm not sure he's going to be able or even want to uproot his life to move here. And then there's—"

"Nash," Porter mutters petulantly.

"Yes. *Totally* mature." I glare at him.

"Look, sweet thing," Hux says softly, drawing my irritation away from his pouting friend. "At the end of the day, if Ziggy wants to be pack, he'll have to make concessions, just like the rest of us. You and Porter are the Omegas. Ultimately, your needs are priority, and we'll work around everything else. If Zig is the man you think he is, he'll understand that and do what's necessary to be with you and this pack we're building."

My bottom lip is sore between my teeth, but my nerves have me a tangled up mess inside.

"And Nash?" I whisper. "He plays for the Storm. I'm not sure if anything even truly exists between us, but if something *is* there..."

Porter sighs beside me. "As much as it pains me to say it, he could always request a trade. It's not like he wouldn't have an in with the owner or anything."

"But two top centers on one team? Barrett would throw a fucking fit."

The guys share a look above my head.

"No. Nope. None of that shit. We're going to be pack, and I want to be included in all of those silent conversations you two have, especially when they concern me or someone I care about."

Hux is the first to respond. "Matthews isn't getting any younger, West. The guy is thirty-eight. They're going to want new blood in and established before he decides to retire."

My heart skips a beat. "Has he said something?"

Barrett's been with the Heat for as long as I can remember. Our team wouldn't be the same without him.

Porter gazes at me with an earnest expression as he absently plays with my hair. "He's dropped a couple of comments here and there, but nothing serious. The guy's still a badass on the ice, but all professional athletes understand that our time in the limelight is finite. We can't play forever. It's probably why he so readily agreed to share the captain spot with me."

"I just..." I release a harsh breath. "I can't even wrap my brain around that right now."

Hux cuddles me close as Porter pulls my feet into his lap and begins to rub the tense muscles there.

"I think we've already got the start of a really good plan. Once we get back from our away games, we can discuss a more definitive timeline and start planning out the logistics. For now, let's just enjoy a quiet night in before it's time to leave you early tomorrow morning."

"How quiet are we talkin'?" I murmur, leaning up to kiss along his bearded jaw.

Porter grabs the remote and flips on the TV, and the announcer's words stop me in my tracks and send my belly plummeting to the floor.

"At the Heat's game tonight, West Carter put a dent in those rumors of her involvement with Porter Hanson and Huxley Mc-Carren when she was seen donning a Nash Daniels Storm jersey, kissing first an unknown fan in the stands, followed by an almost indecent kiss with the man himself. West's rep has yet to confirm or deny her involvement with the divisive Chicago Storm center, but they're trending on social media. #BeautyAndTheBeastIRL has gone viral, ending speculation about her relationship with the Heat's new Omega. Speaking of Porter Hanson, tonight he proved designation means nothing on the ice, winning the game for the Heat with a stunning slapshot into the net during overtime. We'll be on the watch for the latest news on hockey's darling and keep you posted with up-to-the-minute accounts as reports come in."

The news switches over to the weather, leaving us sitting in uncomfortable silence.

"What the hell?" Porter begins. "That hashtag is way better than the one they used for me."

Hux snorts. I groan. Our phones start ringing almost simultaneously.

There goes our quiet night.

## 22

### WEST CARTER

The glass of sangria in my hand is half full, or maybe it's half empty depending on how you look at it. I like to think that I'm a realist, but most of the time, I'm just an optimist in disguise.

*Fuck. How many of these drinks have I had?*

A warm, fuzzy feeling skirts along my skin, which also happens to feel just a little too tight. I'd love to say it's the alcohol, but I know better. My heat is almost here, probably spurred on by Porter's and the flood of pheromones I've experienced over the last week. There's only one problem. The guys are on the road, and I don't want to worry them—they have enough going on with the media and the next two weeks of away games. We officially said our goodbyes at the airport at the butt crack of dawn this morning, so I'm on my own. I did the only thing a girl can do with a dawning heat on the horizon and no one to help her through it—called her besties.

Cadence is on the other end of my cream-colored sectional with her own glass of the fruity drink in her hand. With her big gray eyes and long, wavy dark blonde hair, she's stunning in that *she-has-no-idea-she's-hot-as-fuck* kinda way. Coming from a long line of Alphas, it was a shock to us all when she presented as an Omega. Lucky for her, both of her brothers have wives that were damn near giddy with delight at being able to guide their young sister-in-law. It also doesn't hurt that Bexley and Arden are social media sensations with millions of followers. They pulled her under their wings, giving her a chance to shine on their PackChat profile. That's how she ended up in Chicago with me, studying PR and marketing with a minor in graphic design.

Elliott is in my oversized chair, staring out the floor-to-ceiling windows that surround the living room, giving us a gorgeous view of downtown Chicago at night. The drink in her hand is practically empty, her light green eyes slightly unfocused at the lights sparkling in the distance. Her long dark brown hair is pulled up in a messy bun, her black sweater hanging off her shoulder as she draws her knees up and curls them under her. She graduated with a degree in journalism, much like me, but went a completely different route by landing a job with the *Chicago Daily News* as one of their correspondents. She's serious, professional, and a little bit intense, which makes her someone I can count on to tell it to me straight.

That's why I called my friends. Not only will they help me work through this mess in my head, but they'll help me get drunk while doing it. Seems like a winning combo in my book.

"For the record, I think you should just fuck him and get it over with it," Elle mutters, throwing back the last swig of her sangria.

"Need I remind you that I've already given you that advice and you didn't listen."

Her perfectly plucked brows quirk up as she gives me that stare she's so famous for.

"You act like there's been time in my schedule for that. Like it should've been as easy as penciling him in for a night of wicked debauchery on Wednesday at nine o'clock."

She shrugs. "It could've been. You just chose to go the complicated route, getting yourself bonded and packed up. To each her own."

Cadence rolls her eyes, propping her elbow up on the arm of the sofa and resting her cheek in her hand. "But there's something kind of romantic in the way this is all coming together. These sexy strangers coming into your life, wanting you with a ferocity that only biology can manage to play off as hot rather than creepy as fuck. I want *that*."

"Which part?" Elle asks. "The creepy as fuck part or the sexy strangers bit? Because I'm pretty sure we all know it's not a stranger you've had your eyes on since we were too young to be drooling over knots."

Cadence whips a glare at Elle. "That was a childhood crush, nothing more."

I try to bite back my grin. "C'mon, just admit it. You've been in love with Barrett since we were kids. Elle, how many nights did we spend at Cadence's house, hoping to catch glimpses of Crew, Cohen, and Barrett shirtless and sweaty while they played basketball, so she could pine over B's abs?"

"Too many to count."

Cadence snorts. "Y'all just used me to get closer to my brothers, hoping you'd catch glimpses of them naked. Gag me."

"Betcha Barrett could gag you just fine...if rumors are to be believed, that is," Elle chirps.

"Seriously, I'm so over that. He's too old for me. Plus, you know my brothers. It would never happen," Cadence mutters pitifully.

"He's a great guy, girl. I say you tell those overprotective brothers of yours to fuck off and see where it goes. I think you'd be perfect for each other."

"How'd we even get on this conversation? We're supposed to be solving *your* life problems, not mine."

My sigh is long and deep as I stare out at the city that has been my home for the last four years. Now, everything is about to change, and I'm both excited and nervous about that. I've got two pairs of uniquely different men who want *me* but hate *each other*, split between two cities with close to two thousand miles between them. Part of me knows that Porter and Hux are the safer bet. Our initial connection was powerful and instantaneous. Plus, there's the bond that tells me, even now, Porter is thinking of me. His worry and longing keep sneaking peeks through our connection.

Then there's the other two. Wild cards, I suppose. I know even less about them than I do the two men on the other side of the country, yet my heart beats faster just thinking of Ziggy's dimples and, dammit, Nash's scowl. The look I saw in Nash's eyes as I drove off nearly broke me in two.

Biology is a crazy bastard.

"It's my own fault. I accomplished my goal of diverting the media attention a little *too* well. Now look at where I've got myself. How is it I went from having zero prospects to having too many?"

"First of all," Elle says with a grin, "there is no such thing as too much dick."

Cadence giggles before taking another sip of her drink.

"Secondly, I'm a big believer in destiny. This was all meant to happen, and because you're West Carter, it had to be splashed all over the headlines, with every Tom, Dick, and Harry giving their take on the status of your love life. At least they're no longer worrying over the lack of one."

I groan, dropping my head back on the sofa.

"Look, West," Elle says, standing and walking into my ultra-modern kitchen and grabbing the pitcher off the white marble counter. She walks back over to each of us, filling our glasses up as she continues. "I think you just need to be honest with yourself. You want every single one of those men, otherwise none of this would be an issue. You'd tell Nash Daniels to fuck off and take his Beta boy with him. The fact that you haven't done that is telling. Porter and Hux are going to have to suck it up and give you space to see where that connection goes because denying your draw to the Alphahole is only going to leave a festering wound that will taint the connections you're growing with the others."

Cadence sips her sangria, humming. "She's right. For once, I agree with Elle."

"Are pigs flying?" Elle quips.

Cadence grabs one of my blush fuzzy pillows and chucks it at our friend.

"Apparently. They've got pretty pink wings and sunglasses on. Did you miss them?" Then she turns back to me with an exaggerated eye roll. "As I was saying, you have two weeks before the guys get back. Your heat is practically knocking at your door. I think you should use this opportunity to get to know Nash and Ziggy. See if the feelings stick around once lust is taken out of the equation."

I twist the glass in my hand, looking out at the night sky. "And I...what? Text Porter and Hux that I'm going to let their rival fuck me through my heat just to see if what we have is real? God, that sounds *so* fucking messed up."

"Sounds like the perfect plan to me." Elle studies the glass in her hand like it holds all of life's answers. "You know, we have this preconceived notion of what a pack should look like and how they should come together, but life isn't always neat and tidy. There's nothing stopping you from building this pack in a way that works for everyone. Maybe that means you split your time between here and Slate Creek. Maybe the guys don't have to be best friends. Maybe they just have to come to terms with the idea that the woman they want wants the others too. That she *needs* this odd arrangement to feel whole."

My nose scrunches up. "But that sounds awful. Like I'd be the knot in the middle of the tug of war rope with the two teams always fighting to win me to their side."

"All I'm saying is, a pack can look any way you want it to look. Don't fight to stay within the lines when you could make something even more interesting by ignoring them."

Is she right? Am I trying to force these men into a square hole when they're really a heart-shaped peg? Can we make this work? More importantly, do I want to risk it all just to see if it can?

"I can see the gears turning, West. Whatever you choose, we'll be here in your corner, giving you a safe space to work through all of this." Cadence risks a glance at our friend. "I can't speak for Elle, but know that if you decide you want to move back to Arizona, I'll probably be right there with you. I love Chicago, but I also miss home. My family. My nieces and nephew. I've been working with Jaxon and Locke remotely, helping them with TheOmegasGuide, but it'd be a helluva lot easier being local."

When I glance at Elle, she's staring right back at me.

"What? We always promised we'd stick together. You think I'd just turn my back on that now?" She takes a long sip from her drink, a smirk tilting her lips. "Nah, man. Shit's just getting to the good parts.

I wouldn't miss this chaos for the world. Where you go, I go. End of story."

I bite my bottom lip. These girls have been by my side my entire life. I can't imagine a day without them in it, and as life starts to pull us in separate directions, I pray we can always manage to come back together to fill up our metaphorical—and physical—cups because what we have here is invaluable.

"Just think about everything we've said. I'm sure you'll make the decision that's right for you," Cadence murmurs.

Then Elle adds, "And hopefully get dicked down in the process."

I think of Porter and Hux, traveling…alone. Part of me wonders if they'll use their time together to dive deeper into this new facet of their relationship. For their sakes, I hope they do. Of course, that has images of Hux's knot slipping into Porter's ass playing through my head, and I have to squeeze my thighs together to fight off the ache that blooms deep and wild in my belly. I can feel the heat growing in my core, feel my body's demands start to become impossible to hold off for much longer.

Then the images shift, and it's no longer Porter and Hux. It's Nash looming over me, muscles bulging as he thrusts in hard and deep. I can feel my cheeks flush and my slick flood the space between my thighs.

"We're losing her to heat burn," Elliott snarks.

"We'll stay tonight then give you some space…you know, just in case." Cadence's eyes meet mine, and I know what she's hinting at.

Let the grumpy Alpha come over and help take the edge off my heat. What neither of them realize is that somewhere deep inside, I know that if I do that, I won't be able to walk away when it's over. I'll become exactly what he said I am, *his*, and where will that leave me with the others?

Porter nudges me in the bond, no doubt feeling my nerves right along with my need burning brighter. I try to tuck it all away, so I'm not distracting them from the game, but it's becoming increasingly harder to do as the heat fog slowly descends. And that's what complicates this even more. I don't want my heat to interfere with my decision on how to handle Nash and Ziggy, but my body may damn well not give me a choice in the matter. Will I be able to deny what my body so desperately craves, or will I succumb and be forced to deal with the consequences when I can finally come up for air?

Either way, I'm fucked. Literally or figuratively.

# 23

## NASH DANIELS

Glancing up at the high rise in the middle of the River North portion of Downtown, I fight the unease in my gut. It's been over forty-eight hours since I last had eyes on West, and my desire to see her is battering at my internal walls so fiercely I have to fight back an almost feral need. I'm praying I don't fucking embarrass myself in front of the crowd of strangers passing by.

Ziggy has been scouring the information available, trying to pin down her whereabouts. This is our third lead, and I'm going to lose my fucking shit if this one is a bust like the others. Ever since that kiss in Arizona, my attention has had a single focus: West Carter. I go to sleep thinking of her and wake up wishing she was beside me. Never in all my thirty years have I felt anything close to this level of obsession over a woman, but she's sunk her claws in and won't let go. Now, I need to reciprocate...except with my knot, and hell, if I'm honest, maybe even my teeth.

*Son of a bitch! What happened to Nash "The Beast" Daniels? More like Nash "Pussy Whipped" Daniels.*

"Hey, aren't you—"A man strides toward me, wearing that look of awe that says he recognizes me and is going to want an autograph.

Can't he tell I'm not in the mood to fucking play nice with fans, for fuck's sake? My growl cuts him off, a glare forcing my nostrils to flare and my fists to clench.

"Uh...s-sorry, man. My bad," he mumbles, rushing off in the opposite direction.

*Fuck! So much for not embarrassing myself.*

The large glass door swings open, a doorman holding it for a pretty brunette that looks vaguely familiar, though I can't quite place her. She wraps a scarf around her neck just as her eyes meet mine. They narrow, her head tilting as she takes me in.

Dammit. I don't have fucking time for a puck bunny right now. I need to find my girl.

"Well, if it isn't Nash Daniels," she murmurs, looking decidedly unimpressed.

"Not interested," I grumble.

Her light green eyes narrow. "Good, cuz I'd knee you in the balls if you were."

"Then what the hell do you want?" I ask as she steps closer.

"You've got my girl in a clusterfuck of a situation, *Beast*."

I frown, my brain trying to connect the dots she's so callously throwing down. "What the fuck is that supposed to mean?"

She crosses her arms over her chest, eyeing me with a calculating look. "I take it you're here looking for West Carter?"

The growl slips between my lips before I can suck it back in. Need rushes through me like electricity across my skin, spreading goosebumps in its wake.

The girl smirks. "Yeah. Thought so. Give me one good reason why I should tell you how to find her."

Everything inside me goes still. She knows where West is. My instincts push forward, demanding we cooperate so we can get to her.

"I..." I try to find the right words, ones that don't have anything to do with the vivid images in my head of fucking, knotting, or claiming. Even in my current state, I know none of that will earn me any points. Through the Alpha fog clogging my brain, I finally realize where I know her from. I've seen her and West together on the news. That means there's only one way to pass this test—through good ol' fashioned honesty. "She's gotten under my skin, and I can't get her out. Not even sure I want to, in fact."

She considers me for a long moment, the silent seconds amping up the nerves sparking inside.

"You know she's bonded."

The words have another growl rushing up my chest, but I ruthlessly shove it back down and manage a simple nod, not trusting my mouth to open right now.

"Then what are your plans for my best friend? Bonds aren't reversible, and Hanson and McCarren aren't going anywhere. Can the Beast play nice to win Beauty's heart, or will he carelessly shred the very thing he wants so much into tiny, irreparable pieces?"

Her words bounce around in my head. Logically, I know she's right. I'm not the kind of guy an Omega like West deserves. I'm not a romantic. I don't even know the first thing about courting, and I sure as shit suck at cuddling. But that doesn't stop my instincts from demanding we claim the woman that's like a thorn in our side. When we finally get our hands on her, will we be free of the pain, or will it just dig in deeper and fester like a rotting wound?

*Shit! Maybe I should turn around and—*

"Look, Daniels, for what it's worth, I think you'd be good for her. She needs someone who will challenge and push her. Let the other guys be the ones she turns to when she needs comfort. You can be there pushing for her to keep going when she doesn't believe she can."

"Why are you helping me?" I finally ask, her words playing on repeat in my head.

"Because my friend is a strong woman who deserves to be coddled a little after everything she's been through…"

My brow furrows. "I'm not—"

"*But* she's also in desperate need of someone to get her out of the mental rut she's been stuck in since the moment her mom died. I think you might be the right guy for the job." She shrugs, tucking her hands inside her pockets. "For the record, I've already told her more than once to screw you, so don't fuck this up, all right?"

She turns, heading back for the door. The doorman sees her coming and opens it, holding it for her to pass through.

"Wait! Where do I—"

She pauses without looking back.

"Hey, Blake, can you see that Mr. Daniels here gets to the penthouse to see Ms. Carter? She's expecting him." She flicks a glance over her shoulder, eyes narrowing. "Don't make me regret this."

Then she heads for a waiting Uber and is gone without another glance.

"Right this way, Mr. Daniels," the doorman says, holding his arm out to indicate I should enter.

Deciding I have nothing to lose, I walk into the elegant lobby and follow Blake to the elevators. He presses the button, cutting nervous glances my way.

He's probably seen all the headlines.

*Beauty kissed the Beast.*

*Will the Beast ruin hockey's darling?*

*Who fell first—Beauty or the Beast?*

*Is Nash Daniels the Alpha West Carter has been waiting for?*

Don't people have better things to worry about? Fucking media shoving their noses where they most definitely don't belong.

"Problem?" I growl.

"N-no, sir."

The elevator door opens, and he steps in just far enough to push the button and tap a keycard against the black pad on the wall.

"The elevator will take you up to the foyer outside Ms. Carter's penthouse. If you need anything else, I'll be in the lobby until nine."

I step in and watch the doors close, blocking me off from the curious doorman's stare. Every cell in my body tenses with anticipation. West is almost within my reach. What I'll do once she's there, well, I'm not entirely sure. This isn't some chick flick where the guy apologizes for being an ass and the girl jumps into his waiting arms. I'm no fucking Prince Charming, and I have no intention of saying I'm sorry. She and I will just have to come to terms on what it means to be mine.

The ding startles me just before the doors slide open. I'm staring at two large double doors. The floor is a sparkly marble, and there's a plush cream bench off to the right with a side table along the opposite wall holding a vase full of fresh flowers.

Stalking forward, I press the button on the video doorbell, its chime loud in the quiet of the hall.

No answer.

I pound on the heavy wooden door. "Bright eyes, I've found you, and I'm not leaving until I see you, so you might as well open up."

"What do you want, Nash? Now's not a good time." Her voice is hoarse through the doorbell's speaker, and unease slithers through me.

"You know why I'm here. Let me in."

A whine cuts through the speaker just before she says, "I can't."

Her whine nearly decimates my self-control. My hands land on the wall on either side of the camera, my eyes staring right into it. Everything inside me is going berserk, demanding we get to our Omega and fix whatever is wrong.

"You either let me in, or I will break this goddamn door down to get to you. Your choice."

A few tense moments go by before I hear the click of the lock, then the door opens. I'm pretty sure all the air is sucked from my lungs as my brain damn near ceases to function rationally.

There, clutching the door so hard her knuckles are white, is West, wearing a white cropped cami—her nipples poking through the thin fabric—and black spandex shorts that barely cover her ass. Her bottom lip is being held hostage between her teeth, but those aren't the only things that have caught my attention. It's the scent that hits me the hardest. Spicy sugar plums and vanilla nearly knock me on my ass.

"Fuck, bright eyes," I murmur hoarsely.

She drops her head, her hair creating a curtain around her face. A low keening whimper falls from those plump pink lips I kissed the other night, and my resistance falters. Seeing her looking so fragile instead of the spitfire I've come to expect has this intense protectiveness coming alive inside me.

"West, baby, look at me."

Big blue eyes slowly raise to mine. They're glassy, her pupils blown wide. Her cheeks and neck are flushed, and it's then realization hits.

"Shit! You're in heat," I rasp.

She nods, and my dick is immediately rock hard. Maybe my luck has finally changed. Hanson and McCarren are out of town, leaving West all alone. My fists clench at my sides, the need to grab her and pull her into me at nearly uncontrollable levels.

"Tell me what you need."

Time slows and my chest gets tight while I wait for her to respond. Our eyes are locked, and I watch as she straightens, the cleavage on display rising and falling as she takes a deep breath in and exhales sharply.

I promise myself that if she tells me to go, I'll walk away no matter how impossible that might seem.

Her voice is a mere whisper when she says, "I need you, Nash. Stay?"

# 24

## WEST CARTER

Nash seems just as surprised by the thunderous purr emanating from his chest as I do. He takes one long stride toward me, and panic rushes forward hard and fast. My arm flies up, hand out, prompting him to halt in his tracks.

"Wait. I just…" Another deep breath. "There are a couple of things we need to discuss first."

He nods slowly, blue eyes tracking my every movement.

"The guys will need to know you're here."

One thick brow arches up high on his forehead, and his lips quirk up in a smug grin that looks all too at home on his handsome face. "Dare you to put that call on speaker. I promise to totally misbehave."

I swallow down my chuckle at his bold statement. I know his type. Give him an inch, and he'll take a mile. "Okay. We'll get to that in a sec. Right now, we need to talk through some specifics. Have you ever been with an Omega in heat before?"

He crosses his arms over his chest. "No, but I've heard plenty of stories. The intense sexual drive, the exhaustion, begging for a bite...but you don't have to worry about that, bright eyes. When I claim you, I'll damn well make sure you're of sound mind and fully understand what it means to be mine."

I blink. His sincerity is drowned out by his overwhelming cockiness. *When* not *if* he claims me. It should be a turn off, but *fuck me*, it's really not. Of course, I'm most definitely *not* going to tell him that just hearing those words leave his mouth makes me damn near ready to expose my throat and ask him to do just that.

"And Ziggy?"

His nostrils flare. If he's having trouble sharing with his friend, he's definitely not going to take to sharing with the other guys any easier. Nash is head Alpha in charge—in his mind anyways. It's going to be hard breaking him in to the idea of an equal distribution of responsibilities in a pack.

"If you want him here, I'll let him know where he can find us."

"I do," I whisper, my vision already going a little hazy at the thought of having the two men here with me. "An Omega in heat is a lot for any one Alpha to—"

"You already questioning my stamina, bright eyes?"

Now, it's my turn to wear a smug grin. "Guess we'll see if you're up for the challenge. Hope *The Beast* isn't overly exaggerated...for your sake, of course...and maybe mine too."

His deep rumbling growl sends a jolt straight to my desperate pussy.

"Make that call, baby. I'm not sure how much longer I can hold myself back."

Heading over to the sofa, I grab my cell as the soft snick of the door behind me echoes through the silent penthouse. When I turn, he's shrugging out of his wool coat and hanging it on one of the hooks of the coat rack in the entryway. Something about that image sends a pang through my heart. It's domesticated and familiar, something I can picture him doing as he comes in the door from practice and finds me waiting for him with his favorite drink in hand.

Shaking my head to rid myself of the image, I hit Porter's contact in my favorites. It rings twice before his rich voice comes through the speaker.

"Hey! There's my girl. I was just thinking of you."

"Hey, sugar. You guys up?"

Nash walks over, pulling the phone from my ear and hitting the speaker button. I clench my thighs together as he wags his finger at me.

"Just heading back from breakfast." Hux murmurs something in the background, and Porter chuckles. "Hux is upset we're not heading home to you instead."

I smile, my heart beating rapidly at the rush of affection I feel through the bond. Nash catches me off guard, stepping into me and forcing me back until my calves hit the sofa.

"Everything okay there? You seem...tense in the bond."

I swallow my whine, and slick floods the apex of my thighs when Nash's fingers slide along the exposed skin of my hips.

"Well, I...um..." Nash grips the hem of my cami, lifting it up and over my head. "Don't freak out, but my heat is starting."

Through the phone, I can hear both men cursing, arguing back and forth about whether or not they should ask Coach if they can head home.

"Porter, you know you can't do that. The team needs you. You're just a few games away from the playoffs."

His broken sigh cuts right through me. "You were there for me when I needed you most, hero. I sure as hell should be there for you. Now, I fucking understand what I was picking up on in the bond. No wonder I'm hard as a rock. I'm such a fucking dumbass."

"You couldn't have known. Neither of you."

"I'm so sorry, sweet thing," Hux's gruff voice adds. "You sure you don't want us to pull some strings? I hate thinking of you there alone."

I gulp. It's now or never, but this is the part I'm least looking forward to. "No, the team needs you both, but... Well, there's something else I need to tell you guys."

They wait patiently, all while Nash's fingers dip between the band of my shorts and my skin, dragging the stretchy material over my ass and down my legs until he forces me to step out of them. He tosses them aside and looks up at me. He's on his knees, eyes caressing every inch of exposed skin. I can feel my slick running down my inner thighs, and I bite my bottom lip.

"Hero? You still there?" Porter asks nervously.

"Y-yeah, I'm here. But...um...so is Nash."

Twin growls echo over the line, and I watch Nash's lips curve.

"How the hell did he find you?" Porter mutters.

"You know, I think the better question is..." Nash's mouth closes around one nipple and bites gently before pulling back. "What am I doing now that I have?"

"Son of a bitch!" Porter groans. "The fucker is taking advantage of her heat."

"Hey, it hasn't fully consumed me yet. I'm still mostly clear headed, thank you very much," I grumble.

"Sweet thing, do we need to call someone to escort him out?" Hux asks.

Nash's mouth closes around my other nipple and sucks...*hard*. I feel that shit all the way down in my core as my head drops back.

"You'd do that to her? Force me to leave her and let her suffer through this heat alone?" the wicked Alpha asks just as he leans forward to draw his tongue through the wetness on my thighs.

"Dammit. I hate it that the fucker is right." Porter covers the phone and talks to Hux on the other end of the line, then comes back a moment later. "West, what do you want?"

"I—" A warm wet tongue glides through my slit, and I gasp. "I need..."

"She needs to be fucked before this heat goes into a full burn," Nash snaps.

There's more low conversation, but I can't make out what they're saying. Whether that's because they're purposely talking low enough that I can't hear, or because I have an Alpha's tongue licking my needy pussy, which is more than a little distracting, it's hard to say.

"Let him take care of her since we can't," Hux reluctantly agrees, an edge to his tone that tells me those are the last words he wanted to say.

"Looks like they're smarter than I gave them credit for," Nash mutters against my pussy.

"But make no mistake, Daniels. You better keep those teeth to yourself until we've had the chance to sit down and talk."

"I don't know," he hedges dangerously. "She tastes too goddamn sweet. Might not be able to stop myself."

"Knock it off." I grip his hair, pulling his head away from the spot that needs him most, and the just fucker purrs. "He's already agreed not to bite. He's just being an ass."

Nash's smile grows wider, his lips glistening with the evidence of just how much I fucking liked what he was doing to me.

"Where the hell is Ziggy?" Hux grumbles.

Nash smirks. "He'll be here…eventually."

Muttered curses echo through the room.

"You will never know how sorry I am that I'm not there, hero."

Porter's voice sounds broken, and the need to reassure him suddenly becomes my sole focus—which is saying a lot when a man like Nash is kneeling at your feet with your slick covering his fucking face.

"There will be other heats, Porter. Haven't you heard the theory that multiple Omegas will sometimes sync their heats? Can you imagine?"

His groan is long and low, making my pussy contract with the rush of lust I can feel through the bond. Then I get an idea. Something that might help me feel less guilty about all of this and maybe draw them around to the idea of how this might work between us all.

"When you guys get back to the hotel, go straight to your room, okay? And Hux?"

"Yeah, sweet thing?"

"You take care of our Omega for me. He's bound to get some residual effects of my heat through the bond, and if…" I look at Nash, his eyes going a little wild as my perfume floods the space between us. "Well, if what I think is about to happen, *happens*, then you're both going to be in for a wild ride."

Nash's purr thrums louder through the air, the sound making me clench my thighs together, except I can't, because strong hands are holding them apart. His thumbs circle closer and closer to my sex until one calloused palm slips down behind my knee, lifts my leg, and places it over his shoulder. My pussy is wide open and weeping for him as he licks his lips.

"West, he better fucking take care of you and treat you right, or I'll personally kick his ass when I get there."

"As if you could, McCarren," Nash mumbles, leaning in and taking a deep breath. The purr turns into a low growl.

"We'll see, won't we?" Hux challenges.

"Guys, please. I..." I almost say I love you, but I don't want the first time to be while they're far away and I've got another man's face buried in my vagina. "Don't worry about me. I promise I'll be okay. You just be safe, okay?"

"You too, hero. We'll be home with you soon."

Nash reaches up and presses the red button to end the call before I can respond.

"That's enough of that. Now, you're all mine."

I don't even have time to blink. He dives in, his mouth latching on to my clit so fiercely that I cry out, both hands gripping his hair as my hips buck against his tongue. Tingles shoot up my spine, my orgasm gaining momentum as he works me over with brilliant precision.

He pulls back for air, and our eyes connect. For a split second, he's not the asshole that I've come to know. There's a softness to his features that I haven't seen, and it makes him look boyishly charming.

"You fucking taste like everything I never knew I wanted," he rasps before diving back in with a groan.

"Nash, fuck. *Please*."

"You need to come, bright eyes?"

My moan is loud and needy, heat spiking in my belly. "Fuck yes. Make me come, Alpha."

One of his big hands grips my hip, the other trailing over my ass until his thick finger finds and teases my hole. I whimper, my hips rolling hard against his mouth as the friction pushes me right to the very edge of my sanity.

"Want you to soak my face, bright eyes. Come all over my goddamn tongue," he barks, his sharp Alpha command making my body quake.

I scream his name when he thrusts two thick fingers into my pussy, curling against the front wall and hitting a space that has me seeing stars. My body goes taut as I detonate, his strong hands bearing my weight so I don't collapse to the floor. I'm sure my grip on his hair is painful, and I'm probably suffocating him in my vagina, but he doesn't so much as make a sound. He just continues to eat me out like I'm his favorite fucking dessert.

Lingering aftereffects roll over me, but my pussy is aggressively contracting, the demand for a knot so damn strong that my whine becomes a ragged, broken thing.

"Fuck. You're dangerously gorgeous when you come." He's staring up at me with something akin to awe in his eyes. Then they narrow when he notices my pained expression. "But you need more, right, bright eyes? Tell your Alpha so he can give it to you."

"Please..." I whimper pathetically.

"Words, baby, I need the words. I'm not assuming anything when it comes to you because I'm not gonna fuck this up by being a horny asshat."

My hand caresses his scruffy jaw, watching him nuzzle my palm and along my arm, marking me with more of his scent.

Leaning in, my lips brush against his as I whisper, "I need my Alpha to knot me so deep I can't walk straight for a week. That clear enough for you?"

His nostrils flare and his pheromones flood the room, making it difficult to breathe.

"Crystal." He stands, and in one fluid motion, he picks me up and tosses me over his shoulder. "Your room?"

I point down the hall, and he stalks off, one large palm on my ass and the other rubbing my feet. The incongruity of this man is going to be the death of me. I just hope I get more orgasms and a good knotting first.

# 25

## NASH DANIELS

Her skin is warm under my palm, the fever caused by her heat forcing a pretty blush that makes her impossibly more beautiful. The woman is...incredible? Phenomenal? The best damn thing that's ever happened to me in my shitty thirty years on this earth? I'm not a man who's good with words, but I can guaran-fucking-tee you that they just can't do her justice.

Double doors stand wide open at the end of the hall, and I make my way toward them. Her scent has gotten stronger since her orgasm—less sweet with a spicier tang that has me damn near ready to pound my chest in triumph. *I* did that. I satisfied my Omega. Now, I'm gonna fucking do it again.

Sure, it's a little premature—she's not exactly mine officially—but there's no doubt in my mind she will be. I can't be the only one experiencing this rush or the indelible grip on my soul. She's gotta feel it too, and I'll make sure of that.

Striding into the room, there's a large wall straight ahead with a hall that leads left or right. Unsure which direction to head, I just pick one. Following the shiny marble to the right, I round the corner and see a wall of windows looking out over the city. The sun is shining as Chicago comes alive, people hustling out to start their day.

And I'm about to start mine on a high note. Her room is massive, full of fresh flowers and sparkly touches that somehow contrast against the hard shell I saw out on the ice. She's both softness and strength, and the combination is electric.

The king-sized bed is covered in shades of silver, her pillows stacked neatly against the headboard and sheets neatly turned down... at least until I toss her down. Her gasp of surprise makes my dick throb. I want her making that sound a whole helluva lot more. With her pink hair fanned out over the sheets, her body naked and wanting, slick running down her thighs, she looks like a mythical creature, one who could lure a man to his very death. Even knowing that, it wouldn't stop me. I need her with an intensity that I can't begin to measure.

She draws her knees up and spreads her feet wide, giving me a glimpse of her pretty pussy. When I grab my phone out of my pocket, her brows draw together, creating a valley between her eyes. I pull up my texts, hit the button to record a voice message, and watch her face.

"I'm here with a sexy Omega who just so happens to be in heat. For some godforsaken reason, she wants you here too. Penthouse at 531 Uptown."

I click the microphone button to stop recording and hit send, then shift to the camera app and snap a picture of that glistening cunt to send along to Ziggy. That should get him moving.

"You did *not* just take a picture of my pussy."

"I did. What are you going to do about it?" I challenge, waiting expectantly for that fire to light up her eyes.

Her face relaxes. "Trust you with it."

*Fuck. Me.* This woman is something else. Just when I think she couldn't sink her claws in any deeper, they bury themselves another inch under my skin. The guys are worried about me claiming her, but the fact of the matter is that she claimed me the second she stepped off the ice.

Setting my phone onto the nightstand, I slip out of my shoes and toe out of my socks.

"You're a little too trusting, bright eyes."

Her head tilts thoughtfully. "And I'm not so sure you're the asshole you pretend to be."

"You don't even know me. I'm the biggest asshole there is."

"I think that's what you want everyone to believe, but I see you, Nash Daniels. You can't fool me."

Grabbing the neck of my shirt, I pull it over my head and toss it onto the plush carpet. The entire time, she's watching me, her bottom lip tucked between her teeth. Plenty of women have ogled me. Some for my body. Others for my money. But with West, it's like she sees right through the facade I put on for everyone else, finding the man beneath all the hurt and anger. She's not lying about that. For a split second, I wonder if bringing her into my chaos is a good idea.

But the alternative—letting her go—is simply not an option. I'll drag her into hell with me but make sure not a single fleck of ash tarnishes her perfect skin.

"Having second thoughts?" she murmurs, eyeing me with such seriousness that I swallow down my smart retort.

"Where you're concerned, baby, not a single thing in this world could change the way I feel about you. You're mine. Period. End of fucking story."

One brow arches. "Someone's gonna have to teach you how to share."

"When you're with me, the rest of the world doesn't exist. The others can hang around in the periphery, biding their time until they get you to themselves."

"And now here I am. All yours. Question is, what are you going to do with me?"

My chest is rumbling with a purr so loud I don't even try to fight it.

"Exactly what you asked me to do." My hands go to my belt buckle, then to the button of my jeans. "I'm going to sink my knot so deep inside you that I'll leave an imprint you'll feel every time one of the others fucks you."

She whimpers, her toes curling into the fuzzy blanket. "Fuck, Nash. *Please.*"

"You want this knot, bright eyes?" My pants and boxer briefs drop to the floor, and I kick them away.

She licks her lips, eyes glued to my aching cock that's bobbing in excited greeting. "Yes, Alpha."

Something about the simplicity of that response pulls a growl from my throat.

"Then present for your Alpha, bright eyes. I wanna see that round ass in the air and your needy pussy dripping for my dick."

In seconds, she's on her knees, bending forward until her chest is on the bed. Her pretty little cunt is wet and swollen, ripe for my knot. Animalistic need is building inside. It's intent on claiming her, making her ours, but I tamp that down. That time will come. For now, we'll make her ours in all the other ways we can.

"Mmmm. That's a good little Omega."

She turns her face into the mattress, muffling her whine in the fuzzy fabric, her fingers tangling in the bedding as more wetness seeps out of that tight little hole I can't wait to fill up. Closing the distance between us, my fingertips trail up the backs of her thighs, playing in the thick wetness that's leaking from her sex.

"You're so wet for me, baby."

Skimming over her pussy lips, my thumbs rub and spread them apart to give myself a glimpse of her pink center. My dick is weeping, precum dribbling from the tip as it patiently waits its turn. For now, though, I want her begging for my knot because there's no telling what will happen once I'm finally inside her.

Without hesitation, I thrust two fingers into her warmth, feeling her inner muscles clamping down on me, desperate for what only I can give her. In and out, I stretch her, prepping her for me because I doubt I'll be able to go slow. She doesn't know this, but she'll be my first. And I don't just mean my first Omega. My knot is a virgin, and just the thought of her body tightening around me is damn near enough to have me blow my load and ruin all this.

I climb up onto the bed behind her, fighting to stay in control, but I'm afraid it's a losing battle.

"Nash," she whispers, her tone edged with a whine.

"Shhhh, baby. I've got you." Gripping my dick, I swipe it through her slick, letting my tip tease the edge of her pussy hole.

Part of me wants to draw this moment out and make it special, but the other part is practically feral with his need for her.

"Oh god. Fuck me, *please*, Alpha."

The feral side wins out. In one thrust, I'm balls deep. Her scream ends in a long groan. She's so goddamn tight and warm, sheathing my dick inside her like it was custom fitted for me alone. I don't even realize I'm growling until I reach down, my hands roughly gripping her hips as I pull out and slam back in. The sound our bodies make as they slap together is obscene and fucking filthy, but damn, is it music to my ears.

"Fuck, baby. You're milking me so damn good."

"Knot, Alpha. Knot, please, please, please give me your knot."

"I will. Don't you fucking worry about that," I snarl, feeling the tight rim of her cunt stretching against the swell of my knot with each thrust.

*Fuck! I need that. Need to feel her locking down on my knot until I fill her so goddamn full of my cum that she'll smell like me for days. She'll smell like mine. Like...pack.*

Reality rears up, intruding on the bliss overwhelming my body. It tries to tell me she's an Omega in heat and we're not using protection, but the beast just roars with unabashed glee at the thought. Suddenly, I want nothing more than to breed her, to fill her so full of me that it's spilling out even as I try to push it back in. The image of her round with my kid is something I never in a million years would've said I'd be turned on by, but... *Fuck. Me.* I need that. Want that. Don't give a damn if she's on birth control or if she even wants kids. All rational thought has fled the room, and my Alpha instincts shoot into overdrive.

"I... I... Oh, *fuck*, Nash. Knot me. I can't... I'm not sure I..."

She's mumbling incoherently, and I know I can't draw this out anymore for either of us. One hand moves without conscious thought, gripping a handful of her hair and tugging hard until she whimpers.

"You're mine, West. Say it."

"I'm yours."

"Again!" I bark.

"I'm fucking yours," she snaps back.

There's my little spitfire. When she tilts her head to the side, exposing her throat, I see red. I plunge in hard and fast, my knot hitting the resistance of her cunt until it forces its way through and settles deep inside her. Immediately, her body clamps down around me, squeezing until my vision starts to go black from pleasure overload. My body drops over hers, teeth trailing along the sensitive skin between her shoulder and neck. The urge to bite becomes nearly impossible to deny, but as my release rushes over me, I narrowly manage to stop my teeth from sinking in deep when I bite down. My name torn from her lips is what tips me over that last ledge, and I roar as I come, my dick pulsing inside her.

I can't stop my hips from grinding or my mouth from trailing over her too soft skin, leaving marks in my wake. If I can't bite her for real, I'll mark her entire body to stake my claim. The aftershocks continue to sweep over me every time I feel the tug on my knot. I'm not even sure how long it lasts. By the time I can finally fully breathe again, I'm practically laid out on top of her. Quickly shifting, I pull us both to our sides. Her pussy is still contracting around me, feeling like fucking heaven, with her body nestled against mine. I always thought that spoon analogy was fucking ridiculous, but for the first time, I see the appeal.

Nuzzling into her neck, I kiss the spot where my teeth are imprinted on her skin, both wishing it was the real thing and grateful that it's not. I want her. There's no doubt in my mind about that. But I want her to want me back.

Her hand reaches for me, gripping my neck and pulling me in for a kiss. The position is awkward, but her mouth is just as fucking perfect as I remember. Our tongues slide languidly against each other, and her taste floods my mouth, making me crave more even though I'm still fucking locked inside her.

She drops one last kiss on my lips before her head tilts and her forehead lands on mine.

"That was amazing," she murmurs.

"*You're* amazing."

She grins. "Turns out you really *are* good with your stick."

I cough out a chuckle, the sound unfamiliar and rough. I can't even remember the last time I shared a moment like this with anyone that isn't Ziggy, and even with him, they were few and far between. In a short amount of time, West has begun drawing out parts of me I haven't seen in years. They're a little rusty from lack of use, but maybe with some tender loving care, they can grow as strong and sure as the woman in my arms.

I drop a kiss on her forehead and wrap my arms around her a little tighter.

"You know, they say practice makes perfect."

She sighs, cuddling into me. "I'm more than willing to help you out with that."

"Good," I whisper against her ear. "Because I need you."

And that's God's honest truth.

# 26

## HUXLEY MCCARREN

My watchful eyes are on Porter and, more specifically, the flush working its way up his throat and the muscles bulging in his jaw. Even with two thousand miles between us, her heat is rushing through the bond, and he's feeling every bit of it.

"We're almost there," I promise softly, my hand roughly gripping his thigh as the cab pulls up to the hotel.

"Fucking hell, bro. This shit is..." His head drops back as he exhales harshly. "One touch. One single touch, and I'd probably come in my pants."

Now, I want nothing more than to test that theory because his scent has my dick rock hard, but not here. Not in a dirty cab where we have eyes on us. I want to keep him all to myself.

"I'll take care of that for you soon. We're here."

"Fuck. Not helping," he mutters.

The driver stops, and I make quick work of paying the fare before exiting the car. We're greeted by the doorman, who holds the door as we walk into the elegant lobby, but I don't see any of it. My eyes are on Porter, watching the way he holds himself together as though there's not a damn thing wrong, but I see the tension in his shoulders and the quick rise and fall of his chest. By the time we make it to the elevator and the doors open, he's gritting his teeth.

"You okay?" I ask, pushing the button for our floor.

He slumps against the back wall, his head hitting the spotless glass. "Am I okay that our girl is in heat and our biggest rival is with her right now? Or that he's probably dick deep in that tight pussy of hers, helping her take the edge off? She's already come at least once and..." He groans. "Yeah, I'm totally *not* okay."

"Porter—"

His eyes close. "You don't get it, Hux. I feel every spike in her desire like it's a caress against my cock. I'm getting off to secondhand arousal, and I feel...*dirty*. Like I'm some peeping fucking Tom who's spying on my girlfriend while she's with another man. Fuck. Do you *hear* me right now?"

I step into him, my hand sliding along his jaw until my fingers grip the back of his neck. "West warned us this could happen, especially since the bond is so new. It's not dirty. She knows you're there with her. Did you ever think of that? If you can feel her, then she can feel you too."

When his eyes meet mine, I find desperate need staring back at me. My head dips, and my mouth presses into his. The kiss sparks something hot and dangerous in my blood, and I know we need to get somewhere private, *now*.

The elevator doors slide open, and I grip his hand, tugging him along the hall until we're standing outside our room. These doors are operated by a fucking phone app, so I manage to fumble mine out of my pocket with one hand to access the digital room key. In seconds, the light is green and I'm pulling Porter inside. The door no sooner shuts behind us when I push him back against it, my larger body surrounding his. He makes this sound in the back of his throat, half whimper, half mewl, and I lose it.

Our mouths crash together in an awkward and clumsy mess of lips and tongues. We're both rabid, our hands tugging and pulling off clothes until there's nothing between us. Pressing into him, our hard dicks are nestled together between our bodies, precum leaving trails against our skin.

"Fuck, Hux, I wasn't kidding. I'm—"

He rolls his hips, sliding our dicks against each other twice before his words cut off in a choked groan. He comes between us, hot and wet and thick. A growl forces its way past my lips as he continues to grind his cock into mine.

"I need more," he rasps, and I'm more than happy to oblige.

Leaning in for a bruising kiss, my hand sneaks between us, gathering his cum in one hand while using the other to lift his leg over my hip. The bed is only ten feet or so away, but that's too fucking far. My fingers unerringly find his tight puckered hole, sinking in deep and stretching against the firm ring of muscle.

He gasps, our lips brushing as I pump two digits into his ass. "Holy shit. *Yes*."

"You want my dick, baby? Want me to fill you up the same way our Omega is being filled? Let you both feed off the lust pinging between the two of you?"

He whines, hips rolling against my hand, fucking against my fingers.

"Fuck me, Hux. Do it."

My grin is wicked when I pull my fingers from his ass, gripping my dick. Angling our bodies, the fat head of my cock presses against his ass until it disappears inside him. It's the most erotic feeling, watching my length disappear inside my best friend, feeling him tighten around me as I struggle to hold back and go slow.

"What the hell are you waiting for? I don't want *gentle* right now, Alpha. Fuck me hard and fast and make me yours. "

With a snarl, I thrust forward, my balls slapping against his ass as he cries out against the intrusion. I don't give him any time to adjust. I pull out and slam right back in, making the door creak behind him.

"This hard enough for you?"

"Fuck yes. It's so fucking good, Alpha."

My thighs burn as my body bucks against his, but in this position, I can't get deep enough. Pulling out, I lift him up and carry him to the bed. He's not exactly small, but I'm bigger. I manage to maintain control long enough to crawl onto the bed before dropping us both down onto the plush mattress. His legs immediately pull up, knees wide, so I can find his hole and plunge back inside him.

"Want to see you this time. Watch your face as I make you come on my knot." My hips pull back, then I thrust forward again, hitting deeper and harder. "Can you feel our Omega? Is she as hot and needy as this tight little asshole is for my cock?"

His moan is loud as my hands slide up his arms, holding them above his head and using them for leverage as I fuck into him.

"Fuck. She's..." His eyes close, a whimper escaping when my dick slides out nice and slow, dragging against his inner walls. "I can feel her.

It's almost like we're fucking each other while each of us are fucked by our Alphas. I can't... Goddammit."

I'm almost desperate to feel her myself. Need the connection we haven't yet made with a force that's more powerful than I could've anticipated. My control is weak, considering my best friend...my *Omega*...is milking my cock the same way she's probably milking that asshole's dick. I've been inside her tightness, know exactly what he's experiencing, and I'm jealous as hell he's got her and we don't.

"God, Hux. You should be in the bond with us. It's indescribable."

Those words from his mouth as my dick plows in and out of his ass have my heart doing funny things. I find West's bite mark on his throat and drop my hand to trace it with my thumb.

"Porter..." I can't finish. The words won't come. I don't want to ask him for a bond when his asshole is taking every fucking thrust like a goddamn champ.

His hand reaches up and wraps around my neck, pulling me down on top of him. We're eye to eye, my forearms dropping to rest alongside his head as my hips continue to roll against his body. Going from hard and fast to slow and purposeful has the mood in the room shifting. One minute, we're fucking. The next, I'm making love to the one man who's been by my side my entire life. My best friend. My Omega.

"I'm ready, Hux. You don't need to ask."

In that way we have between us, he knows exactly what I'm thinking.

"I want my bite on you. Need it more than I've ever needed anything in my life."

"Except West."

"I need you both so fucking much it hurts."

"Then bite me, Alpha. Make me yours so you can feel what our Omega is doing to me through the bond."

My chest rumbles with a purr, loud and strong and deep, as my dick slides in and out of Porter's ass. My knot is more than just a little swollen, the anticipation of this moment forcing my body to the edges of its limits. I'm staring down at West's mark, and I know exactly where mine is going to go.

My mouth trails over his shoulder and along the bend in his neck as his chin tilts up, exposing the soft skin there. I lick over the mark, suck on it, and feel his ass clench down on my dick.

"Fuck, Hux, you have no idea how good that feels."

"No, but I'm about to," I murmur against his throat.

I line my teeth up so that the bite marks will overlap, but not touch, matching the way our relationships with the man beneath me intersect and bring us all together. Then I slowly sink my teeth in as my knot pushes against his ass, stretching him around the fullness at my base inch by excruciating inch.

"Oh, god. Fucking *hell*. Hux!" Porter cries out, his body going taut as his ass takes my full knot.

His body locks around me, and I suck hard on my mark, the copper tang from his blood rich and metallic on my tongue. I suck again and again with each thunderous throb of my knot as it swells larger until my release spills inside him. Pulling back, I lick along both marks, out of breath, my heart pounding like a hammer in my chest.

"I fucking love you." Porter grips my face and forces my lips to his.

My soul sings with happiness and relief and contentment flooding through the bond, then, I gasp, sensing surprise and joy and the searing lust lighting up at the other end. It's not as potent as Porter's emotions, but it's there. I can feel West through the connection, and it makes me all the more ready to claim her too.

"I love you too," I murmur against his mouth. "You're mine now."

"Think I always have been, but now we've got her too."

I smile, feeling completely whole for the first time in my life. I've got a pack. One with my best friend and the woman who has changed everything. Sure, there are two more that might be joining us, and I'm still not sure about them, but knowing these two are mine is enough for now. I'll worry about the rest later.

"You're right. Even just feeling her through our connection is like..."

I try to come up with something to describe just how fucking amazing it is.

"There's not a single word in the English language, Hux, that would do it justice. Trust me, I've tried."

There's a rush of pleasure that surges through both of us as our girl no doubt comes two thousand miles away. Porter was right. This is going to be torture.

Rolling us to our sides, Porter's leg slides along my hip. "At least now we can share in the pain of her heat together."

"You know he's going to purposefully try to fuck with our game, right?"

My eyes open—hadn't even realized they'd closed. "What do you mean?"

"You just wait. I wouldn't put it past the jackass to try to plan it so he's fucking her right in the middle of our game to throw us off."

"We've got two intermissions. I'll get you off as many times as I can to keep a clear head."

He snorts. "The guys are gonna love *that*."

"Wait 'til Matthews hears who's with West during her heat."

"Not it!" Porter laughs.

"Fuck. I should've known that was coming."

"You really should have." He kisses the tip of my nose. "Now, let's nap before we have to head to the rink."

He nuzzles into my neck, and my eyes close once again as a purr rumbles loudly in my chest. I fall asleep, wrapped around one of my Omegas and wishing West was here so I could bond her too. I'm done waiting. The next chance I get, she's mine.

# 21

## WEST CARTER

I'm on the bed, cuddled up to Nash's chest, my leg thrown over his and his knot firmly locked inside me after another blow-out orgasm. Am I nuzzling against his jaw like a kitten demanding attention despite the fact that he's passed the fuck out? Yes, yes, I am. I'm an Omega in heat. What do you expect?

Late afternoon sun is shining through the windows, which tells me we've been fucking for hours. The second I felt Huxley light up in my bond with Porter, my heat kicked into high gear. Poor Nash could barely keep up with my demand to be satisfied. This is the first heat I've been able to truly share with someone. Between that and feeling the guys' pleasure from the other side of the country, mine seemed to be magnified tenfold. Now, my heat has settled to a low simmer, but I can still feel that gnawing ache in my belly, the warmth of my skin, and the need building in my full pussy. This short reprieve won't last...and neither may my exhausted Alpha.

Hux nudges me through the connection, and I grin, poking him back. My heart swells at the newness of this link between us. It's faint, which only makes me long for the real thing. We'll get there, there's no doubt about that. It's just a matter of *when*. The sooner, the better in my opinion.

Searching the bond, I find Porter. His concern for me and his love for Hux make my soul feel more settled than it's been in a long time. Piece by piece, these men are filling up the empty spaces within me. I've got two specifically shaped holes left, then maybe the broken-hearted-little-girl-turned-independent-woman will finally be whole.

Nash snores, and I have to bite back a snort. I hate to say I told him so, but... *I totally did*. He's so much *softer* in sleep, the tense lines of his face smoothing out to give him a sort of innocence that's masked when awake. I feel like a creeper, studying him like this, but that natural guardedness would never let me otherwise.

The doorbell rings at the same time my phone buzzes with a notification. There's only one problem: I can't reach it.

Tapping Nash on the nose, I murmur, "Sunshine, I need you to grab my phone so I can check the door."

"Ignore it. They'll go away," he mumbles into the top of my head.

"It could be Ziggy."

He growls. "Fucker's late."

He shifts just enough to reach over to the bedside table for my phone, and his knot tugs on the lock that's keeping us together, startling a moan from my mouth. Fuck. So much for a low simmer. It's already edging back up to a boil.

"Gonna be the fucking death of me," Nash mutters. He hands it over, his eyes already closing as he drops a kiss on my forehead. "Damned if I'm not okay with that."

*Fuck, what this man does to me!*

With a large grin on my face, I click on the app. The sight of the man staring back at me has my belly flipping. There, with a black beanie and scruffy face, is my Beta. I tap the microphone button, a little breathless.

"Hey, Zig. I'll unlock the door, and you can come right in. We're in my bedroom at the end of the hall."

"Now, how the hell am I supposed to turn down an invitation like that?"

I'm smiling like a lunatic as I hit the unlock button in the app. From here, I can just barely make out the soft sounds of the door opening and closing then something rustling, followed by heavy footsteps down the tiled hall. I'm wrapped up in his friend, naked on my bed, and a man I barely know is about to walk into my bedroom. I should feel at least a little self-conscious, right? Except I don't. I'm anxious, with this little flutter in my belly because I'm excited to see him, but I'm not afraid of what he'll think when he sees me. There's just this sort of certainty inside that tells me I have nothing to worry about.

"Whoa! I know I'm just a Beta, but the smell in here is..." Ziggy comes into view around the corner of the wall, wearing dark jeans that show off his long lean legs and a gray henley that emphasizes his broad chest. He smiles, and I feel my pussy clamp down around Nash's now mostly deflated knot when that damn dimple appears. "Oh, pretty girl, you are so damn wicked."

"I'm sure I don't know what you're talking about," I purr, my voice even raspier than normal thanks to my climbing heat.

He nods toward his roommate. "Did you kill him or just wear him the fuck out?"

"I tried to warn him that Omegas in heat were a totally different kind of beast, but he didn't believe me. He thought he was the scarier one."

"Can't a man get a five-minute nap without his stamina being called into question?" Nash grumbles. He glances at the clock, then glares up at his friend. "It's been seven goddamn hours! Where the fuck have you been?"

"Some of us have day jobs, asshole. And next time you send me a voicemail first thing in the morning, how about making sure I'm not in front of my class, using my phone for a presentation? I went to swipe your message away and ended up hitting play instead. The class got to hear all about my sordid plans with "The Beast" and his horny Omega. So...thanks for *that*."

A laugh bursts free right before I hear Nash growl, "Please fucking tell me you closed the goddamn text before the picture came through."

My eyes go wide, and I tip my head back to look at Ziggy with what has to be horror plastered on my face.

"Don't worry, pretty girl, your glistening pussy was safe and for my eyes only."

"Well, thank fuck for that!" I choke out.

"Anyways, I'm a little later than I would've been because I stopped to get some supplies." Ziggy lifts one of the bags. "Some basic toiletries since I'm assuming we'll be here a couple days, some lube, a couple of sex toys that looked interesting, and silk rope."

My pussy contracts at that last bit.

"Fuck's sake, woman," Nash mutters, his teeth gritting against my needy pussy's throb. "What the hell is the rope for?"

"Please tell me you're not all *beast in the rink but meek in the sheets*," Zig scoffs.

Nash's eyes narrow, and I laugh even as I rush to redirect the conversation.

"What's in the other bag, Zig?"

"Chicken wings."

I blink. O...kay, a little random...but then my stomach growls.

"See!" His smug grin is adorable.

"Fucking hell, I need more sleep. Chicken wings and rope. You're a grown ass adult who can't be left on their own for two goddamn seconds."

They bicker back and forth while I grin into Nash's chest. The dichotomy between the two of them is fucking comedic gold, but as much fun as it is to listen to, other needs are demanding some attention.

"I hate to interrupt this little spat you two have going, but I really need to get up and use the bathroom, maybe stretch a little, and... Yeah, I need some of those chicken wings."

"Do *not* encourage him, bright eyes."

Brushing a stray lock of hair from his face, I drop a kiss on his nose. "Sleep. I'll be back."

I start to move, but two strong hands slip under my naked body and lift me from Nash's arms. From full to empty does not make for a happy Omega pussy, but it does make for a messy one.

"Fuck. Your clothes are gonna have some dubious stains, my man."

Ziggy chuckles as he cradles me to his chest, the scent of fresh laundry calling me to snuggle into him as his eyes trail over my body.

"Shit. For the first time, I can fully appreciate the sentiment of 'Afternoon Delight.'"

I giggle, my eyes meeting his.

"You're fucking stunning, pretty girl." His lips brush mine. "You're sure you're really okay with me being here?"

My hand cups his jaw. "You're not going anywhere, Zig. You're mine, remember?"

His nostrils flare, and his eyes flash with a barely banked heat.

"Good. Because I didn't want to eat those chicken wings all by myself."

More laughter bursts free as I point to the opposite side of the room. "Bathroom's that way."

"Yes, milady."

"Son of a bitch. I have a lifetime of this shit to look forward to?" Nash grumbles sleepily.

We ignore him as Ziggy heads toward the open door.

"You're pretty warm. Sure your heat can wait?" he asks softly.

Nodding, I kiss his cheek. "I'll be fine. It sort of got worse when I felt Hux bond Porter. It was so intense I was practically sobbing."

He looks thoughtful. "You think something's off because the guys aren't here?"

I think about that for a minute. I've never been bonded before, so I'm not sure if bonded heats are any different than non-bonded heats, but I suppose that could be why it feels more potent than usual.

"I don't really know. Maybe?"

"Hmmm," he murmurs. "Well, I'm glad I'm here now to pick up at least a little of the slack. Lord knows someone needs to balance out Grumpy Mr. Grumperson out there."

I try to fight the grin and lose. He's just so damn adorable. With the others, there's a sort of tension that hangs around us as we find our footing with each other, but everything just seems so damn easy with Ziggy. He's going to be my partner in crime. I can already tell.

He reluctantly sets me on my feet in the middle of my bathroom, but instead of stepping back, his hands grip my hips and pull me into his body.

"I've missed you, pretty girl."

And with that, his lips touch mine. It's slow and sweet, and while the heat kicks up another notch, I just enjoy the simplicity of the moment with this man that my heart swears we've known forever. When he pulls back, I swallow down my whimper.

"Go use the bathroom. I'll get a shower started so you can clean up a little before eating."

I quickly do as he said, then wash my hands and brush my teeth. I feel almost normal again until I spy Ziggy in the mirror. He's standing in front of my shower, his eyes locked on my butt, looking gobsmacked.

"You an ass man, Zig?"

"I am now. Yours is fucking perfection."

I have a feeling I'll be smiling a lot around Ziggy.

"You think so?" I ask, planting my hands on the bathroom sink, pushing my ass out, and spreading my legs a little wider, giving him a glimpse of my wet pussy.

"Mmmhmm," he hums, grabbing his dick through his jeans.

Slowly, I turn, my hands gripping the cool granite, and lean back.

"You've seen what I've got. Now show me yours."

Bright blue eyes slowly raise, lingering on my breasts before they meet mine. Without another word, he tugs his shirt off and tosses it aside. His chest has a spattering of light hair across his sculpted pecs that forms into his happy trail which leads to something else I can't wait to get a look at. His biceps flex, and while he's not as heavily muscled as the other guys, he's not out of shape either. He's strong and lean and awfully damn cuddly.

When his hands unbutton his jeans, pushing them down his legs, I finally get my first glimpse of what I have to work with. His dick eagerly comes out to greet me, long and thick and absolutely perfect.

"You keep licking your lips like that, pretty girl, and I'll happily fill them up for you."

Just like that, the fire in my blood flares higher. I'm suddenly starving, and most definitely not for chicken. Striding forward, I grab his hand and tug him into the large walk-in shower with its pretty sparkly white tile and silver accents. Steam fills the enclosure, making the space seem otherworldly. Or maybe that's just my heat brain talking.

Sinking to my knees, I let my head fall back until I'm staring into his eyes.

Zig curses. "Fuck, West. I didn't mean—"

I don't give him a chance to finish that sentence. My mouth surrounds the head of his cock, licking and sucking before I take him in deep. He groans, his hesitation forgotten. Long fingers slide through my hair, gripping my head as I bob up and down his length, trailing my tongue across the sensitive underside and lightly spearing it into the hole at the tip. His fingers flex, but he doesn't take control. He's holding back, and I don't want that. I want all of him.

Popping off my current favorite heat toy, I stare up at him with water droplets falling from my lashes.

"Show me what you like, Zig. Teach me. Don't hold yourself back."

"Are you trying to kill me next?" he asks, voice hoarse.

I simply open my mouth wide and stick out my tongue. That's all the invitation he needs. Gripping his dick, he taps it on my tongue twice before sliding it over and around my lips.

"These lips were made for sucking cock." His voice has deepened, his eyes intent and focused. There he is. The man who buys silk rope for the Omega he barely knows because she's in heat. "You were stunning before, but like this... you're fucking heartstopping."

Without any more words, he presses in, slowly at first, testing and teasing. Sensing I'm his for the taking, the nice guy disappears, and the man I'm staring up at thrusts in, balls deep. He hits the back of my throat, making me gag, then he growls and does it again. Over and over, he throat fucks me, one hand around the back of my head while the other cradles my neck, squeezing lightly as he slams in. One or two more strokes and he goes deep, holding me down on him. My nose is nestled in the hair at his base, my lips are stretched around his girth, and I definitely can't breathe, but I'll be damned if I'm not a happy little heat slut.

"That's it. Such a good girl. Take it all. You can do it. Just like that. Fuck."

My hands are squeezing his thighs, slick dripping from my pussy, and I'm so fucking turned on I can't think straight. He forcefully pulls me off his dick.

"Lick the tip, pretty girl. Tongue that hole for me like you did earlier."

I lick the smooth round head of his cock, pressing against the slit at the end, giving it extra attention. He groans, and my belly clenches as a whine climbs up my throat.

"So fucking good, pretty girl. Now, let's go deep one more time before I fuck that greedy little cunt."

He doesn't wait for permission, just plunges forward, his balls slapping against my chin. Without a knot, he can go a little deeper than the Alphas, so I try to relax my throat to take more of him in.

"The sight of your lips wrapped around my dick is so goddamn sexy," he rasps, and the hand on my throat moves up to grip the side of my head. "You're gonna take everything I've got, then swallow around my head. You ace this test, and I'll fuck you so good. I promise."

He does exactly what he said he would. His dick slips down my throat, and I swallow around him reflexively as he begins to thrust fast and deep. The sounds I'm making are fucking filthy—wet squelching sounds that rush out between my moans. Then he presses my face harder into his body, his dick swelling until I gag. Watery eyes stare up at his face that's taut with strain.

"One more second, baby. You feel so fucking good. You've got this."

That one second turns into two, and I can feel the pressure building in my chest. With a growl, he pushes me off of his dick, and I suck in a ragged breath of air, but he doesn't give me a chance to truly catch my breath. In one smooth motion, he picks me up, and my legs wrap around his waist as he spins us and slams my back into the cool tile wall.

"You are so damn perfect. For me, for all of us. You hear me?"

His mouth smashes into mine just as his dick finds my sopping pussy. He thrusts in, swallowing my moan while my pussy squeezes him tight. Pulling back, he pounds into me without mercy, but I don't need any. My body is on fire, desperate for release.

"You're close. I can feel you trying to cut off circulation to my dick. Ready to come for me, pretty girl?"

"Yes, Zig. Make me come."

"One orgasm coming right up." He grins, his dimples making an appearance. "Get it?"

My chuckle is cut off by a shout when he leans back, his long fingers reaching between us to press down hard on my clit, rubbing in little circles that have the world around me going black. I come apart in his arms, the breath stolen from my lungs by an intensely incredible orgasm. As the aftershocks ebb, I gasp in much needed air, feeling him still pumping his hips.

"One more," he demands, his fingertips skimming between my cheeks.

He plunges two fingers into my ass, roughly pumping them in tandem with his cock. It's like lightning zings through my blood at the harsh intrusion, the pinch of pain with the sudden fullness sending me spiraling right into another orgasm. This time, I cry out, my arms winding around his neck as a rough sob slips free. It feels *so* fucking good. My body doesn't even care that he doesn't have a knot. It's so overwhelmed by the incongruity of this man and what he's doing to us that it just sighs in satisfied exhaustion.

He grunts, then a low growl sneaks out as he pulls me down hard on his dick.

"A. Fucking. Plus."

His legs are shaking, and his body continues to grind into me until he leans forward, pressing his forehead into mine.

"Fucking. Perfect."

He's right. This is. These men and what we're building. Unexpectedly, I hiccup, tears spilling out from my eyes.

"Shit. Did I hurt you?" he asks, his voice hoarse and worried.

My forehead rolls back and forth. "Happy tears."

His body relaxes against mine, then he kisses each tear away. "I'm never this lucky," he whispers.

"Your luck has changed, Ziggy Marshall."

"Because of you."

We share a look, one filled with all sorts of things neither of us wants to risk putting into words quite yet. That time will come, and when it does, I'll be ready. My future is finally looking brighter, and I'm ready to grab it and not let go.

# 28

## ZIGGY MARSHALL

Every single muscle in my body is sore—even ones I didn't know existed. It's been forty-eight hours of damn near nonstop sex, and I'm not sure how much juice I have left in the tank. If anyone had ever asked me if there was such a thing as too much sex, I would've laughed in their face. Now, I've discovered death by sex might really be possible.

West is grinding down on Nash's knot, his teeth skimming dangerously across her jaw when I walk back into the room.

"Bite, Alpha. *Please!*" she whines for the millionth time, and I watch Nash carefully.

With every hoarse plea, his control becomes thinner and thinner. That he's made it this long without claiming her proves just how much he's invested in making this work despite his denials.

"Soon, bright eyes," he whispers against her mouth. "I can't wait to sink my teeth into your smooth skin and taste you on my tongue."

Her whimper breaks my heart. This heat has been worse than anything I've ever read about. Whether that's because she's separated from her bonded Omega or because she's not receiving the attention she truly needs with only two of us, I can't be sure.

One thing these last couple of days has proven is that we can't do this alone. West needs and deserves a true pack, one that can share the responsibility of her care to make sure she's never left wanting.

"Knot. Bite. *P-please...*" she begs incoherently.

Like right now.

Meeting Nash's tired eyes, I take pity on the Alpha since he tapped me out to give me a breather. He stills her desperate grinding, his teeth clenched against the cries leaving her mouth.

"Shhhh, baby. We'll take care of you. Zig's back to help."

There are dark circles under her big blue eyes when she turns to look at me.

"Zig..."

I don't know what she was going to say because a fat tear rolls down her cheek as a choked sob bursts out.

"I've got you, pretty girl." I glance at Nash. "Flip her over, Alpha. Her back to your chest."

Watery eyes meet mine as Nash shifts, lifting her off of him. I reach out, and she uses my hand to help her turn over so she's face up on Nash's body.

Climbing onto the bed, I grab the red silk rope from the nightstand and nudge Nash's legs apart. He glares at me in warning, but I don't pay him any mind. Shit's gonna get mighty cozy in here real quick. He better get used to it.

Crawling forward, I reach for one hand, then the other, tying her wrists together.

"Now put them over your head so Nash can tie them to the headboard."

She does as she's told, chest flushed and heaving, while Nash makes quick work of securing her to the sleek white slats of the headboard.

"So goddamn stunning." I stroke my dick to the sight of her strung up and needy.

Leaning forward, I let my tongue play through the slick along her inner thighs. She's tart and spicy, ripe, and ready for an orgasm.

"How much can you take, pretty girl? What are your limits?"

"H-help me learn my limits, Professor."

My dick is instantly rock hard and wanting. Hell. I didn't even know roleplay was a kink of mine, but *damn*. That was hot as fuck.

"Class, today's lesson will test the female Omega's stretching capabilities."

She sucks in a ragged breath of air as I reach forward, shoving one finger, then two, into her wetness. She tries to roll against my hand, but I retreat, forcing her to take what I give her.

"Zig, don't tease."

"Look at me, bright eyes." She glances over her shoulder at Nash. "Trust us. Okay?"

She exhales harshly, then nods.

I swap out two fingers for three despite her pussy trying to clamp down around them.

"How's that feel, pretty girl?"

"Good. *So* fucking good, Professor."

My balls draw up tight at the new nickname, but no way in hell am I rushing this. They'll just need to calm the fuck down.

"Time to test those limits. Tell me to stop, and I'll—"

"Do it. Please, Zig," she begs.

"Fucking hell," Nash groans, his hands roaming her naked body.

Pulling my hand back, I slowly press forward with four fingers, her little hole squeezing around them tightly.

"That's four, pretty girl. You know what's next?"

"Me busting my load without even being inside her?" Nash snarls.

"Someone's getting impatient and not taking the lesson seriously."

She laughs, the sound more than a little hoarse as her body heats to levels we might need to check if we can't get them to come down.

I push my worry aside for now, hoping that this might be just what she needs to get her over the biggest hurdle of her heat.

"All five fingers, baby, here we go."

She's literally gushing at this point, so I'm not even sure why I thought lube would be necessary. All five fingers easily slide in and out, her hips bucking for more.

"You're doing so good for us, pretty girl. You should see your hot little cunt taking my hand. But you can take more, I think."

Her chest is rapidly rising and falling, her fists clenched tightly around the silk rope. She needs to come again, and I think this will push her over that edge. Hopefully, she doesn't pull Nash and me right along with her because I have plans.

My hand meets more resistance as it slides forward to the knuckles, but I pull back and try again.

"Ziggy, I don't think... I don't know if—"

"Relax, baby," Nash purrs, his chest rumbling softly.

I can feel the tension give just enough, so I take the opportunity to press forward, watching her pussy stretch wide around my left hand.

"Oh shit. Oh fuck. More. Less. Something. I-I don't know..."

And then my entire hand is swallowed up by her cunt damn near to my wrist.

"Look at your pretty pussy taking my whole goddamn fist. You're acing this shit."

Pulling back, I see her body stretch around me until my knuckles are visible, then I plunge back in.

"Oh my god. Zig!"

Nash is sucking on her neck, her head tilted back over his shoulder. With her legs spread wide and my fist in her cunt, I almost wish I could take a picture of this moment and hang it on my wall. Pretty sure she wouldn't exactly approve of that though.

My fist is thrusting faster now, in and out, and her legs are beginning to shake. Every time my fist is swallowed whole, she clenches down around me, wanting to lock me within her body. This might be as close as I'll ever get to understanding an Alpha's knot locked inside an Omega. It's a powerful rush, one that has me tilting my fist so that my knuckles brush along the top of her inner wall. Her entire body is shaking now, and I'm about at the limits of my control.

She's the hottest goddamn thing I've ever seen in my life.

"That's it. Give it to me, West. Come all over my fucking fist."

Her hands grip the rope, pulling it taut as her body seizes up. One minute, she's crying out my name. The next, she's squirting all over me, the bed, and Nash until we're soaked with it.

I can't fucking hold back anymore. Carefully removing my fist, I look up. Nash's hands are kneading her breasts as they awkwardly kiss over her shoulder. Using his distraction to my advantage, I take a hold of his dick. He flinches, a growl echoing through the room.

"What the actual fuck, Zig?"

"What? No way you could have lined yourself up in this position, and I'm impatient. Just giving you a helping hand. No big deal."

"No big deal, he says..." Nash mutters, and West's exhausted giggle has me choking back my laughter.

I line him up with West's pussy, and he takes over, rolling his hips until he's filling her up. Their combined moans have me clenching my teeth together so hard I'm surprised they don't crack under the pressure.

Leaning forward, I do the one thing I've been aching to do—lap at her soaked clit, sucking and nibbling, needing her satisfaction on my tongue.

"Shit!" Nash cries out, and I realize I got a little overzealous in my attention, my tongue licking down to the spot where he's seated inside her. Maybe I even licked his dick a little when he pulled out of her. "I swear to Christ, Zig..."

But his complaint cuts out with a garbled moan when I do it again. Now, I don't think I'm bi or anything like that. I just don't give two fucks about who my mouth is on at the moment. It's hot, filthy sex, and at this point I'm too lost to the lust in my veins. I know I'm just a Beta, and we don't get the same feral urges Alphas do, but what I'm feeling right now has to be damn close.

Sitting up, I take my dick in my hand and inch forward until I'm poised at her opening.

"Ready for your next test, pretty girl?"

I don't even recognize my own voice. It's deep and rough, need coiling around my vocal cords and choking me.

"Yes, Professor."

Nash stills, eyeing me down the length of West's body.

"What about you? Any objections? Speak now or forever hold your peace."

"Do it. Make our Omega lose her mind."

West whines, low and deep, when the tip of my cock presses against the hole Nash is already filling. He grunts when I push in, our two dicks sliding against each other. To be fair, this is a first for me, but I'm not hating it. She's warm and wet and impossibly tight. I continue to slide in alongside Nash until I'm fully inside her.

Her eyes are closed, knuckles white on the rope and a low keening whine rushing from her swollen lips.

"Holy fuck, pretty girl. Look at your pussy taking both our dicks. Such a goddamn pretty sight."

She whimpers, her head rolling back against Nash's chest.

"Ready for us to double fuck you now, bright eyes?" Nash growls. Eyes wild, his hips buck involuntarily.

"Yes. *Please*. Fuck me like I'm your good little girl."

Nash's eyes meet mine, and he nods. I pull out slightly, feeling the tug of her pussy trying to clamp down on my dick, then I thrust forward. The movement is so fucking divine, I groan, then immediately do it again, chasing this indescribable pleasure.

"Oh shit. Now, Alpha. I need to be yours *now*. Bite me. Claim me. Please..." She ends with a hoarse cry.

Nash's mouth seals around her throat, and I have a split second to think, *He did it. We're fucked...* before he growls against her skin, his hands gripping her waist so hard she'll probably have bruises. He violently bucks his hips up from the bottom, making his knot skim along my dick. Logically, I should have anticipated this, but in the heat of the moment I just wanted to get my dick squeezed. I didn't consider his knot in this equation. It feels like he's trying to squeeze a goddamn watermelon into her vagina while another cucumber is already filling the hole.

Holy. Motherfucking. Shit. The second he's fully inside, he roars. West screams. And I can't say shit because my orgasm has a stranglehold on my vocal cords. I'm coming harder than I have in my entire life, and I think this really might be the end. Death by sex.

I'm not sure if I pass out or have an out-of-body experience or what, but the next thing I know, I come to with my full body weight resting on West, who's unconscious on top of Nash, who's nudging me with his leg from the bottom.

"Get off, fucker!" he barks.

On weak arms, I push up, my nose brushing along West's jaw. I need to check on her, but I'm pretty sure one arm isn't strong enough to hold my body weight at the moment.

"Pretty girl, you okay?" I whisper, though it's not supposed to be a whisper. My throat is just dry and feels like I swallowed rocks.

"You bastards killed my poor vagina. It's never gonna be the same again," she rasps with her eyes still closed, but I see the grin she's trying to hide.

"But it felt fucking fantastic, didn't it?" I prompt more than a little smugly.

She releases a long wavering sigh. "It did, dammit."

Nash's eyes are closed, his hands blindly reaching up to untie her arms.

She whines as she pulls them down. "Fuck. That's a weird ass feeling."

Nash rubs her arms as he yawns. "Yeah. So is shoving my knot through my girl's tight hole while another man's dick jacks me off inside her."

I can't help it. I burst out laughing, which just shimmies our dicks that are trapped in her body, then West follows suit.

Nash growls, "You two are fucking trouble!"

We just laugh harder.

# 29

## WEST CARTER

How is this real life? Ziggy's in my kitchen cooking breakfast in his boxers, and Nash is in the shower. It's like this is a morning that's played out a million times before, yet the newness gives me a flutter in my belly each and every time I catch sight of the guys in my space, caring for me in ways I had no idea I was missing so damn desperately. I've been soaking it all in while I can even though a part of me is sort of waiting for the moment my happy little bubble bursts. Is that my past talking or just pessimism I didn't know I had rearing its ugly head? I can't be sure. I hate it, but there's a small part of me that wonders if it was just the sex haze. Maybe what exists between us doesn't feel as real for them as it does for me, not that the guys have done anything to make me think that. They've been incredible.

My heat lasted an insane five days. It was nonstop sex, sex, and more sex. With Ziggy having to work and Nash having to step out for practices, it was a rough ride, but we made it through, and now the last week and a half have looked like this—domesticated bliss.

"You hungry, or are you *hungry*, pretty girl?" Ziggy wags his eyebrows with the spatula in his hand.

I smirk. "Do you really want my answer to that?"

"You just want me for my body."

Walking up behind him, I wrap my arms around his waist. "I want you for so much more than that, Ziggy."

"Aww. You—"

"I mean, you also make a really mean omelet."

The spatula stops in midair, and he shoots me a glare over his shoulder. My giggle rings through the kitchen as his free hand comes up to grip the one resting on his chest to keep me from running away.

"Is that all I am to you? Personal chef and a big dick to sit on?"

"While your cooking is top notch and your dick *is* mighty comfortable..." My chin rests on his back. "Having you here with me means more than you can ever know."

He turns from the stove, wrapping his arms around me. "West, you came into my life and filled up an emptiness I didn't know existed. I will never be able to put into words how grateful I am for that." My heart is pounding in my chest, feeling fuller than it ever has...and then his hands shift to my butt. "I'm also incredibly grateful for this ass."

I giggle, burrowing in and holding him so damn tight.

"Food's burning, jackass," Nash grumbles, walking into the kitchen in just a towel.

"Shit!"

Ziggy turns back around to the stove as my eyes trail over Nash, taking in the sheen on his skin that reminds me of all the sweaty moments we've had. And because my pussy is a hussy where they're concerned, it clenches needily.

"You keep perfuming like that, and I'll say fuck breakfast and eat you instead."

I grin as I feel slick fill the apex of my thighs. "Don't you have a meeting with Coach Tomlinson this morning?"

One brow arches. "Yes, but if you think that's a deterrent, you're wrong, bright eyes. Just won't have time to play with my food, that's all."

A groan slips out, and Ziggy hums.

"You're lucky I didn't make waffles today. West with a side of whipped cream and berries sounds pretty fucking sweet right now."

"Tomorrow." Nash steps over to me, his fingers brushing along my jaw until his large hand cradles my head. "Because now I'm starving for spiced plums and whipped cream."

He kisses me, and there's an undercurrent there that's different. The heat is undeniable, but this is softer. Not much, mind you, because this is Nash after all, but enough that I'm almost holding my breath.

"Breathe," he whispers against my lips.

When my eyes open, I find his locked on mine. There's a moment when the anticipation has my belly doing flips.

Then the doorbell rings.

"Who the hell is that?" Nash growls.

"I don't know." Stepping out of his arms, I head for the door, peek out of the peephole, and gasp.

"Well?"

I whip open the door and find Porter's huge smile staring back at me. In two seconds flat, I launch myself at him, his strong arms catching me midair and spinning me around.

"Fuck, hero, I missed you."

He smells like mint chocolate and tea. Hux's spice mixes with his in a combination that shouldn't necessarily work but somehow does. Before I can say anything, his lips are on mine, his tongue diving into my mouth. It's beyond hot and over way too fast once a choked sound leaves his lips.

"You taste like *him*," Porter murmurs.

"Maybe that's because my tongue was just in her mouth."

When I spin around, Nash is glaring at the two men in my doorway, arms crossed over his naked chest.

"Still here, Daniels?" Porter asks.

"Someone had to be."

Ouch. Tension rises in the bond, Porter's anger hitting me sharply in the heart.

"C'mere, sweet thing. Ignore them. I need to hold you for a minute." Hux snags my hand and pulls me into his broad chest.

I snuggle in, wrapping myself up in my other Alpha whose purr is rumbling so hard my cheek tingles. Then he sighs, his body relaxing against mine.

"What are you guys doing here?" I whisper.

"After last night's game, we switched our flight to be able to get here this morning so we could come straight here instead. Wanted to see if we could convince you to come back to Arizona with us so we could spend some time with you."

The growl behind me has my shoulders tensing.

"What makes you think you can just walk in here and drag her to Arizona?" Nash snaps.

Ziggy's hand lands on Nash's shoulder. "Nash—"

"She's my bonded Omega," Porter snaps. "I have every right to want to be with her."

"If you think I'm going to let you steal her away, you have another thing coming."

Hux tenses against me. "She's not a goddamn toy, but you two are definitely acting like fucking toddlers."

"Guys—"

The two groups of men start arguing back and forth, ignoring me and my attempts to calm the situation. My stomach clenches with a feeling that's too close to nausea for my comfort. I knew it was coming. That perfect little bubble I've been living in is popping under the reality of dealing with two separate groups of men who aren't pack. Hell, they aren't even *friends*.

Nash takes an aggressive step forward, and Porter meets him halfway.

"Back the fuck off, Daniels. You've had her for two goddamn *weeks*."

"Eat shit, Hanson. You can't force her to leave. I dare you to try."

Back and forth, voices raise. Anger has flooded the room, making my chest ache.

"Shut the fuck up, all of you!" Ziggy yells. "You're upsetting her."

They don't listen. Suddenly, my future is laid out before me. I'll be a pawn stuck between these men. They're proving right now that the beef between them is larger than their feelings for me. And I only wish I was talking about their dicks because right now they're sure acting like some.

Sadness and fury build inside me, part my own and part influenced by Porter, but he doesn't seem to notice.

"She's *ours*, Daniels. I have the bond mark to prove it."

"You might, but your Alpha sure as hell doesn't. So fuck off. She's mine."

"Guys!" Ziggy shouts.

Porter gets in Nash's face, slinging insults until my grumpy Alpha has had enough and shoves him...*hard.*

"Don't fucking touch him, asshole," Hux growls, stepping up beside Porter.

Ziggy tries to hold Nash back from swinging at Porter, but it's a losing battle. There's going to be a brawl right inside my front door, and I've had enough. My fists clench at my sides, and my gut churns. This is never going to work. They'll always be at odds, and nothing—not even me—will be enough to change their minds.

"Out!" I shout over the growls and snarls, but they don't hear me, so I take a deep breath and scream, "Get! Out!"

My body is shaking with dread and anger so deep I'm either going to punch someone or start sobbing. The room has gone quiet, with all eyes turning to me, though they continue to dart glances at each other.

"Hero, don't—"

"You heard what I said. All of you. *Out.*"

"West," Hux begins, spearing me with his big brown eyes, and I feel the first furious tear roll down my cheeks.

"I would like you all to leave," I rasp.

Ziggy steps forward, studying me with such intensity I can't even face him. I look away, my lips starting to tremble. "I think we should do as she says," he quietly states.

"Fuck no! I'm not—"

Ziggy's eyes snap to Nash's. "You can, and you will. For West."

Nash's eyes meet mine. Fear and frustration stare back at me.

"Bright eyes, please..."

His tone has softened to the point where I almost don't recognize it, and my heart is breaking a little inside. The future I had just found and grabbed onto with both hands is now searing my palms, a painful burn that will leave scars in its wake.

"It's never going to change, is it? I'll always be stuck in the middle of this war between all of you. Nothing—not even my feelings for all of you—will make a damn bit of difference. Just...*go*."

"You heard her. Everybody out," Hux commands, grabbing Porter's bicep and trying to guide him to the door.

Porter takes one step toward the door before he turns back, marches over to me, and slides his hand behind my neck, kissing me with the force of a man who's desperate to imprint himself on me so I don't forget him. Not like I can. We're bonded, and that means I have some very difficult things to think about.

Nash watches the entire interaction, nostrils flaring and his fists clenched tightly at his sides. I ignore him.

Porter pulls back, dropping one last kiss on my forehead. "I won't be far, hero."

He stalks towards the door, past Hux, and into the foyer. The Alpha stares at me, a lost expression on his face as he tugs me into his chest, squeezing me tightly.

"We'll figure all of this out. I promise."

He kisses the top of my head and follows Porter into the foyer. I hear the ding of the elevator and their low murmurs, then it goes quiet. They're gone. When I turn, tears trailing down my face, I study the bulge of Nash's jaw muscles. He's struggling to rein himself in. *If only it weren't too late.* Without a word, he heads for my bedroom.

Ziggy steps forward, wrapping two strong arms around me and tucking me in under his chin.

"It'll be okay, pretty girl."

The tears fall harder. "I don't think it will, Zig. They're never going to get along. I'm not enough to—"

"You're more than enough. Everything will work out. You'll see."

I squeeze him tighter, needing to hold on to something so I don't fall apart completely. When did I grow so dependent on these guys? I've survived on my own for years, but the second they arrived, my instincts forced my hard-earned lessons to take a back seat to their demands. Except this time they may have gotten it wrong, and I'm the one that will suffer for it.

Heavy boots trudge down the hall, and Zig squeezes a little harder before he pulls back, gripping my chin and forcing me to meet his gaze.

"You have my number now. Call me if you need anything, you hear me?"

I nod, more tears falling.

He drops a soft kiss on my lips, and when his arms slowly slide away and he heads for the front door, I almost call him back. Almost tell him he's become important to me. That I need him. But the scent of spiced rum and vanilla hits me strong and sharp.

When I force my eyes to Nash, his are like a stormy sea filled with so many emotions I can't begin to name them all.

"I love you, West."

My breath catches, and another tear rolls down my face. "Nash..."

His nostrils flare, and he shakes his head. "Never thought I'd say that to a woman. Ever. But here I am. I just..." He looks away, brows furrowing. "You want a pack, but as today has proven, I don't think I'm built for pack life. As much as it kills me to say it, you deserve an Alpha who can give you everything you need because you're an amazing woman, West Carter."

"But you said I was yours," I whisper around the whine building in my throat.

"I'll always be yours, but I think it's best if..." He grits his teeth, taking a deep breath in and exhaling. "If you let McCarren make you his."

It's like he took a sledgehammer to my heart. It shatters, leaving nothing but pieces too small to ever put back together again. I hold back my sob and force myself to keep it together just a little longer. When he steps into me, I bite my bottom lip to keep myself from begging him to stay. Loving me is one thing. Wanting to be with me is another, and he's already said he's not sure he's man enough to do that.

With blurry eyes, I watch him lean into me. "Ziggy was right," he whispers in my ear. "This is the one thing I can do for you, bright eyes." Then he closes the distance between us and kisses my cheek.

It feels like the end of something great that never had a chance to really even begin.

He steps back, a low growl rumbling between us before he simply walks away.

I don't turn. Don't speak. Just wait for the click of the door to close before I release the ragged breath I've been holding. The sob I've been fighting breaks free. My body sags, and I drop to the floor, wondering where everything went wrong and if I'll ever be okay again.

# 30

## HUXLEY MCCARREN

"I'm telling you, Hux, something's wrong."

Porter is pacing back and forth in our temporary living room while I'm splayed out on the surprisingly comfortable sofa. My head is thrown back on the cushions, and my eyes are closed to avoid watching him wear a hole in the carpet. Porter's scent is more bitter chocolate than mint, his stress flooding the room, leaving a tart flavor on my tongue. After the blowout at West's place, no way in hell were we going to just fly back to Arizona. Thank fuck we had a bye week. Instead, we found an AirBnb down the street from her penthouse, so we'd be close by in case she needed us.

I sigh. "It's only been six days. Her group text asked for a little space, and we agreed to give it to her."

Even though it was the hardest thing I've ever had to do. Not talking to her every day has been hell. My instincts are pushing against my sensible nature, demanding we go over there and tell her how we feel. They don't care that we're respecting her wishes or that she's avoiding all of us because we acted like immature, insensitive dickheads.

"You don't understand. She's gotten way too good at blocking me out of the bond. She wouldn't do that unless something were wrong, right?"

"Babe, I think you need to calm down."

My phone buzzes in my pocket, and I lift my right ass cheek off the sofa cushion to grab it. Forcing myself to open my tired eyes, I raise it to my face and frown.

**Ziggy: Need you at West's apartment.**

**Me: Is everything okay?**

Bubbles appear at the bottom of the screen as I try to keep my nerves at bay. Why is he with West? Didn't we *all* agree to give her space? Well, all of us except Nash because that asshat had the balls to walk away from her.

**Ziggy: She needs her Alpha, and considering the situation, I didn't think Nash would be a good choice.**

*Her Alpha.* Damn straight I am.

**Me: On my way.**

Anxiety spikes sharp and fast, my imagination running wild. *Fuck.* Maybe Porter's right. Maybe something *is* wrong.

"What is it?" he asks, pausing in front of me.

For a brief moment, I consider lying to him because he's anxious enough as it is, but this is *Porter,* my Omega and my best friend. We don't lie to each other, and I'm not about to start now. Flipping my phone around, I show him the text.

His eyes whip up to mine. "I'm coming with you."

I'm shaking my head before he can finish the sentence. "I think you should stay here and let me go alone. We're only down the street. If I need you, you can be there in a matter of minutes."

His hand skims through his hair, eyes a little wild. Misery is alive in the bond, and it kills me to see it etched all over his handsome face.

"I don't know what to do," he whispers.

We're both a little lost, but we need to start having some real conversations about how to move forward. All too soon, reality is going to rear its ugly head. We'll have to go back to Arizona, so we've only got a matter of days to figure this shit out.

"Look, Porter, I think we need to talk about where we go from here."

"I'm not fucking leaving her."

"I'm not saying that."

"Then what the hell are you saying, Hux? Right now, our girl is hurting because of us, and everything we almost had in our grasp is falling apart. Fuck knows that doesn't mean I'm going to give up on her, unlike the *asshole* who rejected her for some bullshit reason."

"I think you need to talk to Nash." I stand, watching surprise flash across my best friend's face. "We both do, but you two have the biggest beef. The faster we can clear this shit up and come to some sort of understanding, the faster we can get back to our girl."

He's staring at me like he wants to argue, but he knows I'm right. The only thing holding us back right now is *us*.

How many times did our dads give us that talk when we were kids, filling our heads with the infinite possibilities laid out before us? Sure, back then it was about getting a scholarship, or going pro, or winning a championship, but this particular lesson doesn't just apply to hockey. It applies in *life*. Never more so than when it comes to the woman we will do anything to win back. I'll take that over a championship any day.

Stepping toward him, I grab his hand. "Just think about it, okay? I miss her."

"And you think I don't?" he rasps.

"I know you do. I can feel it in the bond. But we're the only ones who can fix this, and you know it."

Leaning forward, I press a soft kiss to his lips. "I'm going to go over there and see what's going on. Just keep your phone on you in case I need you."

He nods, and with one last look, I'm out the door and on my way down the busy Chicago streets, passing business folks in their fancy suits and ties, cars honking at each other, and the smell of fresh baked bread from the mom and pop bakery thriving on the corner. While I've never been a fan of the city, preferring the mountains and dry air, I can see why West is so fond of this one. The hustle and bustle, the food, the energy.

But she needs to come home.

The doorman at West's building recognizes me, holding the door open as I walk up.

"Good evening, Mr. McCarren."

I simply nod and make my way toward the elevator. The ride up to the penthouse is filled with nerves and anxiety and even a little bit of excitement. I haven't seen her in almost a week after being gone for two before that. The need to hold her is stronger than anything I've ever felt before.

A loud ding indicates my arrival, and I step into the foyer. Rather than ring the doorbell, I shoot Ziggy a quick text letting him know I'm here. Seconds later, he's opening the door and holding it open so

I can walk in. He looks tired and haggard, with dark circles under his eyes and rumpled clothes.

"What's going on, Ziggy? You're making me nervous."

He runs both hands down his face.

*That can't be good.*

"She's in the bathroom, but she'll barely talk to me. She needs you."

I swallow harshly, a sense of foreboding kicking up in my gut. "What am I going to find when I walk in there?"

He looks down the hall before turning back to me, his lips pursed for a moment before he whispers, "A scared, broken-hearted Omega."

*Scared? Why the hell would she be scared?*

Turning to walk down the hall, he stops me with his hand on my bicep. "Just promise me something."

I nod because my own fear is starting to rise, and it's got a stranglehold on my throat.

"Fix this." He stares me down, daring me to argue. "We need to be here for her. Now more than ever."

"I promise."

His shoulders relax a little.

I glance down the hall. "Did she call you?"

A small hint of my Alpha side rears up in indignation that she may have called the Beta instead of us, but I shove that shit down. I refuse to let some voice ruin what I just promised to fix.

"Her friends called when she wasn't answering her phone. One's out of town for work, and the other is in Arizona visiting family. They were worried when she sent them a nonsensical text, so they hunted me down at the university. They gave me the codes to get in and check on her because she's been alone here for six goddamn days." He shakes his head. "I'll stay until I know she's going to be okay with you here, then I'll slip out and give you guys some time alone."

"Thanks, man."

"Good luck. You have my number if you need me."

Making my way down the hall, I see the double doors are open. The closer I get, the stronger her scent gets, except it's not the rich spice I'm used to. It's tart and bitter. She's hurting, and my instincts are rioting inside. We shouldn't have waited so long. I should've been here, forcing her to let us in rather than allowing her to withdraw from us.

Loving someone doesn't mean you give them everything they want. Sometimes it means giving them everything they don't even know they need.

The wall straight ahead is covered in a silvery wallpaper that glints a little with the light coming through the myriad of windows I can make out just beyond its edges. For a second, I'm not sure which way to go, then I hear her whine, low and keening. My feet are rushing forward before I can consciously think about what to do or say.

Coming to a dead stop in the doorway of a large, luxurious bathroom, I get my first glimpse of my girl. She's leaning back against a large jacuzzi tub, her knees up and her body curled around them. Her forehead rests on her arms, shoulders shaking with quiet sobs that damn near rip my heart out. Her hair is in a messy bun, her body encompassed by an oversized hoodie that barely covers her ass on the cold tile.

"Hey, sweet thing," I murmur. Her head whips up, eyes red and puffy, with tears pouring out them.

"Huxley?" she whimpers.

"It's me, baby. Can I come in?"

She blinks, almost as if she's not seeing me. She looks so small. Lost. *Fragile.* I can't stay away anymore. Striding forward, I scoop her up off the floor and cradle her in my arms. Hers wrap limply around my neck like she doesn't have the strength to hold on to me. She nuzzles against my jaw, her breath ragged as her sobs start anew.

"West, you're scaring me. Tell me what's going on and why you're not answering your friends' calls. They're worried about you."

She hiccups, pulling back until I'm looking into her bloodshot eyes. Slowly, she draws one arm toward her until her fingertips poke through the end of her sleeve. There's something in her hands, and it takes my frantic brain a second to process what I'm seeing, then my eyes dart back to hers.

"You're as white as a ghost," she says hoarsely. "How do you think *I* feel?"

The thin stick in her hand has a little oval screen with one word. *Pregnant.*

Words are still failing me, my mind whirring a million miles an hour. It can't be mine. I wasn't here for her heat. That means it's... *Nash's*. The man who walked away from his Omega. *Rejected* her. I know shit all about the chemistry between Alphas and Omegas, but even I understand that the ramifications of what he did are far reaching. Now that she's carrying his baby...

Okay, so maybe that's a little Alpha-centric of me. My logical brain knows that the baby could also be Ziggy's, biologically, but right now, it's the Alpha hindbrain in control. It doesn't care about logic. It only cares that another Alpha, one we barely tolerate and, honestly, didn't have a reason to give a shit about, is likely responsible for fathering this child with the woman we love.

*Fuck.* He may not want her, but I do, without question. Sure, she's pregnant with another Alpha's baby, but to me, that doesn't mean shit. She needs me, and I will stand by her no matter what. Now, I just need to find the right words to reassure her that everything is going to be okay.

*Say something, dammit!*

"You know this doesn't change anything, right? You're ours and so is that little one growing in your belly."

A pained sob escapes. "But it's *his*, and he doesn't even want me."

"But we do," I say softly. "We'll be there with you every step of the way. I promise."

"Porter's going to freak the hell out." She sniffles. "I don't even blame him. I should've been more careful. I'm *bonded* to Porter, and I should've taken him into account before I went off and got myself knocked up by an Alpha he despises."

"West, look at me. Porter might be surprised at first, but you're his *Omega*. He'll fucking love that baby like his own because he or she is a part of you."

"How can you be so calm about this?" She wipes her sleeve across her eyes, drying her tears. The life changing stick waves in her hand as she says, "I'm pregnant with another Alpha's baby, Hux! One who very clearly wants nothing to do with me or this pack. Now, I'm going to have to share my baby with an asshole who'd rather walk away than try to be nice for once in his goddamn life. *God*. Past heat-me is a goddamn idiot."

Part of me settles as I start to see the angry flush pinkening her cheeks.

*There's my girl.*

Sure, this isn't what we had planned, but isn't that par for the course with us? We'll get through this *together*. I have no doubt that as soon as Porter gets over his initial shock, he'll come to the same conclusion. They're both ours, regardless of DNA. Now, more than ever, I know we have to work through our differences for both the woman in my arms and the little one growing inside her. And Daniels really is a jackass if this doesn't help him see that this is where he belongs.

"You're not an idiot. We were for not being here when we should have been then acting like giant dicks by showing up and expecting you to drop everything to come with us. Daniels may be an asshole, but in some ways, he was right. We didn't take into account his feelings on the matter either."

"You guys had games. I understood. It's not your—"

I grip her chin, forcing her eyes to mine. "A game is *never* more important than you. Do you hear me?"

A single tear trails down her face, and I drop my forehead to hers. My heart is going to explode out of my chest if I don't give in and tell her exactly how I feel about her.

"I love you, West. You don't have to go through this alone. Let us help."

She whimpers softly. "I love you too."

My purr rumbles between us, my lips touching hers softly. She wraps herself around my neck, squeezing me so tightly I can barely breathe, but I don't care. I've got my woman in my arms and her lips on mine. I'm one happy fucking Alpha.

When she pulls back, she's studying me intently.

"You really mean it? You don't care if the baby is Nash's? I was worried that you guys wouldn't want me—"

I growl, cutting her off.

"Not one fucking bit. I meant it when I said you're mine. That's not conditional." I kiss her again just because I can. "But you're gonna need to tell him. He deserves the chance to dig himself out of the hole he dug."

Her face scrunches up, and I just know she's about to argue, but then she surprises me.

With a hefty sigh, she says, "I know. And I will, I promise. But right now there's something else I need."

"What's that, sweet thing?"

She takes a deep breath, exhaling slowly. "I need my Alpha to make me his. Officially."

I growl. "Fuck, West."

Big blue watery eyes meet mine. "Please, Hux. I don't want to wait anymore."

"Me either, baby."

With purposeful strides, I carry her out of the room, and she points to the left as we exit. My need for her is growing by the second, the demand to make her mine singing in my blood. I've been so consumed by her and the situation that I haven't paid much attention to my bond with Porter, but a flash of anger suddenly surges through our connection. My footsteps falter.

"Hux, that was Porter," West asks, her voice hoarse from crying. "Is he okay?"

Before I can reply, Porter soothes us both through our bonds, his guilt followed by a rush of affection.

"He's fine, or he would've called."

She looks at me dubiously.

"Trust me?"

"With our lives."

Something about that simple statement does weird shit to my chest.

"Good, because I'm gonna take such good care of you both! Starting right now."

My dick is already hard and weeping for her, but he's gonna have to be patient. I set her on her feet next to the giant king-sized bed. Sunlight is shining through the windows as my eyes scan down her body. It's then I realize the sweatshirt she's wearing is mine—one she must've stolen from our apartment. The sound that leaves my lips is somewhere between a purr and growl, rough and needy. I fucking love seeing her wearing my shit almost as much as I love taking it off of her, but not yet. I need to do something else first. If I'm going to be her Alpha, I need to take care of her in *all* ways.

"When was the last time you ate, baby?"

She blinks, a pretty blush tinting her cheeks. "I had some crackers this morning. My stomach has been a little upset, and I thought it was nerves."

"I'm going to make you mine..." She bites her bottom lip, and I damn near take her right then and there, but I keep a firm grip on my control...and her bottom lip, saving it from further torture. "But first, I'm gonna feed you. We'll eat in bed then see how you're feeling."

"Hux..." Her voice cracks as a single tear leaks from the corner of her eye. 'Thank you."

"You don't ever have to thank me for taking care of what's mine." I kiss her forehead. "Get comfortable. I'll be back in a few minutes."

Walking out the door, I shoot a quick text to Porter.

**Me: Hey, you good?**

**Porter: Yeah. Ran an errand. I might be a little while. How's West?**

**Me: She's better. I'll let her tell you all about it later.**

**Porter: Think she'd be willing to let me come over and see her?**

**Me: I know she would. I'll text when it's safe to head this way.**

**Porter: 10-4. Give her a big hug from me in the meantime.**

**Me: You got it!**

Knowing both of my Omegas are okay, something within me settles. I'm doing what a good Alpha should do. I'm taking care of them and making sure they have what they need. Now, how do I get this message across to Daniels so he can pull his head out of his ass and make our girl happy again?

# 31

## PORTER HANSON

Huxley's words play through my mind on repeat.

*We're the only ones who can fix this, and you know it.*

He's right, but I'll be damned if that isn't a hard pill to swallow. Nash and I have had a rivalry since I joined the league. To be honest, I'm not even sure what started it. I just know the guy's an asshole. Any time you put us in the same room, shit gets explosive.

But now we're in love with the same woman. I've seen the way he is with her, the way she softens those harsh edges, making him *almost* likable. *Almost* being the key word. Not that the fucker is aware of her effect on him. He couldn't possibly be, or he wouldn't have walked away. The fact that he did so easily... Well, I'm not sure what that says about him.

Even when I thought I was a Beta, I knew I'd treasure the members of any pack I wound up in, especially my Omega...if I were lucky enough to have one. Now here I am, with the possibility before me, and I'm willing to toss it away just because the guy is a little egotistical? Fuck, maybe a *lot* egotistical, but I can't say I'm much better, now can I? Where does that leave us? Like Hux said, we're the only things in our way, so can I leave it all behind in order to move forward?

Of course, regardless of how I feel, West seems awfully attached to the jackass. Otherwise, she wouldn't have kicked us all out when we were throwing tantrums in her living room like toddlers. Now, after almost a week without her, I've reached the limits of my sanity. Ziggy said West needed Huxley, and I need West, so there's only one thing to do. Swallow my pride and try to make amends. With one quick text to Ziggy, here I am, standing at Nash's door, hand poised to knock.

The door suddenly swings open, an angry Nash staring back at me.

"What the fuck are you doing out here staring at my door for fuck's sake?"

My anger boils over even though I'm frantically trying to keep a lid on it. "Why are you always such a dick?" I bark.

Hux startles in the bond, and I feel West peek through the block she's been maintaining all week.

*Shit. So much for making things right. Way to fuck it up already, Hanson.*

I try to soothe my emotions, guilt swallowing me whole for interrupting their time together. Sensing their calm in the bond, I return my attention to the angry Alpha practically snarling at me.

"Hanson, I don't have the time or the energy for your shit right now. Go the fuck home."

He tries to shut the door, but I stick my booted foot in to stop him.

"Wait. I'm sorry. Just...hear me out."

"Make it quick. I've got a bottle of Jack calling my name."

I frown. For the first time, I take in his haggard appearance. With a week's growth of beard and tired eyes, he looks like hell. Smells like it too—a mix of booze and sour vanilla that damn near turns my stomach. Maybe his decision to walk away from West wasn't as easy as I had assumed it was.

"Why'd you do it?"

His eyes narrow. "Do *what*?"

"Why'd you reject her? That woman is the best thing that's ever happened to you, and you know it."

He grits his teeth so hard I can practically hear the crack of the enamel from here.

"Thought you'd be happy. Now, she's all yours."

"Look, Daniels, I know we have a history and you're not my biggest fan, but even you have to know that I'd never be happy about anything that would hurt the woman I love. And make no mistake, I love West with everything I've got."

He looks away, tension evident in every taut line of his body.

"I love her too, believe it or not." His voice is so low, I almost don't hear the words, but then his piercing blue eyes clash with mine. "That's why I left. She doesn't need my shit weighing her down when she's got you guys."

I blink. Nash Daniels being *noble*? Are we in an alternate universe right now?

"Did you ever take a second to consider that she loves you back? Maybe she doesn't care about your shitty attitude or your heavy ego weighing her down."

"If you're trying to convince me to change my mind, you're doing a fucking lousy job of it."

I sigh. He's right, but maybe that's because there's just this naturally antagonistic energy surrounding us anytime we're within a few feet of each other.

"Why do you hate me?"

He blinks slowly, tired eyes looking back at me. "I don't hate you."

"Well, you sure as hell fooled me."

Even his growl sounds exhausted.

"Look, I'll say this once and only once. I'm not a nice guy, okay? I'm a fucking prick who doesn't trust anyone and never lets anyone get close. I—"

"But you let Ziggy in. He's your roommate *and* friend, right?"

I watch his shoulders droop, the fight all but leaving him.

"Since you're obviously not going to let this go until you've said your piece, come in so we're not arguing in front of all my nosy ass neighbors."

He holds the door, letting me pass. His apartment is ultra-modern with very few personal touches that make the place a home. No pictures of family or friends. No books filling the floor-to-ceiling bookshelves that should give me insight into the man before me. It looks like he just moved in, but I'd guess he's been here a while.

"You want a drink? I'm going to need one to deal with this conversation."

He heads for the kitchen without waiting for me to respond. I can feel my irritation spike, but I take a deep breath and exhale. He said it himself, he's not a nice guy. Maybe his shit personality just is what it is and it's not personal. Maybe that's my problem. I've been thinking it was an issue with me when in reality, he's just a dick to everyone. In a way, I almost pity him. That's a damned lonely way to live.

"I'm good, thanks."

# HE'S SO SLICK 259

He grunts, then I hear the cabinets open and close, the sound of liquid splashing and a cap being replaced before he stalks into the living room and crashes down on the large white leather sectional like his legs refuse to hold him up anymore.

I slowly make my way to the opposite side, sitting forward and placing my elbows on my knees. Neither of us speaks for a long moment. Maybe there's no way to salvage this situation at all. I start to wonder if this was a mistake, then my brain starts trying to figure out how to break the news to West.

"My family is full of think-for-yourselfers," he begins, staring into his glass of whiskey. "I was the youngest of ten kids from six different men. We were raised by a single mother, with little supervision and zero role models. All of my older siblings are shitheads. Some of them are into drugs or prostitution, others alcoholics, and a few are wasting away in prison. Early on, I learned from their mistakes and started to rely solely on myself. Kept my head down and stayed out of trouble. I hated being at home because who knew which father-wannabe-of-the-week would be there, so I started hanging out at the ice rink a couple blocks from our shithole apartment. An old man noticed me lingering around and offered me my first job, picking up garbage from the stands, when I was maybe ten. I'd spend my afternoons watching the figure skaters practice then would stay and watch the young hockey teams while I became an unpaid cleaning crew. That old man noticed my interest, and when I was in middle school, he handed me a pair of used skates and told me to get my skinny ass out there to see if I could do it. When I got a scholarship my senior year and told him I was off to Boston University, you should've seen the smile on his face. He was the first person to ever believe in me, and when I signed my first professional contract, I anonymously paid off his house. He knew it was me though. That old man showed up at my first game and gave me a hug afterward because I scored the winning shot."

He takes a long sip of his drink, his bitter scent making my nose itch. I stay silent, worried that if I say the wrong thing, he'll go cold on me again and I won't get the information I need to help turn this entire thing around.

"He died about six months later, right around the time the leeches that are my family started coming around to ask for money. They weren't subtle about it either. They knew I had done well for myself in spite of them and were fully willing to take advantage even though they'd done jack shit to help me get to where I was."

"You can always tell them to fuck off, you know."

A cruel smirk tilts his lips just before he takes another long swallow of whiskey. "That would be the smart thing to do, right? Except they threaten blackmail or suicide or some other ridiculous thing, and I cave each and every time. I shouldn't give two shits about people who wouldn't cry or show up at my grave, but for some dumbass reason, I do."

For the first time, I see that his dickishness is directly linked to his need to protect himself from being hurt more than he already has...and I'll be damned if I'm not starting to feel even sorrier for the man. Nash Daniels is an asshole, but that's because he's never had people in his corner. "West loves you. You have to know she'd never expect anything from you above what you're willing to give."

He nods, tosses back the last of the alcohol, and stares at the empty glass with his brows furrowed.

"I'd give her everything, even my very life if she asked it of me."

"Then what the hell is the problem? I don't get it."

"It's not her I'm worried about. It's *you*." He looks up at me then with blue eyes the color of a stormy sky. "I'm not sure I can ever be to you what you'd need me to be. I'm not used to sharing, and I can't guarantee I can play nice when forced to. Not sure if I can bite back my sharp retorts or curb my anger where you're concerned, and that would put West in the middle, forcing her to pick sides. I won't do that to her."

I stare at him in shock, not having expected him to give a damn about me whatsoever. And sure, maybe his ultimate concern is West, but there's still a nugget of concern for me there as well. That's a start.

"What do you think I need you to be?"

He looks confused for a second. "In a pack, even with unbonded Omegas, Alphas hold a certain sense of protectiveness and friendship, with the connection between the other members tying them together, albeit loosely. Hurting you would hurt her, and I don't want either of those things on my conscience. I've got enough already."

"But look at us right now. We're having a conversation without screaming at each other or slinging insults back and forth. We're talking like normal, rational adults."

He does that slow blink again like he's only just realizing that we are indeed not stabbing each other in the back.

"West isn't here. There's no competition. No demand for her attention."

"You don't think it's possible for us to maintain a little civility now that we have an understanding of each other? You're a dick, and I'm a smug asshole. We both own our flaws and give each other a little bit of grace. Seems like a decent start to me."

He's still staring at me when he sets his glass down. "And what about McCarren? He's the kind of Alpha West deserves. Strong, caring, seemingly kind, and protective. What can I provide that he doesn't?"

*There it is.* Nash Daniels is insecure. Of course, I don't tell him that because it would just end in another fight, possibly with fists involved, and that's not why I'm here.

"You can just be yourself. West doesn't expect anything from any of us except maybe a little of our time and affection. Be yourself. She seems to love the ass nugget vibe you give off."

His lips twitch before he cuts that shit off.

"But I'm serious. We can make this work. I…" I run a hand over my hair, looking out the large windows at the city just beyond the glass. "I *want* to make this work. For West, and for all of us. I think we need each other more than we know."

At first, I wasn't sure our pack needed two more members. I liked the idea of keeping it small and close. But now that I've seen there's more to Nash than I expected, the idea of all of us finalizing our pack appeals to my Omega instincts. Maybe it's the image of a home bustling with life and family. Maybe it's the thought of having extra hands around to help keep the burden of pack from resting solely on our shoulders. Or maybe it's simply the idea that this is what West has been longing for, and I'd do anything to make it happen for her. Bottom line is that my decision has been made. Nash and Ziggy belong with us.

"And how do you think that's going to work? West splits her time between here and Arizona, flying back and forth around our game schedules? That sounds like a jealousy and possessiveness clusterfuck in the making."

"I'm willing to give it a shot if that's what West wants. Of course, I'm pretty sure we could all find a place in either location to call home then travel to other places as time and schedules allow."

As soon as the words leave my mouth, I know that's what I'd want. One central home base where we all live, and we can work around everything else. We can even house hunt together, finding something that works for everyone. Excitement fires up in my veins at the prospect of looking for a pack house. Thinking back to my childhood and all the years Hux and I spent surrounded by love and chaos and laughter... Damn, I didn't realize how much I missed that until just now.

Nash runs both hands down his drawn face. "I think you're giving me too much credit, Hanson."

"And I think you're not giving yourself enough."

His eyes find mine. "I may not be a fan, but I can see why West is. You and McCarren are good for her."

"And so are you. You just have to decide if she's worth the risk of letting the rest of us in, knowing there will be some speed bumps along the way that we can navigate together."

"She's worth it. That's never been in question."

"Then know that I think you are too. You may never be my Alpha, but I think we can eventually be friends...even when my team beats yours in the championships."

He snorts. "Good fucking luck with that."

The air between us seems lighter than it first did, our paths to becoming a pack no longer shrouded in darkness and poisonous vines ready to take us down. We're clearing the way to a future, and I only hope he can see the final destination with the same clarity that I can.

"Just think about everything I've said, okay? We both want what's best for West, and I really think that's all of us as pack."

He eyes me for a second before he simply nods, then he swallows harshly.

"How is she?" he asks quietly.

I try to fight my grimace. "Ziggy called Hux over to her apartment because West needed him."

"Is something wrong?" he growls, sitting forward like he's ready to leap from the sofa and run straight to her door if he had to. "And what the hell was Ziggy doing over there?"

"I'm not sure. I wanted to go with Hux, but... Well, he didn't want me there. He said he'd text if anything was wrong, and I haven't heard from him, so I'm assuming everything is okay."

He relaxes slightly, his eyes darting to the cell phone that's sitting silently on the arm of the sofa.

"You could call her, you know."

I watch the bob of his Adam's apple before he shakes his head. "I'm not sure she'd want to hear from me right now."

"I bet she'd love to hear from you, but let's hold off until Hux gives me an update just in case."

He nods, then gives me a questioning look.

"What?" I ask.

"I haven't eaten in... Hell, I don't even remember the last time I had food. You want to stay for some pizza?"

I tamp down my shock, determined to accept this olive branch whether I'm hungry or not.

"I could eat."

He grabs his phone and dials a number. When he starts to give his order to the woman on the other end, I have to fight back a smug grin. I did it. I've forged what is the start of a potential friendship between the surly Alpha and myself, with West as the catalyst for it all. My phone buzzes with a text, and I see Hux's name on the screen. I reply quickly, getting excited for a whole new reason. I might actually get to see my girl. Things are finally looking bright, with the future we wanted so desperately not so far out of our reach after all.

# 32

## WEST CARTER

For the last hour, Hux and I have shared the yummy mac 'n cheese he whipped up with some of the leftover pulled pork from one of the food delivery orders I barely ate. We're in bed, talking about nothing and everything—our favorite bands, what we wanted to be when we were kids, the one thing we wish we were good at but aren't. Little tidbits about ourselves fill the tiny holes in what we know about each other. We've strayed away from the harder topics like Nash and the baby, saving that for later when reality chooses to make a reappearance.

The vision I had for my life veered off course the second I met these men. Instead of a wealthy, sophisticated pack that would take me in and pamper me like the Omega I'm supposed to be, I found these rough-around-the-edges hockey players who need me almost as much as I need them. It isn't some unbalanced scale, where they give and I receive. It's a mutually beneficial connection, where each of us comes to the table with our own strengths and weaknesses and we work together to build the life we want for ourselves. It's give and take, perfect imperfection. Maybe it's not what anyone would call a fairytale, but it sure feels a little like one.

"You're quiet all of a sudden," Hux murmurs, eyeing me cautiously.

"Just thinking about how we so often have these skewed ideas of what life should be like that we miss how wonderfully messy real life can be."

His grin is a little lopsided. "Messy is kind of our specialty."

I chuckle. "It is. Never a dull moment around here."

He looks thoughtful for a moment before he grabs the empty bowl and sets it aside. "None of us are perfect, but I think we're perfect for each other."

"I agree. What we're building here is real. None of that fake shit the media wants everyone to believe is true."

"Bexley reached out to Porter, by the way. We didn't get a chance to tell you about that. Barrett set up a call, and she wants to do a series on TheOmegasGuide about the perception of designation in professional sports."

"That's amazing. Porter will be perfect for that."

"He said he'd do it..." His eyes are serious on mine, his fingers tangling with my own on top of the blanket. "But only if you agree to join him."

"Of course I'd be there to support him. I think the work Bex and Arden have done to shed light on issues facing our society is invaluable."

He smiles, dimples appearing under the dark hair of his beard, and not for the first time am I struck by the rugged beauty of this giant man.

"He asked if I thought you'd be okay with him coming by later..."

Nerves skitter through me. I love my Omega, but I'm terrified of what I'll see in his eyes when I tell him the news.

"Hey, don't do that. He... Well, he cares about you a lot. You have absolutely nothing to worry about. It will all be okay."

When Hux says it, I almost believe him. His fingers squeeze mine, and the first small sparks of need coil in my belly. Getting to my knees, I crawl over until I'm close enough to lift one leg, straddling his much longer ones on the bed.

"I can feel him in the bond, cautious little peeks now and then to see if I'm okay. That you're okay. Is it selfish that I want to feel you in the bond too? To know that you're really okay with all of this as much as you tell me you are. I..." I can feel the nervous ramble building in my throat, nearly threatening to choke me with the need to give him an out before he makes an irreversible decision. "I was worried that I'd ruined what we had. That my wanting Nash and now me carrying his baby would change how you felt about me. That I was being greedy by wanting it all. I'd understand if you want to take some time to be sure of me. I still want you to be my Alpha, but I also don't want to guilt you into something that you're not ready for or—"

His large hands grip my hips, pulling me forward until I'm sitting on his lap. I can feel the long hardness that nestles in the cleft of my pussy and hear the low rumbling growl he's failing to fight back.

"You're not guilting me into anything, West. I decided, practically from the first moment I laid eyes on you, that you would be mine. Wanting another Alpha and having his baby isn't going to stop me from taking what I've already claimed as my own."

My eyes go glassy as he leans in and kisses me so sweetly, I can't help but lose myself in him. His hands grip the bottom of his sweatshirt that has ridden up my thighs, slowly pulling it up and over my head, forcing our mouths to part. I'm not wearing anything underneath, and when his eyes trail over my body, his nostrils flare. His scent is rich and strong, making my pussy drip with need for him.

"I can't wait until you're swollen with our baby," he whispers against the curve of my breast as he leans in and pulls a sensitive nipple into his mouth. "Can't wait for your breasts to be full and ripe so they can feed her."

He sucks harder, his words and the draw from his mouth making my pussy contract around nothing. The whine builds in my throat, and I try to swallow it down to no avail. It slips free, the responding purr in his chest making my hips roll involuntarily.

"Hux," I rasp.

"I can smell the change in your scent. That cinnamon is tinged with a little vanilla and something rich and exotic. It's fucking intoxicating."

He laps at the other nipple until he closes his mouth around it, the sharp, deep suction forcing a long moan to burst free.

"Mmmm. The thought of nursing from you is getting me so hard."

I gasp, finding the thought both scandalous and more than just a little sexy.

"I'll have to share them when the baby comes, but for now, these perfect breasts are all mine."

He goes to town, licking and sucking and biting my nipples until I'm a writhing mess above him. My pussy is sliding along his length encased in silky sport shorts. The friction feels amazing, but I need more.

"Hux, *please*."

"I've got you, sweet thing." One hand releases me to grip the waistband of his shorts. I rise up just enough that he can shimmy them down and let his long, thick dick spring free. "Sit on my dick, baby. Ride your Alpha."

I've never been so eager for anything in my life. Holding myself over his erection, I slowly slide down until his fat head is stretching my hole open and pressing into my pussy. My hands are gripping his neck to steady myself against the need to impale myself on his dick. Instead, I press down steadily until he's as deep as the position will allow.

"God, West. You feel so damn good," he murmurs, leaning forward and trailing his lips along my throat.

One large arm is wrapped around my waist, with his hand tightly gripping my hip. The other one has skimmed up the middle of my back, splaying out between my shoulder blades. When I give in to the need to move, rising up just enough to slide back down his shaft, his fingers flex, a choked sound leaving his lips.

"Just like that, baby. Fuck. You're such a good girl for your Alpha."

The Omega in me preens as my hips start to roll. The teasing thrusts are shallow and slow, my body being held against his while he nuzzles into me, marking me with his scent. Our movements are sensual and smooth, not harried or rushed. We're loving each other in a way that makes my heart sing while my body sighs with pleasure. With every slow grind onto his cock, I feel the swell of his knot pushing against my center, begging for entry.

"Hang on, but keep riding me, sweet thing. You're doing fucking amazing."

I don't have time to ask him what he means. All of a sudden, he starts to lean me back, my body weight supported by his massively strong arms. The tilt of my hips shifts his dick until it's skimming along my upper walls with each slide of his thickness inside me. When his mouth once again takes a nipple and sucks hard, I mewl, the sound low and needy, and my pussy clenches around him.

"Fuck yeah," he growls, his lips brushing my breast.

My hands slide through his long hair, holding him to me as he continues to suckle in sync with every glide of my hips.

"Oh my god," I groan, savoring the tingles rolling up my spine.

"That's it. You're squeezing me so fucking good. Tell me when you're ready for my knot."

I'm ready now, but I can't seem to find the words. I'm so lost in him and what he's doing to my body. My hips have lost all sense of rhythm as they urgently grind down on him.

"Now, Alpha. Knot. *Bite...*" I manage to choke out.

He growls, the hand at the top of my back sliding up to grip my shoulder. Using his touch for leverage, he pulls me down onto his knot. The stretch is divine, the tight ring of muscle fighting against the thickness at his base until it finally gives. He slides in, and my breath catches as he begins to swell inside me, setting off an orgasm that rolls across my body like a wave, crashing against the shore only to be immediately swept up in the next.

"Mine," he snarls, seconds before I feel a fiery sting on my breast then a harsh pull on the spot his teeth have claimed.

I scream, acute pleasure rushing through my veins. I barely hear his roar echoing around us. Barely feel the first lick of his tongue as he tends to his mark. Barely feel the warm wetness on my cheeks as I cry out of pure unadulterated happiness. I'm too busy focusing on the flood of emotions through our new bond. Love. Elation. Happiness. Pride. And a sense of wonder that has another rush of emotions overwhelming me.

Through it all, Porter appears with excitement he can't contain. He's relieved and thrilled and so many other things it's impossible to count them all.

"I love you, West," Hux murmurs, drawing me up to wrap himself around me as he buries his face in my hair. "Fuck, I had no idea..."

He never finishes the thought, but he doesn't have to. I get it. Our mutual bonds all overlap, strengthening what was already there until it's incredibly powerful. We're officially pack, and together, nothing and no one can tear us apart.

"I love you too."

He kisses me softly, then pulls back and lets his forehead rest on mine. He doesn't even have to ask. I can sense what he wants in the bond, and I want it too. It's time I fill our Omega in on what I've gotten us all into.

"Call him. He should be here."

Hux meets my nervous gaze. "I know you're worried, but everything's going to be okay."

I nod, incapable of words. I believe him, but that doesn't stop my heart from beating overtime as I try to come up with a way to tell one of the men I love that I'm pregnant with his rival's baby.

## 33

## WEST CARTER

The crowd in the arena is supercharged tonight. The Heat is preparing to play the Sentinels, and this is the first time the four of us have been separated in the last few days. Porter's been at my side and extra clingy since receiving the news of our little puck nugget. Those are his words, not mine, for the record, but we've all sort of picked up on it and I'm pretty sure it's sticking.

Poor kid.

Instead of the anger and hurt I was expecting, Porter quickly recovered from his initial shock and immediately went into uber-Omega mode, pulling up a popular baby site and adding tons of shit into a cart for us to sift through later. Bottle warmers, breast pumps, an odd little bottle contraption that latches on to a man's pec to emulate the act of breast feeding to give Mommy a break. Personally I can't wait for that one only so I can snap photos of Porter using it.

Did my handsome, badass hockey player turn into a sucker for fuzzy baby blankets and little stuffed pucks with silk taggies on them? He sure as hell did. One big puddle of ooey gooey Omega sweetness once he learned he was going to be a daddy. Go figure.

I can't stop my grin even though I'm not even entirely sure I'm not dreaming all of this.

Of course, my dad is over the moon, already in preparations for—gag me—those GILF years he's been harassing me about. I'm pretty sure he's going to try to use my baby to get chicks by really laying on the doting grandpa bit *hard*. I'm not sure how I feel about that. He was angry when we told him that Nash was no longer in the picture, but when he found out that the angry center didn't know about the baby yet, he gave him a little bit of grace—as only a wonderfully caring man can. Though an *I can get rid of the body* reference might have been made in case the asshole doesn't come around when he finds out.

And don't get me started on Ziggy. He's been researching BDSM safety during pregnancy, like which ropes are safest to use and in which positions, and always seems to have a fucking bucket of chicken wings handy. Not that I'm upset with that last bit. Seems little one is a sucker for buffalo sauce.

Huxley has been the doting Alpha, making sure I have what I need, that I remember to eat even when my stomach is queasy, and ensuring all of the proper doctor appointments and reminders get set.

Between the three of them, I'm never left wanting, but there's still an asshole-shaped hole in my heart that doesn't seem to heal no matter how many days pass. He's there on the periphery of my thoughts, along with the need to tell him about our baby giving me a guilt ulcer.

Or maybe that's just morning sickness.

I *will* tell him, but part of me is holding out hope that he reaches out to me first. Just the smallest hint that he still thinks about me would ease some of this all-consuming hurt inside. It's not going to happen, of course, because this is Nash we're talking about here, but a girl can dream.

Ziggy and I are in the suite, waiting for the game to start. He's holding my hand, but he's constantly glancing at the phone in his other as if he's waiting for a text.

"You waiting for a call or something?" I ask.

His eyes dart up to mine. "Nope."

My lips purse as I give him a *do-I-look-dumb-to-you* look.

"I was just...waiting on a text from Nash and didn't want to bring it up and upset you."

Just his name has my belly doing somersaults.

"Oh." I clear my throat. "How's he doing?"

"He's struggling, but he'll never admit that."

I bite my bottom lip, attempting to contain the whine that wants to escape.

"Hey, pretty girl, don't cry."

He swipes at a tear I wasn't even aware had rolled down my cheek.

"I'm sorry. I... I should probably call him and set up a time to talk."

He stares at me with something like pity flashing in his eyes, and my stomach pitches. I swore all the guys to secrecy, wanting to handle this on my own terms. I got us into this mess, and I'll damn well be the one to dig us out of it. They all reluctantly agreed and are letting me figure it out at my own pace. In the meantime, my poor belly is taking the brunt of my emotions.

"I'll be right back. I'm going to use the restroom and maybe swing by the concession stand to grab a pretzel. Need anything?"

He shakes his head. "Want me to come with you?"

"No, you wait here. I'll only be a second."

Standing from the chair at the counter table in the suite, I make my way out the door and down the hall on autopilot. I'm not paying attention to where I'm going or what I'm doing, just blindly walking while wondering how in the hell I'm going to get through this. My heart is broken, and despite the efforts of three amazing men, I can't ignore the fact that one is missing.

I somehow manage to find the bathroom and quickly go about my business, washing my hands then splashing a little on my flushed face. Ultimately, I decide to skip the pretzel since my stomach is in no shape to consume anything at the moment. Arriving back at the suite, I'm getting ready to pull on the door when it suddenly opens. I'm hit with Nash's rich rum and vanilla scent, and he appears as if I'd conjured him out of thin air.

"Nash?" I gasp.

"West? What are you doing here?"

"I just went to use the restroom. What are *you* doing here?"

My brain is malfunctioning, the sight of him too much for my fragile emotions to deal with.

"I was...um...in town for some business and wanted to stop in and see Ziggy before the game."

"Oh. I see." My chest feels tight, like I can't draw in enough oxygen.

*Of course he's not here to see you. He rejected you, remember?*

"You look...*beautiful*," he whispers. "Arizona sun suits you."

I don't know how to reply to that. Instead, we stand there, drinking in the sight of each other, until I clear my throat.

"Well, I'm glad you're here. I need to talk to you about something important."

"I'm not staying, actually. I've got a plane to catch if I want to make it back to Chicago in time to rest up for the Storm's game tomorrow.

Maybe we could get together next week to talk? I'll give you a call when I figure out my schedule."

"Right. Of course."

My hands are wringing together in front of me as I fight to stave off my tears just a little longer.

"Take care of yourself, bright eyes."

For a brief second, I think he's going to lean in and kiss me, except he doesn't. It was just my brain's wishful thinking. Instead, he turns and walks down the hall and out of sight. I stand there, staring after him, wondering when this will ever get easier. Porter and Hux both appear in the bond to check on me, witnessing my misery happening in real time. They're angry, and my attempt to soothe them fails because I'm breaking inside.

"Hey," Ziggy says, appearing in the doorway. "C'mere."

He tugs me into his chest, and I lose it, the first sob breaking free when his arms wrap around me. He pulls me into the suite, carting me over to the plush sofa where he sits and drags me into his lap.

"It'll be okay. I promise."

"You can't promise that, Zig."

"Just trust me, alright?" He tucks some stray hair behind my ears, then brushes off the tears still lingering on my cheeks. "Look, the game is starting. Let's watch the guys kick some ass."

Focusing on the screen above the sofa, I stay cuddled with my Beta throughout the entire first period. The guys are leading by two, and the opposite team can't do shit on offense. With clock counting down, the Heat have the puck with Barrett in control. He flies down the ice, skirting the goal to pass the puck to Porter. Between the two of them, they go back and forth, keeping the other team on their toes. Porter shoots it back to Barrett, then the other team's left defenseman barrels toward B and doesn't stop until they're both crashing into the wall with such force that the entire wall of glass shakes. I sit forward, hearing Barrett's cry of pain from here.

My eyes locked on the screen, I see him slide down to the ice, clutching his shoulder in pain. The team's doctors skate out to check him over, but he's not getting up like he usually does. This is bad. Really bad.

"Ziggy..."

He's rubbing my back as we wait for the Heat's center to get to his feet, but he never does. Once a stretcher appears in the tunnel, I'm on my feet, rushing out the door with Ziggy on my heels.

The crowds pass in a blur, and I'm running down the team's hall until I see them wheeling Barrett through the tunnel. I'm up next to the stretcher, reaching for B's good hand, as I walk with the group.

"Hey, loser," I murmur, trying to keep it light, but my voice cracks instead.

"Sugar plum..." His voice is hoarse with pain.

"You're gonna be alright, B. You're too damn stubborn to let this take you down."

"They think I either dislocated or fractured my shoulder. Either way, it's not looking good for the rest of the season. Fuckers will have to win the championship without me." His smile is more of a grimace, but he tries. "Speaking of stubborn..."

I shake my head, grinning even as my eyes get glassy. "Nope. We're not talking about me right now."

"You manage to wrangle that feral Alpha yet?"

"Not yet. No."

"You will. You're too damn stubborn to let him walk away."

The EMS team turns the corner, and I stick by his side the entire time. They're heading for the arena's rear door, probably where an ambulance is waiting to whisk my friend away.

"You need me to handle anything at your apartment? I can feed Puck for you."

"Old bastard misses you. He'd like your company, I think."

"I miss him too. Miss all of you, actually."

He eyes me through bloodshot eyes. "You coming home to us, sugar plum?"

"I... Yeah, I think so."

They push through the rear doors where an ambulance is parked next to the curb.

"Good. 'Bout time. Team needs you."

"Hey, B. There's something else I need to tell you before they steal you away."

"Sugar plum, if you tell me you found yourself *another* rival Alpha, I might just have to kill myself."

I chuckle, but the sound is part sob. The EMS team pauses, letting me lean in so I can whisper in B's ear.

"My little puck nugget needs Uncle Barrett, so heal fast, okay?"

He pulls back, shock and pain plastered on his face.

"No fucking way!" His eyes are wide, mouth hanging open in shock.

"Yes way."

"West..."

"I'll be okay, B. Just wanted you to hear it from me and not the media."

"I love you, sugar plum. Make sure those boys of yours spoil you rotten."

"Duh!" I chuckle weakly.

They push him forward and lift him into the open double doors. In seconds, the ambulance is pulling out of the parking lot with its lights whirling.

Warm arms wrap around my middle, and I turn into them, needing the hug more than I need anything else right now.

"He'll be okay, pretty girl," Zig says softly, dropping a kiss on my forehead.

"He will, but he's not exactly in his twenties anymore, Zig. What if this is the end for him? I can't imagine the Heat without Barrett Matthews on the ice."

"Let's wait to see what the doctors say before we jump to any conclusions, yeah?"

My exhausted sigh is swallowed by the night. "Okay."

He guides us back inside and up to the suite. Intermission is almost over, and the rest of the game goes by in a blur, with the entire team no doubt playing for their fallen teammate. Porter is on fire, scoring two more times, earning himself a hat trick. Hux blocks two attempts at the goal by the Sentinels.

When the final buzzer sounds, the Heat win the game four to zero. With the playoffs right around the corner, the Heat and Storm are neck and neck, so they'll no doubt play each other heading into the championships. I'm both excited and anxious to see all of my guys out on the ice again even though I'll have to cheer one of them on silently.

## 34

### WEST CARTER

For close to a month, I've waited for Nash to reach out, but his schedule has been crazy as the road to the playoffs narrowed, or at least that's what I tell myself. There have been media rumblings about the Storm's star center, but no verified reports. I'm starting to wonder if he's looking for a trade out of Chicago...and away from me. Not that he seems to remember I exist. I've given him space. Ignored the need to talk to him or see him. I refuse to be the desperate girl begging for attention. He knows where I'm at if he wants to see me. I'm done trying...even though the voice in my head keeps reminding me that we have something very important to discuss.

The guys have been amazing despite my mood swings and random bouts of tears. We've started to talk about where we want to call home, and while Arizona was the ultimate winner, I also couldn't quite let go of my ties to the Windy City. The idea of severing that last connection to Nash is like a stab through the heart. Maybe it *would* be better if he left the Storm. Then I could finally give up this little spark of hope I'm keeping alive inside me.

We're back in Arizona with the Heat facing off against the Storm for the last regular game of the season. Tonight's winner will head into the playoffs. My anxiety is through the roof, both because I'll get to see Nash for the first time since that brief run-in a month ago and because the guys have been acting super shifty. Lots of whispered conversations. Secret lunches they think I don't know about—*as if*. Late-night phone calls and a bazillion texts. I don't know what they're planning, but it has me on perpetual pins and needles, waiting for who the hell knows what to happen.

It's hours before gametime, and I'm walking down the tunnel with Barrett. He wouldn't tell me why or give me any hints. He only said that there was a surprise waiting for me on the ice, and I needed some light gear and my skates.

"You know I don't like surprises," I grumble, side-eyeing my best friend.

"You'll like this one. Trust me."

He's been on the team's injured reserve list, his shoulder dislocated but healing nicely. He thinks I don't notice the strain on his face or the worry in his eyes, but I do. He loves this game, and the game loves him, but all players know they'll have to hang up their stick for good at some point. He's at a crossroads, and I know whatever he decides, it won't be easy for him.

We pause at the edge of the rink, the area darkened with only the upper thoroughfare lights illuminating the space.

"I want you to know that I'm proud of you—for the woman you've become and the pack that you've created for yourself."

"B, I—"

"Shhh. Let me get this out, okay?"

I nod, fighting back tears.

"I knew one day I'd have to share you with the men who would become your new family, and at first, I wasn't thrilled with how it was panning out. First, Hanson and McCarren. Then Daniels and his weird ass friend. But now..." He sighs, tugging me in for a big hug with one hand. I have to maneuver the stick to avoid breaking his nose. "Now, I'm glad you have them in your corner. You deserve to have strong, capable men at your back, ready to support you through this thing we call life. I approve, sugar plum, and can't wait to be the doting uncle to that little puck nugget of yours."

I snort as the first tear falls. "I didn't get them all, B. I tried, but in the end I wasn't enough."

"You were, and now it's time to prove it to you." My brow furrows as he turns me toward the rink. "Go on out there. Your surprise is waiting."

With one last glance at my friend, my skate hits the ice and I make my way toward the center. It's dark, with just enough light to make out something in the middle of the rink. Then a spotlight appears, and I have to blink at what I'm seeing.

In the center of the ice, arranged on a red runner, is a small circular table with some sort of glass dome placed on top. When I skate closer, I make out a single red rose through the glass, placed in a thin vase that almost makes it appear as if it's floating inside.

My brain can't quite figure out what it's seeing, but my heart begins to pound in my chest regardless. Then I hear the sound of metal sliding across the ice and turn, my stomach in my throat. Nash skates toward me from the tunnel. He's in a plain black jersey, his helmet and stick in his hand. He skids to a stop, only a couple feet between us.

"Hey, bright eyes."

"Nash?" I whisper. Is he just an illusion that will disappear now that I've said his name out loud?

"I'm sorry I haven't called. There were some things I had to work through first."

He looks solid and steady, like the last month hasn't been as hard on him as it has been on me. Part of me wants to hate him for that, but the rest of me just wants to drink in the sight of him to shore me up for when he inevitably walks away again.

"Did you get them all sorted out?"

The right side of his lips quirks up. "I did." He inches closer. "You once asked me if I was confident in my stick game. I'm here to prove just how confident I am."

My head tilts in confusion. "I don't know what that means."

"The beast wants to challenge the beauty to a shootout. The person with the most goals after three shots wins."

I blink. "You want to go up against me in a shootout? Right now?"

"That's just what I said, isn't it?"

God, why does he have to be so sexy when he's being an asshole?

"What's the prize?"

"You."

My mouth opens, then closes, my brain stuttering. I can't quite figure out the angle he's playing right now, and any words freeze on my tongue.

He's more than willing to help me figure it out. "I win, and you're mine. You win... You're still mine, but I'll let you pretend it was your decision."

My eyes meet his, the cocky smugness plastered on his handsome face forcing a slow grin to curve across mine. I'm pretty sure my heart is going to explode out of my chest, but then the main lights come on.

Down at the goal, I see Hux, fully suited up and smiling at me through the bars of his helmet. Right behind him, on the other side of the glass, are Porter and Ziggy.

*So this is what they've been up to. Maybe surprises aren't so bad after all.*

"You up for the challenge, bright eyes?" he asks, the first hint of nerves evident in the slight rasp of his voice.

"On one condition."

"Name it, and it's yours."

"After the game, we all sit down and have a long talk about where we go from here."

"Deal."

I pull on my helmet. "Time to show me just how good you are with your stick then, Daniels."

He grins wickedly. "I'm damn good, as you well know."

We take our positions, and he drops a puck on the ice.

"Ladies first."

Shaking out my shoulders, I take a deep breath and exhale. He's got to know that I win either way, but I'll be damned if I don't want to prove that I can play with the big boys.

With my stick in my hand, I move the puck down the ice, seeing Hux get in position. He damn well better not take it easy on me. I dribble the puck down the floor, weaving my way toward him until I'm within shooting distance. I start to circle to the right, but spin and head left, throwing Hux off. He's not prepared for my slapshot into the net, barely missing his gloved hand.

I grin widely, turning and heading back down the ice.

"That's one. Your turn, Daniels."

"Don't look so smug yet, bright eyes. I'm a star center, need I remind you."

"Your humility is obviously the *star* of this show," I quip sarcastically.

"We'll see just how humble I am when I make you mine."

My breath catches as he rushes down the rink at speeds that astound me, and I've been around the game my entire life. With ease, he gets the puck past Hux, then returns with a triumphant grin.

"Game's not over yet!" I call out.

Now that Hux is warmed up, the next two shots miss, but it's my turn again and I'm determined to beat him, just to hold it over his head for the rest of our lives.

The puck slides down the ice, tapping against my stick as I aim right down the center. Hux prepares himself, but at the last second, I swing around the back of the goal and tip the puck into the net right between his legs.

I throw my hands in the air, my guys cheering behind me.

"One more shot, Daniels. Don't cave under the pressure."

"It'll take more than a little slip of a woman to have my nerves getting the better of me."

"Guess we'll see."

He scoffs playfully, and even though the urge to say fuck the game and drag him into me is alive in my chest, I want to win just the teensiest bit more. With graceful ease, he handles the puck, and when he's just about down to the goal, making his final move toward the net, I release my secret weapon.

Could I pick a more romantic moment? Sure. Could I make it cute and sweet like all those baby announcements I watch on PackChat? Absolutely. But *this*, this just fits us. What better way to tell my beast that we're having a baby than to throw him right off his game? If I know Nash's inner, hell, mostly outer asshole as well as I think I do, he'll look back and appreciate the ingenuity of choosing this moment.

With a massive grin on my face, I shout down the ice, "You're going to be a daddy, Nash Daniels."

His footsteps falter, his stick scraping across the ice and missing the puck entirely. He skids to a stop and spins around, eyes wide, shock written across every line of his face. The stick drops to the ground, then he's barreling toward me faster than I can blink. I remove my helmet, watching as he does the same and tosses it aside.

"What did you just say?" he rasps.

"I'm pregnant," I whisper.

He reaches for me, tugging me into his arms. Mindful of my skates, my legs wrap around his padded waist as he spins us on the ice.

"Fuck, bright eyes. I'm so fucking sorry," he murmurs against my jaw, nuzzling me and marking me with his scent. "I shouldn't have been a jackass. I should've—"

"No, you shouldn't have, but you're here now." My stomach tilts just a bit, and I really don't want to get sick in the middle of the rink. "Any chance you could stop spinning us now? Puking is *not* how I want to remember this moment."

"Shit! Sorry." His big hands bracket my face. "How are you feeling? Are you both okay?"

"We're good. Better now that you're here with us."

His purr rumbles against my chest. "I'm never leaving either of you again."

"We'll figure out the details later. Right now, I just need two things."

"Name it, and they're yours."

"I need you to kiss me..."

"Duh. And the other?"

I grin. "I need you to say, 'I lost to West Carter because her stick game is better than mine.'"

"I fucking love you, bright eyes...but I'm never saying those words. *Ever.*"

I laugh right before his mouth crashes into mine. He tastes of vanilla spiced rum, and I wish I could devour him whole.

I hear the cheers of the other guys and feel my entire world settle into place as my grumpy Alpha carries me off the ice and down into the tunnel. Opening the first door he finds, he strides in, setting me down on my skates. It's an empty office of sorts. A simple desk and plain office chair fill the space, with a clean white board covering most of the wall.

"Strip," he demands, the full force of his Alpha bark in his tone. "I need to be inside you. Now."

I'm unlacing my skates, tugging them off and tossing them aside as he starts to do the same. I shimmy out of what I've got on until I'm standing before him naked.

"Put your hands on the desk and hang on, bright eyes. This is going to be quick."

I spin around, planting my palms on the cool wood. His heat warms my back once he steps into me, his strong hands gripping my hips and lifting me up onto my toes to get me in the right position. One second, I feel the fat head of his cock at my entrance, and the next, he slams home, his knot edging my hole. A whine slips from my throat. Anticipation is amping up inside me, needing his bite to finally feel complete.

"Fuck, baby. You feel so goddamn good."

He pulls out and thrust in again. Over and over, he fucks me until my toes are curling against the concrete and my hands are gripping the desk so hard my knuckles are white.

"I need to see you," he growls.

Flipping me around, he lifts me onto the top of the desk. He forcefully pushes my knees to my chest, leaning forward and plunging right back into my sex. I cry out, his thick length hitting deeper in this position.

"You mine, West?"

"Yes, Alpha. Yours," I manage to choke out.

He growls, plunging in harder. The sound of skin slapping against skin is loud in the complete silence of the room.

"Say it again," he barks.

"I'm yours. Please, Alpha, bite me."

"Where do you want it, West? Want me to sink my teeth into that plump lower lip you're always torturing? Or maybe the breast that Hux didn't claim? Or maybe here..."

He leans down, kissing the inside of my knee then licking up my inner thigh.

"What about right here?" he murmurs against my skin, continuing to roll his hips back and thrust forward as he kisses up and down my leg.

The spot is sensitive, like there's a direct line to my greedy pussy, and a deep whine rushes out.

"Does my little Omega like that?" He skims his teeth across the tender spot again. "Fuck, you taste so goddamn sweet. Want to sink my teeth in and make you mine."

"Do it, Alpha. Bite me."

"But what if I want to bite you somewhere that I can kiss any time I want, reminding you who you belong to—what you mean to me?"

His hand releases my leg, sliding up my arm until he reaches my wrist. He drops the softest, sweetest kiss there, and my heart goes into a free fall.

"Nash, please," I beg.

His chest rumbles as his hips smack into my ass, his knot stretching the outer ring of my cunt in a way that makes me mewl like a kitten. He pulls out almost all the way, hovering there for a moment before he sinks his teeth into my inner wrist at the same time he buries his knot inside me.

Fire burns through my blood as my orgasm consumes me, my body going taut. I bite down on my lower lip to keep from screaming when Nash's knot swells even larger, locking inside my body until we're practically one.

His growl is a perpetual rumble from his chest as he grinds against me. He's tending his mark with long, slow licks that have my pussy contracting around him with each one.

"God, bright eyes, I can't believe you're really mine," he murmurs reverently, leaning up and sliding his arms under my back.

He lifts me and, holding on tightly, walks us around the desk and drops into the chair. My arms are around his neck, my legs straddling his. Our bodies remain locked together, our combined scents soothing in a way I never would've guessed. As we sit tangled together, I'm settled by the closeness, feeling warmth in the bond and a rush of congratulatory wishes from Hux and Porter.

"Thank you," he whispers against my lips.

"For?"

"Giving me another chance."

"I love you, Nash Daniels. I would never give up on you."

"I don't deserve you."

I grin and kiss the tip of his nose. "I know."

His smile transforms his face, just like he's transformed my life.

## 35

### WEST CARTER

We're walking to the suite when I hear someone call my name. Turning, I find Bexley and Hawke walking beside Arden and Cohen.

"Hey guys! I didn't know you all were coming tonight!"

They walk over, the girls and I sharing hugs, then I introduce them all to Ziggy, who's standing beside me.

"Barrett got us tickets. Said we shouldn't miss tonight's game because it was sure to be a great one," Cohen says with a smile.

"How's he *really* doing? He puts on a brave face for me, but I know better."

Cohen sighs. "He's doing okay. Doctors say it's healing nicely and he might be able to play in the championship. He just has to take it easy, which we all know is impossible for Barrett."

I roll my eyes. "You're not kidding."

"But we want to talk about you and this new pack of yours." Bex grins. "Porter agreed to work with us, and we were hoping we might be able to convince you to join him."

"I'd love that, actually."

Bex claps her hands together. "Yay! I'm so excited. Arden and I have loads of ideas for the series, and we can't wait to get started."

"We figured we'd wait until after the season's over to give you all a little break. Does that work for you?" Arden asks.

"That should be perfect. We're going to start house hunting soon, so we'll be in the area more frequently once the season ends."

"Oh my gosh, you're moving back here?" Bex asks hopefully.

"Yeah, I've been in talks with my dad to join the team officially. We're going to work out the details over the summer."

Hawke smiles. "Well, then welcome back, West. The girls have been dying to hear the story of how you all got together. Maybe you can have a girls night and fill them in so they can stop with all the conjecture."

I laugh when Bexley elbows Hawke, who barely flinches.

"I'd love that."

"Any chance you could convince Cadence to move back too?" Arden asks hopefully.

"The girls have already said where I go, they go, so I'm pretty sure you'll be seeing a whole lot more of all of us soon."

Arden leans her head against Cohen's shoulder as he wraps his arm around her. For so long, I've watched their packs with envy, longing for what they've found. Now, I have it, and my smile feels almost too wide for my face.

"Are the rest of your packs here?"

Cohen nods. "Bastian and Locke are getting food then meeting us at our seats. Axton and Shaw are scoping out the merchandise, and Camden and Crew are talking to a group of fans that managed to recognize them while the rest of us snuck off."

"Well, I hope you all enjoy the game. Let's do dinner the next time we're in town."

"Drag that sister of mine with you, and you've got a deal."

I grin at Cohen. "You got it, boss man."

He cringes at the old nickname. "Never was a dull moment with the three of you around."

"Imagine how much more trouble we can get into now!"

Cohen groans, and Bex and Arden laugh.

"C'mon, let's save the other two before they start a media frenzy none of us want," Hawke suggests, taking Bex's hand.

"Enjoy the game, guys!"

"You too, West." Bexley and Arden share knowing grins. "We can't wait to meet your pack."

They walk off, and for a second, I want to run over and ask what's so amusing, but knowing them, it's something silly like watching me fawn over my own pack of hot guys after drooling over theirs for so long. Teenage crushes are embarrassing. What can I say?

Ziggy and I head back to the suite. The game is just about to start, and for the first time in a month, I feel like I can sit back, relax, and watch my guys battle it out on the ice.

"You look happy," Ziggy murmurs in my ear. His arm slides behind my back to grip my hip as he buries his nose in my hair.

"Maybe because I am." I tilt my head back to look up at him. "You were all in on this?"

He nods, dropping a kiss on my forehead. "He didn't want to come to you until he knew he could be what you needed."

"He already was," I murmur.

"But he couldn't see that. It took a conversation with Porter for him to understand that we all wanted him here too—dickishness and all."

I chuckle. "Well, thank you. I know it's not going to be easy, and we have a lot to talk about after the game, but I really believe this is how it was meant to be. Now, the logistics of it are going to take some finagling. If we're buying a house here, then he should get a say. We'll have to work around game schedules and travel plans, but I know we'll find a way to make it work."

He just hums and squeezes me a little tighter as he walks toward the front of the suite. Stepping just outside the enclosure, the thick metal railing is in front of us when we look down at the ice, waiting for the game to begin. I step forward, wrapping my fingers around the thick metal bar.

The announcer welcomes the crowd to tonight's game featuring the Phoenix Heat and the Chicago Storm, and when he notes a special change to tonight's lineup, the crowd goes wild with anticipation. My forehead creases with confusion as the lights dim and the spotlight hits the tunnel while the Heat's music blares through the speakers.

"First up, your starting right wing for the Phoenix Heat, number nine, Porter Hanson."

The crowd cheers as Porter skates out, waving at the crowd until he stops on the marked line.

"And at left wing, number five, Flint Campbell. Followed by the right defenseman, number twenty-four, Nixon Brooks. And your left defenseman, number seventy-four, Rafferty Sorensen."

The crowd is on their feet, cheering for each of the men as they skate out to the line. The anticipation amps up once Hux steps up to the entrance, large and fierce. Only I know he's really just a cuddly koala.

"Fan favorite and your starting goalie, number thirty-three, Huxley McCarren."

Hux does a little circle around the rink, waving at the fans. Then the lights cut out, and shock filters through the stands. I can't blame them. I'm shocked too. This is definitely different from what usually happens.

"And now, a change to tonight's starting lineup for the Phoenix Heat. For the first time in orange, cream, and black, wearing number fifty-five, is your new starting center for the Phoenix Heat..."

Music pounds through the arena as a silhouette appears backlit from the tunnel. My heart stops when the spotlight kicks on.

"Nash 'The Beast' Daniels!"

The roar of the crowd is nearly deafening. I can't take my eyes off of him. He skates toward the line of men, stopping just beside Porter and Huxley, then they turn around. The light pans over the backs of their jerseys as the cameras zoom in so the audience can see *Carter* stitched onto the back of each one.

"We love you, pretty girl. We're yours, and we want everyone to know it," Ziggy whispers in my ear.

At some point—I have no idea when—he changed. When I spin around, he's wearing a huge grin and sporting a new Heat jersey. He does a slow twirl, and I see that he's got my name on his back too.

My breath catches, and my hand flies up to my mouth as tears pour down my face. He pulls me into him, tipping my chin up to his.

"I love you too," I rasp.

"Good. Now kiss me for the camera since Nash can't interrupt us this time."

I laugh, but he catches it with his mouth as his lips smash into mine. The crowd cheers while our kiss is plastered all over the screens throughout the arena.

# HE'S SO SLICK

My heart is overflowing. I've found my pack, and just like they all promised, things just might be okay after all.

So I broke one of my rules and did a hockey player...or three.

Guess rules really are made to be broken, but only if he's so slick you can't help yourself.

## 36

### ZIGGY MARSHALL

Nash walks into the living room, coming to a grinding halt when he takes in all of us spread throughout the living room.

His eyes lock on West. "You said we were having a romantic night in."

She blinks those big blue eyes at him, glancing at the three of us laid out on the carpet, then back to the Alpha who looks ready to lose his shit.

"I did."

"There is *nothing* romantic about three men in sleeping bags with personal pan pizzas on their chests, watching some chick flick that Ziggy no doubt picked out."

She sucks her plush lips between her teeth, a hand going to her belly which is jiggling slightly as she valiantly tries not to laugh.

"It's romantic because there's food, candles, and our entire pack is home. What more do we need?"

He growls.

"Look, I knew if I told you what was really happening, you would make an excuse to be late." Her tiny hand reaches for his. "Just give it a try...for me."

*Fuck. She's going to play that card. He's a sucker for it, and she knows it.*

"I'm not laying my ass out on the floor, and neither should you. Your back's been bothering you, and that won't be fucking comfortable. You and I can lay on the sofa. I'll give the movie five minutes, and if they say *like* every five seconds, I'm out."

"Fine. Now come here and sit down with me."

He grumbles the entire walk from the doorway to the sofa, carefully maneuvering between us to reach it. He lifts West up, settling her in his lap. You can physically see the stress of the day melt away with the simple touch of her skin on his.

"What's this shit about, anyways?" he asks, nuzzling into her hair.

She grins. "This pampered ice skater who's forced to train with a washed up, grumpy hockey player. They end up falling in love and living happily ever after. Kind of like us."

His brow quirks up. "Are you calling me washed up?"

"Notice he didn't argue with the grumpy part," I add helpfully.

Hux snorts. Porter chuckles, lifting his hand for a high five. Our palms connect, and Nash growls.

"I fucking hate the lot of you sometimes. Your amusement in the bond is like nails on a chalkboard."

"Man, that must be weird." The entire room goes silent. I look at the others, all of them staring at me with wide eyes. "What did I say?"

My eyes dart to West's, and there's shock written all over her face.

"Fuck, Zig. I'm sorry. I—" Her voice cracks.

Shit. I didn't mean to make her feel guilty. The thought just popped in my head, and I opened my big mouth. The need to soothe her forces me to sit up and face her so she can see that I'm really not as bothered as she's now assuming I am.

"No. Don't be sorry. We've all been going a million miles an hour, looking for a house, going through the buying process, renovating, trying to get things done before baby gets here, and me interviewing with Arizona State University. It honestly hasn't occurred to me until literally right this second. I... Well, I'd like to be able to feel you all in the bond." I shrug.

Huxley tilts his head back, his eyes meeting Nash's.

"What the hell are you looking at *me* for?" the other Alpha demands.

Hux rolls his eyes. "He was your friend first. Just thought I'd give you dibs."

Nash and I glance at West at the same time, seeing the guilt there. She's beating herself up for not thinking of this sooner. Fucking hell. Maybe I shouldn't have said anything.

"I'm going to have to do this, aren't I?" Nash grumbles. "Fine. Get up. Let's make this quick."

"What?" I rasp.

"You want a bond. You're going to get one."

"Just like that?"

"Look, do you want to be part of this pack or not?" Nash barks.

Quickly, I set my pizza on the floor and slip out of my sleeping bag. Getting to my knees, I crawl over to where West and Nash are sitting.

"So, how do we do this?" I ask softly.

"Give me your hand."

# HE'S SO SLICK

I raise my left hand just as West grabs a hold of my right, squeezing lightly.

"You *have* washed this thing, right?" Nash asks, staring at it dubiously.

I nod even though I'm not a hundred percent sure when the last time I washed it actually was. "Yup."

His eyes narrow. "Why is that not convincing?"

Porter groans. "Just bite him already."

"You know this is irreversible, right?" Nash asks, his voice lowering slightly.

I nod again.

"And you're going to feel the full force of his grumpiness through the bond," McCarren adds with a smirk.

"I can handle it. Have for years," I retort.

Nash rolls his eyes. "Gee, thanks."

"You're welcome."

"For fuck's sake." He lifts my hand.

"Wait, have you thought about where you're going to bite me? Like, there are huge ramifications to bite locations, and sometimes unintended consequences that—"

I feel the piercing bite through the skin on my pinky. I gasp, eyes going wide as West leans forward, dropping a kiss on my cheek.

"Do you feel it, Zig?" she whispers reverently.

"I-I do. It's incredible. I... I feel *you*."

She's love and light and warmth, her feelings trickling through my connection with Nash. I can even sense the other guys, though more faintly, through the connection with West.

I'm sure I'm like a livewire in the bond. My emotions are cascading in all directions.

"Jesus, you keep that up, and you're going to give me vertigo," Nash mutters.

Then he sucks my pinky into his mouth, and I know I shouldn't, but a groan slips out unbidden. Nash growls, no doubt sensing my sudden spike in desire. I'm not really into him or anything, but the bond mark is *sensitive*. What can I say?

"You suck like a pro," I quip.

Porter nearly chokes on his beer, and Hux bursts out laughing.

West's giggle makes my heart damn near burst with joy.

Nash grunts. "Don't get any ideas. The dick tonguing was a one-time thing."

Porter and Hux whip around.

"Dick tonguing?"

"*He* did the tonguing. Not me," Nash quickly clarifies, a distinct flush working up his throat.

"Mmmhmm. But you liked it," Hux murmurs wickedly.

"My dick is for West and only West. None of you horny fuckers get any ideas."

He licks my pinky one last time before he slumps back on the sofa. West is still laughing, and the happiness filtering the bond fills me up until I'm close to bursting with peace and love.

This is what I've been waiting my entire life for, and it's so much more than I could've anticipated. I see our future laid out before us. Family. Kids. Love. And sure, a whole heap of troublemaking with the one woman who holds my heart.

I can't fucking wait.

# Epilogue

## NASH DANIELS

**FIVE YEARS LATER**

West skates backward, grinning at Porter. He's holding Navy's hands, but she's really just placating him. The little spitfire can already skate solo, but since she loves her daddy and likes to make him smile, she plays along.

Finally letting go of her hands, he claps like any proud father would when she manages to skate right into his arms. He lifts her up, spinning her in circles, and her laughter makes my heart feel like it's going to burst out of my chest.

"He's such a sucker." Zig laughs. "That girl's been skating without help for at least a month now."

"Let him have his moment. Can't help it if my daughter takes after me and is a little badass on the ice."

"Don't let West hear you say that," Hux chuckles, coming to stand beside us near the bench. "Pretty sure she'd take full credit for Navy's skills considering she's the one that was always taking her out on the ice, even when she was a baby."

We're all quiet for a moment, watching Porter pull West into a hug with him and our little girl. The trio stand out on the ice with the lights blaring down on them, and it's one of the most perfect moments I've ever seen. But fuck if I'll tell Porter that. Don't need that shit to go to his head.

The Omega and I have come a long way. Sure, we still bicker, but it's more sibling banter than *I'll slash your throat in your sleep* fighting, so I figure we've done well.

"Season's getting ready to start," Hux murmurs, sliding a look my way.

"Got a point?"

"How many do you think you have left in you?" he asks softly.

I shrug. The thought of not playing hockey leaves a burning hole in my gut. Sure, my body isn't as quick to recover as it used to be, and hits hurt a helluva lot more. And yes, I miss the close-knit family dynamic like fucking crazy during the season, but I always assumed an injury would finally take me out. Not me being sentimental.

"Don't know, but it doesn't feel like it's time to let go quite yet." I glance over at my packmate, assessing the strain on his face. "What about you?"

"At least one more season, maybe two, but I kind of want more time with our family. The game takes us away too much, and I feel like every time I come home, Navy's grown a foot and has learned some new amazing skill, and I... Fuck, I want to be there for them all, ya know?"

I nod, because I do know. We miss out on a lot during the season, but not playing the game I love is a hard pill to swallow as well.

"What are you guys discussing so seriously over here?" West asks, skating up to the wall. I didn't even hear her coming.

Hux tilts his head in my direction. "Wondering if the old man was ready to hang up his skates any time soon."

I shoot him a glare. "Old man? You're only a fucking year younger than me, bro. Eat shit."

Hux and Zig laugh, but West studies me carefully.

"You thinking about it?" she asks softly.

Her pink hair has long since gone full blonde, but she still looks exactly like she did the first time I saw her take her helmet off. Beautiful and full of the fire that always stirs the one inside me that lives for her.

"Not yet. But maybe soon."

She nods knowingly, sensing my peace through our bond.

Porter skates up with Navy in his arms. "Did you see our little skater out there? She did amazing!"

"She sure did." Zig holds out his arms. "Now come see Daddy Zig."

Navy giggles and holds her little arms out. Her jet black hair, shaped into mini buns on the top of her head, bobs as she's passed from one dad to the other, giggling when the playful Beta blows raspberries down her neck.

"Hey, guys, you all still here? Figured I'd miss you."

Maxim Carter walks up in navy blue dress slacks and a gray quarter-zip sweater. The man doesn't look more than mid-forties, but I know better. I've learned a lot in the last few years, mostly from the man that raised an amazing daughter like West. I can only hope that I'm half the man he is when my child is grown.

"Papa!" Navy squeals, holding her hands out to her grandfather.

"Hey, little puck nugget!" He pulls her in and spins her around. "Wanna go grab a pretzel with Papa?"

"Yay!" She claps. "Bye, Mama. Bye, Daddies."

She waves as they walk away, the legendary Maxim Carter playing Itsy Bitsy Spider up Navy's legs. West gets this mischievous look in her eyes I've grown to recognize...and secretly love. Don't need to be giving her any ideas either.

"You know, hockey season's roughly six months. That's cutting it awfully close if we head into the championship," West states matter-of-factly, looking at all of us expectantly as she skates out into the center of the ice.

I cross my arms over my chest, wondering where she's going with this. I can feel her excitement and nerves in the bond, but I can't figure out what's stirred up this particular reaction.

"Cutting what close, bright eyes?"

"Nothing. It's no one's fault. The slapshot was just a little too accurate, that's all."

My eyes narrow, and the others step up beside me.

"What the hell does that mean?" Porter asks, glaring at the gorgeous woman skating in circles like she's a professional figure skater.

"Look, sometimes one or even *two* get past the goalie. It happens." She sucks that lower lip into her mouth, her grin fighting to break free.

"Is she making any sense to you guys?" Hux asks, confused.

"I know you've all heard the old saying, *he shoots, he scores.*"

"Spit it the fuck out already, woman!" I bark.

"How do y'all feel about maybe adding a couple new players to the lineup?"

For a second, I stare at her in confusion, then the lightbulb goes on, my breath catching in my lungs.

"No fucking way!" I growl, making the others turn to look at me.

I'm rushing out onto the ice in my street shoes, wrapping my arms around her and lifting her up so I can smash my mouth onto hers.

"Someone fill us in," Porter whines in true Omega style.

"The team will have a couple new fans next season," she says, staring down at me with the most beautiful smile on her face.

"Holy shit! You're pregnant?" Hux shouts, sliding out onto the ice to join us in our huddle.

"Wait, really?" Porter asks excitedly. He skates out to us and wraps us all in a huge hug.

"But she said a *couple* new fans..." Zig begins, eyes widening, then he laughs. "Twins, pretty girl? We're having *twins*?"

He unsteadily makes his way out onto the ice, and it's hugs all around as I stare into the blue eyes of the only woman that's ever managed to capture my heart.

West Carter is a little fucking brat...

But I love her anyway.

*Want more of the* Knot Pucking Mine Omegaverse *crew, with appearances from some of your favorites? Stay tuned for Barrett's story, coming soon. Any guesses who his leading lady may be? Email them to me at sinclairkellyauthor@gmail.com.*

# About the Author

Sinclair Kelly is a paranormal & contemporary romance author who writes to give all of the feral characters in her head a voice. She's fluent in sarcasm and dry humor. She lives in sunny Arizona with her loving husband, three adorably exhausting kids, and a feisty Australian shepherd puppy named Havoc. She loves reading, writing, coffee, vodka, tattoos, wine, donuts, broody asshole book boyfriends, badass FMCs, sangria, and all of the friendships she's made since she began her writing journey.

**Want more Sin?**
www.sinclairkelly.com
https://linktr.ee/SinclairKellyAuthor

**Other Books by Sinclair Kelly**

**Knot Yours Omegaverse Series**
I Think Knot
Knot A Chance
Knot My Problem

**Standalones**
Fighting Fallon
Landry

**Sinner's Mark MC Series**
Saint
Rogue
Ace
Trip (Coming Soon)
Squire (Coming Soon)

**The Ghost Girl Series**
A Fate Unknown
Twist of Fate
It Must Be Fate

**Land of Legend Series**
If The Broom Fits
If The Wand Sparkles

If The Throne Calls

Printed in Great Britain
by Amazon